THE MYSTERY OF JULIA EPISCOPA

THE VATICAN CHRONICLES BOOK 1

JOHN I RIGOLI
DIANE CUMMINGS

THE MYSTERY OF JULIA EPISCOPA

DEDICATION

In memory of Delphine

For Scott and Jordan

ONE

Herculaneum, Italy, AD 79

A s the small boat pushed out from the shoreline, it jerked and rolled in the choppy black waters. On deck, the woman struggled to keep her balance. She strained to see the old man with the small dog in his arms, barely visible now on the sandy shore. Just as he faded from view, she saw him turn away and head home to their villa.

The woman's two wide-eyed daughters trembled as they looked at her. She placed a steady hand on each one's arm. "Everything will be fine. We'll return in a few days." She prayed it would be so. The woman beckoned her steward forward and took from him the cloth bag she needed to keep in sight. She cast her eyes skyward, blinking away falling ash and soot that clung to her blue cloak turning it a dusky gray. Then she turned, straightened, and steeled herself for the days ahead.

This day had begun like any other. Julia Lucinia and her daughters, Livia and Flavia, had planned a trip to the markets. The old man, known only as Scribe, intended to accompany them. He needed to purchase ink and papyrus for his writings. However, just as the lunch bell tinkled, the house tottered, rocking back and forth as if being torn from its very foundation. The girls, already in the dining room, screamed. Julia rushed in breathless, and the old man appeared on her heels.

"What's happening?" Julia's face was white with horror.

"Girls, Julia," the scribe said, "gather your belongings quickly. You must get to Neapolis. I'll take you to the boats."

Vesuvius had been spitting and coughing for the past several days, but nothing of this magnitude had jolted the small community of Herculaneum for as long as anyone could remember. The scribe saw danger, and he wanted the family well away from it. Neapolis lay far enough from Herculaneum that Julia and her girls would be safe.

A moment before leaving home, the scribe hurried back to the library and returned carrying a single scroll.

As Julia stuffed it inside her cloth bag, she noted the cup on the mantelpiece and reached for it.

"Yes," the scribe said, "they should stay together."

Clutching Yarrow, the family dog, the scribe and the house steward shepherded Julia and her daughters down to the waterfront. The steward would accompany the women. It was never done for them to travel by themselves.

The marina had become crowded with citizens scrambling toward the boats. The old man urged his charges forward onto one of them. The steward followed.

Julia then motioned the scribe aboard.

"The smoke seems to be thinning and heading away. I'll be fine here," he said, yet he doubted his words.

Flavia reached for Yarrow, but the little dog yelped and clung to the scribe. "He wants to stay with you," she said.

An hour later, the hypnotic blue of the bay of Neapolis came into view. Julia scanned the rocky, sunny shoreline where emperors and the wealthy came to play at their extravagant villas. She saw the boardinghouses clustered near the shore and knew that they would need to move quickly to locate lodging suitable for three women of their station. Good food could be had at one of the many cook shops that lined the beach-front.

Instead of thinning, the smoke began to thicken, and the atmosphere darkened. When Julia turned to look toward home once more, the deep red glow at the mouth of Vesuvius caught her attention. Almost simultaneously, the explosion came, so deafening that it silenced her daughters' screams. She watched as the terrible eruption spewed rock and ash high into the sky that then fell back in a great cascade that crept down the sides of the mountain.

Julia gasped. Her daughters, though grown now, huddled close to their mother. The steward surrounded the three as best he could.

Once on shore, Livia and Flavia settled into bed. Julia watched all night as the volcano spewed out more molten lava every few seconds. She couldn't know then what damage Vesuvius had unleashed on her home. But twenty-four hours later, when another eruption more powerful than the first reached the coastline of Neapolis, there could be no doubt. Herculaneum, the town that lay at the foot of the volcano, the one she had just left behind, was no more—the town destroyed, her villa buried, and all those who had stayed behind dead and gone.

It was beyond thinking that her friend, the scribe, was dead, but she knew that he was. She allowed herself only a moment of grief as the knowledge that she would never return to the life she had known overcame her. She was a woman alone now, heading into a future unknown, one she would have to forge anew.

TWO

"**V**al, come here a minute."

"What is it?" Valentina scooted back from the table and rose from a pint-sized chair she had been using to peruse piles of old documents in the small, tucked-away space called the Ancient Manuscripts section of the Vatican Library. She smoothed her knee-length black skirt. Her heels clicking on the polished marble floor, she crossed to Erika, her friend and colleague, who was sitting a few feet away at the other end of the table, her eyes fixed just inches from an ancient parchment.

"Look at this. There's a name change on this tag." As Erika looked up, a tiny line across her otherwise-smooth brow gave intensity to her concentration. "I didn't see it at first because the tag is nearly worn out. Here, take a look." Erika grabbed the arm of the magnifier attached to the table and pulled it toward the document. Valentina moved in closer and bent over. With their heads nearly touching, the two scientists scrutinized the *titulus,* the small tag that the ancients attached to a scroll to identify its writer.

Valentina brushed a white-gloved finger across the tag, spreading a thin layer of dust onto the tabletop. "You're right,"

5

she murmured. "It looks like someone inked over part of the original name."

Erika pulled the magnifier down to within inches of the document. "Look here, the Latin a in the name Julia has been covered over with the Latin *ūs*. Same with the last name: Episcopa changed to Episcopus. You can tell because the ink doesn't match."

"Neither does the handwriting," Valentina said.

"It looks as if the original name was Julia Episcopa, but now it reads Julius Episcopus. Weird. This is really messy work if a scribe was just correcting a mistake."

Valentina Vella and Erika Simone were seasoned classical-historical archeologists with advanced degrees in a half-dozen dead languages. They were currently working on a Vatican project.

A familiar face showed at the door to their softly-lit workspace.

Erika was the first to look up. "Paula? My goodness, I didn't expect to see you here." She got out of her chair, welcomed Paula in, and gave her a kiss on each cheek. The two women had had a casual tryst several years back and had remained friends after their brief romance was over.

"Wow! Paula," Valentina said. She, too, got up and the two exchanged kisses. "Hey, take a look here at something kind of crazy." Paula was also a well-known archaeologist.

"What have you got?" Paula asked.

"Look at this tag," Valentina said, taking Erika's chair.

Paula bent over, her eyes just inches from the tag, and then she sat down in Valentina's chair for a closer inspection, fingering the tag and observing it from different angles. "Hmm, it's odd. A name change. Have you read the scroll yet?"

"Not yet, we just discovered the tag," Erika said. "And what are you doing here, so far away from home?"

"Research for my second book," Paula answered.

"I hope it goes better than the first one," Erika said wryly.

Paula gave Erika a pained look, then smiled ruefully. Paula Kirkpatrick, an American, was the author of a book called *The Invisibility of Biblical Women in Modern Readings*. A particularly conservative American bishop had failed to appreciate Paula's book and had her sacked from her teaching post at Georgetown University. She'd faced almost a year of unemployment before landing a job as professor of divinity at Oxford.

"Well, I hope so, too," Paula said.

"Okay, how about we read this thing?" Valentina said. "Erika, do you want to do the honors?" All three women could easily sight-read dead languages; this one was in ancient Latin.

"Sure. I'll give it a shot." Valentina stood and Erika took a seat. The scroll was small, about the size of a fashion magazine. Its left corner was tattered. "I hope I can…. It's turned so black with age."

While Erika remained at the table, poring over the document and trying to make out the writing, Valentina took a few steps away. Something at the edge of her memory tickled for recognition. *I've seen that hand before. Whose is it?*

Erika started in, stumbling at first to make out the old and damaged letters. Then, she found her rhythm.

To the most holy Clement,

I request a meeting in Rome with the bishops Lexus, Terentius, and Porcius on a matter of some urgency. I recognize that this request is most unusual but it is a matter of great urgency. If my fellow bishops are outside of Rome, I would strongly urge that they be called back into the city. There is a matter that must be attended to as soon as it is convenient.

I remain ever your humble servant,
Julia Episcopa, District of Trastevere

"Good heavens," Erika said, looking up. "What do we have here?"

"It appears to be a letter to Clement," Paula said. "Quite a demanding letter."

"Clement? As in, the fourth pope?" Erika squinted and looked at the bottom of the scroll.

"Who else would it be? It's signed by a bishop and it concerns other bishops," Erika said. "But an episcopa," she added, accenting the *pa*. "A female?"

"It can't be. It's not possible." In her work as an expert in ancient languages Valentina had examined hundreds of Church documents, many of them the earliest in Church history. She was certain that no woman had ever been a bishop.

"It's awfully odd," Erika said. "What do you make of it, Paula?"

"Well, my first thought would be that this is a hoax or a forgery," Paula said before Valentina interrupted her.

"That's it," Valentina said, returning to the table and hovering over the small scroll again.

"That's what?" Erika and Paula said in unison.

"This is Julia Lucinia's handwriting."

"What?" Erika raised an eyebrow in surprise. "Is it?"

Paula narrowed her eyes.

"I'm sure of it," Valentina said.

Julia Lucinia had been an upper-class first-century Roman woman married to a wealthy nobleman. Valentina and Erika knew her well. More than a year before, they had translated a cache of mid-first-century scrolls that had been found in an excavated villa in Herculaneum. Many of the documents had been written by Julia Lucinia.

Valentina turned again to the document. "We're looking at something strange, and I don't know what to make of it. This letter is written by Julia Lucinia. I'm sure of it. But the idea that Julia Lucinia came to be Julia Episcopa? It's preposterous. There's got to be an explanation."

"What do you think, Paula?" Erika asked.

"Of the letter, we can rule out forgery because Val recognizes the hand. But Julia Episcopa was Julia Lucinia? Good heavens, that brings up all kinds of questions. Perchance we have found a female bishop for the first time?"

"Whoa. I don't think we can make that leap just yet," Valentina replied. "There may be a dozen other explanations. I wouldn't even dare discuss this as a possibility unless we had irrefutable evidence. One letter…it could be just one giant mistake."

"Who are you working for?" Paula asked.

"Ricci," Valentina said.

"Paula rolled her eyes. "Let's get out of here."

THREE

"**W**hat did Cardinal Ricci hire you for?" Paula asked after the three had taken seats at Il Ragno d'Oro on Via Silla, a lively family restaurant near the Vatican.

"To investigate the role of women in the first-century Church," Erika said. "More to the point, we're looking for the equivalent of what would be women priests today: bishops and elders—female ordination, basically. Not that the cardinal thinks we'll find any. He's sure we won't."

"This have anything to do with Augustine cracking open the door to the subject of women priests?" Paula asked. "The pope wants backup for his idea?"

"You bet," Erika said. "He's already cited the presence of deaconesses, but he seems to want to know if any woman was positioned higher than that rank. He ordered the red caps in the Holy Office to convene a commission to study the idea and advise him."

"I can imagine how that went over," Paula said.

"Yeah, the uproar could be heard in all corners of Rome," Erika said with a laugh.

"The liberals and conservatives were at each other's throats,"

Valentina chimed in. "The liberals hailed the pope's move, but the conservatives charged him with pandering to feminists and other radicals."

Paula laughed. "I can just see Cardinal Ricci elbowing his way into the directorship to make sure the outcome will be what he wants. He's had his eye set on the white cap and the red Gucci shoes forever."

The waiter came and, with a flourish, set down three steaming plates of pasta and clams. "*Altro?*" he asked. The women smiled and shook their heads. As the waiter departed, they lifted their forks and joined in a distracted silence as they dined.

Halfway through their meal, Erika put her fork down. "What do you think is behind that tag?"

"That the scroll was written by a man...or a woman." Valentina laughed.

"Maybe you did find a lady bishop." Paula smiled.

Valentina raised her eyebrows. "Are you looking to be excommunicated? Ricci would brand you a heretic for uttering such blasphemy."

Erika's sky blue eyes twinkled, a smile playing over her lips. "It would be so worth it. Imagine, after so many years and so many scholars having worked in these archives, you and I find a woman bishop. Just think." Erika was just warming up, but a laughing Valentina cut her off.

"*Quando voleranno gli asini.*" When donkeys fly. Valentina pushed her plate aside. "I need to visit *il bagno*," she said.

"I'll join you," Erika said.

The thirty-something twosome had met at an excavation site as grad students and hit it off. When their graduate studies were complete, with a PhD for each of them, their decision to partner in business came easily because neither saw themselves as nine-to-fivers in dreary academia.

After they squeezed into a tiny bathroom, Erika said, "I haven't seen Paula in quite a while, but I can see that she hasn't completely recovered from the nightmare of losing her job at Georgetown."

"I agree. She looks drawn and thin, and maybe she's too eager to push back against the Church that she sees has, well, bullied her," Valentina said.

"Yeah, she does see it that way," Erika said.

"Okay, all set?" Valentina said as they washed and dried their hands.

"Yep."

Returning to their table, they found Paula tapping a finger on it. "Oh look, I'm not jumping to conclusions," she said. "Just thinking. It's possible. We know women took leadership roles in the early Church. The letter's signed 'Episcopa.' You can't be close-minded, for goodness sake."

"I'm not going to risk my reputation or my career unless we find something more." Valentina shot a warning glance at the other two.

Paula ignored Valentina and speculated, "If Julia Lucinia joined the Christian movement and rose in the ranks to be ordained a bishop, it would belie Holy Office claims handed down century after century. No women priests, ever."

"If she was a bishop, wouldn't it follow that there were other female priests?" Erika noted.

"That would be a logical assumption, of course," Paula said.

"We've got no hard evidence, ladies," Valentina countered, "and this is not a battle we want to be in the middle of. Remember, the Holy Office has its knives out over this issue as we speak."

"And Cardinal Ricci would be a dangerous man to cross," Erika said.

"You two were hired to find just this sort of evidence. What's wrong with you?" Paula's voice rang with the challenge she just expressed. Paula pushed her plate aside and placed her tightly folded hands on the table. "You may be on to something earth-shattering, world-changing even. I don't think you can ignore it and still consider yourselves scientists." She let out a deep breath, unclasped her hands, and set them in her lap.

Erika glanced at Valentina, wondering at her silence, and then turned back to Paula. "I can't get my mind off that altered tag.

Who? And why? Usually, a change just corrects an error. But somehow this seems different."

"I know," Paula said. "It could be a simple correction, or someone might have known exactly what he was doing and tried to turn the female writer into a male."

"Now there's a wild thought," Erika said.

"Not that wild, really. Every day we find new scrolls hidden in caves and private libraries. Some of them are revealing some surprises."

"So you're suggesting that Julia could have been purposefully disappeared and erased?" Erika said. "That could explain the tag, I suppose...."

"Oh, come on. You two are building a vast conspiracy here, based on one letter. This is absurd." Valentina's taut expression showed her objection to where this argument was leading.

"Maybe. This is simply one idea to add to the pot." Paula narrowed her eyes and thought for a moment. "I think you should go after this woman. Find out about her, and see what happens. If you could bring an ordained woman bishop of the first century to light...dear God. What would the Church say about that?"

Valentina held up both hands to stop her. "Paula, this is our careers we're talking about. Even if we can prove this beyond a reasonable doubt...." She ran out of words.

"I get it," Paula said. "But listen, the Church assigned you a job: to search out and report. You need to report what you find, not what Cardinal Ricci *wants* you to find."

Valentina said nothing.

Erika sighed. "Well, where to from here? Can you help us, Paula?"

"No. My book, with its rather timid suggestion that women are being screwed by the Church, has already got me labeled as a radical. You don't want to be associated with me." A faraway look implied that Paula was reaching for something in her memory.

"What is it, Paula?" Erika said.

"I've got something. I'm remembering.... I have seen a document written by one of Clement's secretaries referring to a woman named Julia around AD 96. I couldn't further identify her, but this could be your 'something more.'"

Valentina considered. "The date lines up with the letter. When Clement was pope."

"I'll look for it," Paula said.

FOUR

Rome

Valentina placed an arrangement of multicolored tulips on the L-shaped counter dividing her small kitchenette from the large, open *salotto*. She glimpsed out her balcony window at the small piazza two levels below and smiled to herself when she saw two young boys arguing over a skateboard, their mothers in hot pursuit to break things up. Back in the kitchen, she double-checked the refrigerator to make sure that her housekeeper had picked up the wine, prosciutto, and fresh fruit.

Valentina smiled to herself. While being in a long-distance relationship had its drawbacks, it made every coming together feel like the first time. She moved into her bedroom and slipped out of her dressing gown and into a knee-length pencil skirt that accentuated her curves. Checking her wristwatch, she hurried to the bathroom mirror and touched up her make-up, applying a bit more lipstick than she'd usually wear.

She slipped into a pair of stilettos, grabbed her bag, and hurried out the door, walking briskly down the street to where her Alfa Romeo was parked, taking care not to catch a heel in the rough, cobblestoned streets. She was running late, but so, too, was Luca's plane on this crisp, early spring Saturday morning. She should arrive at Leonardo da Vinci-Fiumicino Airport in plenty of time to avoid his having to wait. Valentina had a thirty-five-kilometer ride ahead of her, and as she motored onto the six-lane autostrada, she punched in her favorite jazz station.

Valentina had been single-minded in her pursuit of a career, and she was at the top of her profession. She'd had little time to pursue relationships in university, and as an expert in archaeology and linguistics, she'd spent half her life traveling across the globe, consulting for institutions, museums, and universities. Settling down had simply never occurred to her.

Until Luca Pallavicini came along.

While vacationing at her family's château in the quiet mountainside village of Le Châble, Switzerland, Valentina had met the man at a hotel bar and fallen in love. One year her junior, Luca came from nobility in Padua. He had studied in Vienna and then entered the Foreign Service. He currently called the City of Music home.

Luca was tall and handsome—a blue-eyed blond who was refined, intellectual, and sexy as all get-out. Their relationship was far from conventional, but it worked well for both of them. As a member of the diplomatic corps, Luca had little choice in his assignments, and they were both simply grateful that his current placement was a short plane ride away. And though she'd never say it to Luca, Valentina wasn't entirely certain that she'd be happy sacrificing her independence for a wedding ring.

She was looking forward to seeing Luca this weekend, and not just for the obvious reasons. The discovery in the archives was weighing on her. She needed a break, she needed some romance, and she needed to talk to someone she could trust.

As she pulled up at the arrival curb for Austria Airlines, she saw her lover emerging from the doorway. She thought, *How much better I like the arrivals than the departures.* She smiled to herself.

Valentina popped open the trunk of her Alfa and got out just as Luca arrived to chuck his bags inside.

"*Ciao, tessora,*" Luca said, wrapping an arm around Valentina's waist and pulling her in tight. He kissed her neck and her lips and held his eyes on her, leaving her breathless. "Let's get out of here."

Easy banter made the drive back to Valentina's flat short and sweet. Once inside, they reached for each other. It would be several hours before they found themselves at a favorite, out-of-the-way haunt, where the seafood was his favorite and the crepes hers.

During dinner, Luca sensed Valentina's distraction. "So what's up, *amore?* You seem far away."

Valentina recounted finding the scroll with Julia's signature. "Luca, this could be the find of a lifetime, but I don't want to step into the hornet's nest of Vatican politics. I don't know that we should pursue this."

Luca put down his fork and eyed Valentina. "That doesn't sound like you."

"Luca, my profession is littered with the corpses of academics who have crossed the Holy Office. And they have a special place in career hell for women who make inconvenient discoveries. A female bishop would be very inconvenient."

Luca reached across the table and took hold of Valentina's wrist. "You were assigned to find evidence as to the role of women in the church. You found it."

"Maybe. Maybe not. It's just a piece of parchment, so far."

"So, you follow the evidence and risk your reputation, or you play it safe and sacrifice your scientific integrity?"

"And live to fight another day." Valentina met his gaze. "If I don't come to the conclusions that Cardinal Ricci expects, he has the power to destroy my career, Luca."

Luca moved his hand to cover hers.

"By the way...did I tell you this?" Valentina asked, a sparkle in her eyes replacing the look of worry that had been there.

Luca laughed. "No, but it must be something good, by the look of you."

"I've been tracing my genealogy."

Luca laughed again. "Well, that's a change of subject. What does it have to do with...?"

Valentina laughed for a change. "This might sound a little silly, but my roots go back to an ancient Etruscan tribe—same time period as when this Julia lived."

"Does it."

"Yes, if you can believe that. I don't know, but I feel a bit connected to this woman. I want to know more about her, find out who she was. I feel I may even owe her that."

Luca drew back. "Owe her that?"

"Yeah, I don't know why. Just a feeling."

"It seems you've made up your mind, then. If the look on your face is any indication, I'd say that your heart is with looking into it."

"Yes, it seems so."

"Then you've made up your mind?" Luca asked.

"No, I haven't gotten *that* far."

On Monday morning, when the cabbie's car horn sounded to summon Luca, he said, "Let me know what you decide."

"I will. Call me tonight. Tuck me in." She wrapped her arms around him suggestively.

"I wouldn't miss it." He smiled, kissing her. "I know you'll do the right thing, whatever it is." Luca gave her a last kiss on the top of her forehead and off he went.

Valentina weighed her choices for another two days. It wasn't just her career on the line. Erika, who was always too impulsive, could see her career ruined as well. Their business, their laboratory, could all be lost. But she was a scientist, and she simply could not sacrifice her integrity, consequences be damned. She'd need to find a way to keep Ricci out of the loop for a while.

Valentina picked up the phone and called Erika. "I think we have to find this woman," she said.

Unsurprised, Erika said simply, "We can't do this on our own, you know."

"No, we'll need help. And I know just the person who's going to give it to us."

FIVE

"Ati," Julia called out while fidgeting with two bracelets on her dressing table. "Where is my veil?"

"Calm down, daughter." Vesia Lucinia stepped into Julia's spacious, second-floor bedroom. "It will not do for you to become overexcited."

"Oh, fiddle-faddle, Mama. A girl doesn't get married every day!"

Vesia gave her daughter a sideways glance. "Come. Sit with me. There are things we must speak of."

"Oh, Mama, not now," Julia said with a tap of her foot. "It's almost time."

"Yes, it is, and that's why you must listen to what I say."

Julia relented, heaving her delicate arms upward. Vesia led her daughter to the edge of the bed, where they sat down side by side.

"Julia, I want to be sure you know what to expect tonight." Vesia probed her daughter's face.

"Mama, please, you embarrass me. I am no longer a child. I know...."

"Still, I want you to be sure of your duties." Vesia cast her head down, looked at the hands folded in her lap, and then raised her eyes to her daughter's. "For me, the marriage bed has been a joyous place, but that is not so for many wives who find their marital duties most…uninviting. I do not know what it will be for you. I hope for the best. But if it is not, know that you must endure your duties, for heirs must be born. In time, after you have produced children, your husband will likely take his pleasures elsewhere."

"Surely not, Mama. I will love my husband, and he will love me. My marriage will be like yours and *Apa's*."

Vesia sighed. "You are still young, little one, and there is much you do not yet know."

"I will make Marcus a good home."

"Julia, you are a good girl, but you have always had a mind of your own. If you really want to make Marcus happy, you will put aside your headstrong ways and become an obedient wife to your new husband. It is expected of you and foolish to do otherwise."

A petulant look crossed Julia's face before she acquiesced. "You will see, Mama. He will be happy. We both will be happy."

Julia's mother looked skeptical. "I hope so. Now, time to get dressed." Vesia flicked her hand and rose with authority. She strode to a large cupboard that held the long, white gown Julia would wear to the altar.

Earlier, Julia's maid, Cassia, had powdered her mistress's face and piled her long, thick, brunette tresses tight and elaborately high on her head. As Julia slipped off her everyday *tunica*, letting it fall to her feet, Vesia stood by, holding the white, woolen wedding dress, ready to help her daughter into it.

At her mother's insistence, Julia had woven the dress herself. She had not been eager for the task. It was a tedious undertaking that provoked Julia's characteristic impatience. Many young brides-to-be were buying their wedding costumes, and Julia did not see why she could not do the same. But her mother had refused to allow it. "You must be proficient in all skills if you are to keep a husband," she had said.

Vesia knotted Julia's dress at the waist and fitted a garland of flowers to her hair. She kissed her daughter and then drew a sheer, flame yellow veil, a symbol of her virtue, over her face.

"I will leave you now, Julia. Wait here for your father." Vesia squeezed her daughter's hands and started toward the door. She gave one backward glance to her only living child and double-checked to see that all was in place and she had done her job well.

Vesia had tried to teach her willful daughter about the duties necessary of a Roman noblewoman, but she often ended up frustrated as Julia's determination won out. Knowing their daughter well, Vesia and Julia's father began to arrange her marriage as soon as she came of age, clearly aware that it would take some time to find a match.

And they were right.

For two years, Julia had exasperated her indulgent parents by rejecting all suitors brought before her. Now that she was seventeen, they had finally found success. In her parents' eyes, the perfect man had come along, and they would brook no refusal from their daughter. Her father put his foot down and ordered her betrothal to a thirty-year-old Roman nobleman, sight unseen.

Although Julia had put up a fuss, the notion of marrying Marcus Aquillius secretly thrilled her. He was descended from rulers of the empire, and she could anticipate a life of style and ease, moving about the many estates the Aquillii owned throughout Italy. While she had yet to meet her betrothed, in the way that young girls romanticize, she decided she loved him.

Julia looked around the bedroom that had so delighted her in the mornings as it caught the sun through a small window. Now, though, in late afternoon, her room seemed shrouded in shadows, almost as if it were fading from view. *It's as if this room is disappearing,* Julia thought. *I will probably never see it again.*

"Julia, you look lovely," her father exclaimed upon entering her bedroom and taking in the soft, pretty features that shone beneath her veil. *She's a beauty,* he thought. *This is but a glimmer of the woman she will become. Soon, she will be the most beautiful woman in Rome.*

"Let's go, little one." Gavius held out his arm.

"*Apa...*" Julia ventured, second thoughts entering her head.

25

"Now, never you mind. Everyone gets cold feet." Giving Julia a soft caress with his eyes, he said affectionately, "It pains me to give you away. But this is a great day, and you will be very happy." Casting a sideways glance at his daughter, he added, "You *must* make a success of it. Now, let us join our guests downstairs."

Cassia waited for her moment. She hadn't much time and dared not be caught. The kitchen staff, bustling about readying the meal for the first wedding feast, would be in a near panic. They would pay her no mind.

Cassia slipped silently out of the kitchen entrance and crept around the side of the house before taking off and running toward the stone wall that separated the house from the olive grove. Darting behind the wall, she hurried toward Quintus.

The Lucinius family had taken Quintus and Cassia into service just a few months apart, when he was fourteen and she only thirteen. Their attachment had formed right away, and over the next two years, their affection deepened. Quintus and Cassia had been scrupulous in their demeanor, though, and no one suspected their bond. As slaves, they would have found trouble in a relationship not approved by their owners. Now, though, they wanted to marry, but it would be impossible. Cassia's move to her mistress's new home would separate them.

Quintus was gathering firewood to keep the cooking ovens burning when he saw Cassia running to him. Even on this cold winter afternoon, he sweated under the load of wood he was carrying. Later, he would tie the stacks of wood into bundles and carry them over his shoulders to the kitchen.

"We must run away," Cassia sobbed as Quintus held her.

"And where would we go?" Quintus asked, stroking the back of her head. "How would we live? We would get caught, and we would die."

"We could find a way," Cassia said sorrowfully. "I could speak with my mistress," she said more hopefully.

"You must not," Quintus replied. "You know that you cannot stay and I cannot go with you. There is no other choice. You must leave with your mistress."

"I cannot."

"You must."

"But I cannot, truly. I cannot go away from you. I'll…I'll…."

Quintus broke away, gripped Cassia's shoulders, and fixed his eyes on hers. "Please, Cassia, do not think of putting yourself in danger. This is our lot. Go now. Please!" Quintus gave Cassia a little push as he released his hands. "Go."

Holding back gulping sobs, Cassia turned away and dragged herself toward the house.

Quintus watched, feeling a stone land upon his heart.

SIX

The Lucinius family shrine looked beautiful indeed. White flowers lent a sweet fragrance to the room, and many stanchions holding candles cast a soft glow in the early evening haziness. Incense burned, and garlands of grapes swagged from posts. A flute played as guests assembled in the atrium, their finery swishing and their quiet words of greeting to one another adding a low hum to the air. At the signal of a loud high note, the audience fell silent. The groom's parents and Vesia took their seats, and then Julia appeared on the arm of her father. Quiet echoes of "Oh!" and "She's beautiful!" sounded as father and daughter strode down the aisle. Gavius released his daughter at the altar and gave her a kiss.

Julia stood alone there and waited. And waited. As the minutes elapsed with no sign of the groom, she gulped in shame. Guests began to look around nervously, their loud whispers punctuating the air. Julia glanced at her mother, whose warm smile had frozen, and to her future in-laws, one of whom looked worried, the other embarrassed. When thirty minutes had passed with Julia still standing at the altar and guests turning restless with no sign of the prospective groom, Julia, with tears blurring her vision, gave a beseeching look to her father.

Gavius rose heavily. He turned and gave a long look to the Marcus's parents before addressing his guests. "I regret to say—"

At that moment, laughter and shouting was heard coming from outside. Marcus burst in, his wedding party in tow. Outfitted in a wide-striped toga, he nodded his apologies as he strode to the altar.

Gavius looked startled, but immediately came to himself. He shouted, "What is the meaning of this? Your lateness is intolerable. There will be no wedding today." He would not turn his beloved daughter over to a rogue.

Halfway up the aisle to the altar, Marcus stopped in his tracks, his faint smile dissolving.

Marcus's father leaped to his feet. "No, no," he shouted. "Surely there is an explanation, a reasonable explanation. My son…he would never behave dishonorably. *Numquam.*" Never.

Marcus's mother dropped her fan and slumped to the side. Her sister caught her and propped her back up.

"Please, hear him," Marcus's father pleaded.

Gavius turned to his wife, whose expression hadn't changed. With a barely perceptible nod, she indicated she wanted to hear Marcus out.

"Speak, then," Gavius said. "What purpose had you to arrive late for your wedding?"

Marcus strode to the altar and faced Gavius and Vesia. "Forgive me, please. The aqueduct at the city gates flooded the entrance and then stopped working altogether. A mess to clean up and then repair. I could not leave our citizens without water. *Ita paenitet me.*" I am sorry.

"So, you see," his father said, puffing his chest out, "you cannot blame the boy. He was doing his duty."

Gavius was not naïve and he doubted Marcus's excuse, but he turned to Vesia, who had put on a smile again. As the guests adjusted themselves and turned their attention toward the altar, Gavius said solemnly, "There *will* be a wedding today, and a celebration feast to follow." At that moment, Gavius decided he must seek out his lawyer to insure his daughter's future.

During the exchange between parents and bridegroom, Julia had all but been ignored. When she ventured a first look at her groom, she thought, *Oh! He is handsome indeed.*

"Where is Cassia?" Julia stomped her foot in annoyance that her maid was missing from the downstairs room. She stood beside her cloak, which hung on a hook. She needed Cassia to fasten it onto her shoulders before she stepped out on this cold night.

After the ceremony was complete and the bride and groom had shared cake at the altar, a raucous celebration began. Servants laid out platters of food and passed vessels of wine. Marcus danced once with his bride and then with all the other young virgins. Now the hour was late, and the guests were waiting for the new bride to emerge, after which they would all form a procession toward Julia's new home.

Cassia crept in.

"Where on earth have you been? I've been waiting for you." Julia's anger showed in her tone. It also showed from her hands planted firmly on her hips. "This is my wedding day, you know."

"Yes, mistress. I'm so sorry."

"Well? Where have you been?"

"In the…kitchen…?" Cassia answered.

"In the kitchen?" Julia wanted to know. "Is that a question? You're not sure where you've…?" Julia noticed the red coloring Cassia's cheeks. "Cassia, what is it? You've been crying?"

"Oh no, mistress, I haven't." Cassia turned her face away as far as she dared.

"You have been. I can see it. I demand you tell me what's wrong."

"I'm sorry, mistress," Cassia said. "It's just that it will be difficult to leave this house and the friends I care about."

Mollified, Julia said, "You will soon fit in at the Aquillius house. Don't worry. And remember, we'll be fitting in together."

"Yes, mistress."

Julia had treated her maid with kindness since Cassia had been assigned to her the year before. The wall separating mistress and maid had begun to crumble as Julia confided secrets to Cassia, and Cassia, an intelligent girl, had responded with clever observations.

"Well, fasten my cloak and let's go now. They're waiting for us," Julia said.

Cassia opened the door and Julia appeared, to the cheers of all the guests. She risked a peek at her new husband as he came forward to offer his arm.

A young slave boy carrying a pine torch led the procession to Marcus's home near the Capitoline Hill. The bride and groom and their parents and guests followed. Arriving at their destination, Marcus carried Julia over the threshold, while their families congratulated one another on what promised to be a most successful pairing.

Julia lit a torch, doused it, and tossed it among the guests. Then Julia said goodbye to her parents.

She entered her new bedchamber and sat down at her dressing table. Cassia removed her hairpins, letting dark curls fall to below Julia's shoulders, and then she left the chamber, quietly closing the heavy wood door behind her. Changing into a simple tunic, Julia ventured toward the great canopied bed. She climbed in and pulled up the thick coverlet.

Marcus caught his breath as he laid eyes on the bride he was seeing for the first time. Even through her veil, he could see her very large, dark eyes and her beautifully curved lips set against dove-white skin. She was petite and trim, though curvy enough. Her long swan neck displayed a determined-looking jaw. *She's damned beautiful,* he thought. *This marriage might turn into something more than a political alliance.*

Marcus Aquillius was still boyish at age thirty. His close-cropped dark hair framed his best features: an aquiline nose and smooth, pale skin. However, his coal-black eyes told the real story of Marcus Aquillius. Cold and unresponsive, his eyes seemed to say to others that he dwelled in a world only he was the center of, with everything else of little importance.

Now, in the early morning hours, disheveled and drunk in overindulgence, he had only one thought. *Best get to it.* He smirked.

It was late morning when Cassia woke her mistress. As she finished dressing Julia, there was a sharp knock on the bedroom door. Julia nodded for Cassia to answer it.

An unusually tall, unpleasant-looking man breached protocol and took a step into Julia's bedroom.

"I'm the house steward," the man said imperiously. "My name is Draco. Come. I'll show you the house."

Julia took an immediate dislike to this creature, noting his curiously heavy brows and a nose that looked as if it had gotten the short end of too many fistfights. She also noticed how he immediately sized up Cassia, giving her one long, slow look from head to toe. It was clear Julia would have to assert her authority early—now.

"No, please point the way to the dining room. Then you may go." Julia's tone was cold.

Draco flinched and raised his chin with a jerk.

As he began to retreat, Julia said, "Wait."

Draco stopped in his tracks with his back to her. "Yes?"

"My husband? Where is he?"

"He left early," Draco said.

"I see." Julia let a beat pass before she said, "Steward, you will face me and address me properly."

Draco slowly turned around. "Yes…Mistress."

"And *do not ever* set foot in my bedroom again. Now, go." Despite his near-threatening demeanor, Draco would be no trouble for Julia. Her mother had taught her well how to deal with servants.

"Let's you and I look around," Julia suggested to Cassia.

The house was very fine. Julia and Cassia walked past the bedrooms, each with brightly colored walls and vibrant tile floors, before coming to a hall with long windows and a mosaic floor that gleamed jewel-like. Farther on was the atrium. One of the walls displayed a painting of a bright yellow bird drinking from a small reflecting pool. Long stone benches faced each other in the middle of the room. The *tablinum* showcased portraits of ancestors and housed family records. They made a quick tour of the kitchen and lavatory before Julia sent Cassia to the servant quarters and sat down in the dining room, which had been prepared for breakfast.

As Julia rose from the breakfast table after finishing, she donned a hooded cloak and exited a side door for a walk through the gardens, bleak at this time of year. When she felt a presence behind her, she whirled around to see Draco ducking behind a wall.

SEVEN

Yigael Dorian sat with his feet up on a brown leather ottoman in his sparsely furnished apartment in the Jewish quarter of Jerusalem. He stroked the gray-and-white-striped tabby sitting in bliss on his lap while sipping a cup of fresh espresso made from the one luxury item he possessed: his Rancilio Silvia espresso maker.

Yigael was in a funk. He wasn't good with time on his hands, and he had plenty of that. Today was Friday, when lovers were anticipating Saturday night trysts and busy families were making weekend plans. At age fifty-three, Yigael had no lover, no family, and no plans. His wife, Ruth, and son, Abel, had been killed in a café bomb explosion thirteen years back, an event that tormented him as much this day as it had the day it happened.

After serving his two obligatory years of service in the Israel Defense Forces, Yigael had pursued his doctorate in archaeology and linguistics at Cambridge University. It was there that he met and married Ruth. A brilliant academic, he rose rapidly in the ranks of the Israel Antiquities Authority (IAA), leading major excavations throughout the Middle East. IAA provided the perfect cover, then, when the Mossad tapped him for intelligence work. Becoming a spy was a calling Yigael didn't covet, but having come from an ardent Zionist background, he had been taught that no one would protect the Israelis but they themselves. Driven by an unquenched thirst for vengeance over the death of his family, Yigael stepped away from any serious archaeological work and volunteered to take Mossad's most dangerous and deadly missions throughout the Middle East. A strong, husky man, but small in stature, Yigael moved stealthily into and out of kill zones with no notice. No one ever linked him or the Mossad to the hits he carried out.

Yigael was on leave after two espionage assignments failed. As an officer of the counter-terrorist unit, Kidon, he planned a hit on an Afghani war lord and sent two officers into the field. Unfortunately, the hit simply achieved the death of an innocent goat farmer and his family. Afterward, he led a group of Mossad officers into Syria to take out a scientist believed to have been working on chemical weapons, but the building he worked in turned out to be a hospital, and the "scientist" a medical doctor. The state of affairs had become so complicated that Yigael no longer knew who the bad guys were. Or was he the bad guy? He had been proud of his early achievements, but these latest missteps had depressed him.

"So where to from here?" he asked Abra. "I don't know."

Abra turned her yellow, almond-shaped eyes up to her adored master and purred. Yigael had picked up the scrawny little stray at Geha Junction. Barely six weeks old, the pathetic urchin had been cowering in a narrow alleyway. Yigael had reluctantly carted her home and installed her in his small flat. He had rescued her, but in a certain way, she had rescued him as well. If there was any peace in his life, it was through this small feline, and he had developed a real soft spot for her.

As Yigael sipped the last of his espresso, he spoke, as he often did, to his dead wife. "I'm making the world a safer place, aren't I?" He wanted so badly to hear her answer.

"How can the world be a safer, more peaceful place when violence continues?" he asked himself. *There will never be an end to all this. The world has always been at war. It looks like it always will be. So what am I doing?*

Over the weekend, Yigael came to the slow realization that no amount of killing his political opponents would avenge the murders of Ruth and Abel. He missed them as much as ever, but none of the retaliations had brought him peace. For the first time, in the isolation of his small Jerusalem flat, with Abra by his side, Yigael broke down and sobbed for the loss of his family. Somehow, the outpouring of his anguish settled him.

On Monday morning, he got up and donned a freshly pressed, dark gray suit and navy tie. He stepped outside, hailed a cab, and directed the taxi driver to the Har Menuchot cemetery at the western edge of the city. Yigael felt trepidation as he approached his family's tombstones, but as soon as he stood before his two loved ones, peace fell over him. At his son's gravestone, Yigael moved his lips for several moments before placing several small stones on top. Then he moved to the site of his wife. He brushed off her tomb and carefully laid down more stones. Yigael stayed for many minutes, and then thoughts began to pour in, unbidden. For the first time, he was sure that the words he was hearing were coming from his beloved Ruth: *"Yigael, find the joy in your life again. It is time. You needn't grieve further. I am fine."*

Then he heard Abel's voice: *"I am happy, Abba, and you should be, too."* Then his mind went blank. The words ended.

Yigael waited, yearning for further communication, but no words came. The energy he had felt coming—from where?—drifted away.

The next day, Yigael resigned from the Mossad and renewed his contract with the IAA.

One week later, having dropped Abra off with Esther Berlin-sky, who ran a boarding kennel and who adored the little tabby, he hopped on a plane for Paris.

Yigael stepped out of a light-blue cab at the Marriott Rive Gauche Hotel and Conference Center on Boulevard Saint-Jacques. He walked through the grand hotel's front entrance and checked in. Refusing a bellhop, he rolled his bag to an elevator and rode to the third floor, where he exited the elevator, turned a corner, and made his way down a long hallway to his room. He unlocked the door, placed his bags in a corner, and sat down on the edge of the bed.

With Mossad now in his past, Yigael was returning to his first passion: archaeology and the annual archaeology seminar.

Yigael freshened up, washing his face with warm water, toweling dry and changing into khaki slacks and a cobalt blue shirt. The conference was not scheduled to start until morning. With some free time, he headed for the bar and a coffee. Choosing a corner booth in the cozy ambiance of dark wood and leather, Yigael felt ready to relax.

Then he saw her.

In the center of the room on a barstool sat Valentina Vella enveloped in changing lights. Having immediately spotted Yigael when he entered, she swiveled, stepped down, and headed straight for him. Without a word, she took a seat across from him and crossed her elegant legs.

"Well, well," Yigael said, scrutinizing Valentina with his steely black, half-closed eyes. "I guess I shouldn't be surprised to see you at an archaeology conference."

"No, but that's not why I'm here. How are you, Yigael?"

"I'm well. And you?"

"Still mad at me?" The two had not seen one another since they had disagreed on the interpretation of an ancient text and had written opposing opinions for an archaeology publication. The academic response to the quarrel had supported Valentina's view, to the consternation of Yigael.

"No," Yigael answered. "I never should have been angry with you. Sorry." He looked right at her.

Valentina examined Yigael, taking his measure. *I have never known him to sound like this—vulnerable, somehow softer, and more human. Could that be possible?* Valentina knew the long and short of Yigael's life and career. As longtime friends, Valentina worried about Yigael's inability to emotionally move on from his deep grief. The two hadn't worked together in several years. She had tried numerous times to lure him back into archaeology, but she had failed. Therefore, while tracking him down this time, she was surprised and heartened to find that he was here at the archaeology conference.

Yigael asked baldly, "If you're not here for the conference, then why have you come to Paris?"

"To see you, of course," Valentina answered.

Yigael's eyebrows snapped up. "Whatever for?"

"Dinner tonight. We have a reservation at Lasserre. Eight o'clock."

With that, Valentina slid from her chair, picked up her small clutch, and walked purposefully toward the door.

EIGHT

Heads turned as the tall, auburn-haired woman stepped through the front entrance into the elegant Lasserre. Valentina was dressed to kill in a stunning black, long-sleeved, knee-length cocktail dress with a V-neck and a pattern of black beads at the waist. Red suede stilettos and a wide platinum bangle inset with tiny rubies finished her look.

The maître d' led her to the table she had requested, the one with the most privacy, in the corner beside the gold, ceiling-high drapes. Yigael, always early, was waiting for her. A snifter filled with single-malt Scotch sat half-consumed on the white linen tablecloth. Yigael stood, acknowledging his colleague's presence, and the two seated themselves.

"I'm going to have the fish," Yigael announced. "The braised sea bass. And you?"

"Please, Yigael, give me a minute here. I'd at least like to get a drink in my hand."

"Yes, of course. You look lovely, Valentina. How is Luca?"

Valentina smiled. "Ah, too far away at the moment. Just left for Vienna."

After ordering a champagne cocktail, Valentina perused the menu quickly. "I think it's going to be the spiced duckling with roasted figs. Yes."

The two spoke little as they tucked into a dinner considered the best in Paris. Ordering a *soufflé au chocolat* to share and knowing that they would have to wait at least twenty minutes for its puffy emergence from the oven, Yigael said, "Well, haven't you kept me waiting long enough?"

Valentina laughed. "I couldn't interrupt this gastronomic delight with conversation." She was amazed when Yigael told her that he had left the agency, though he provided few details.

"Quite," Yigael agreed.

"We have a new project," Valentina revealed.

"We?" Yigael asked grimly.

"Mhmm. You and me," Valentina said.

"Right," Yigael said. "And just what do you have in mind?"

"A dig. Potentially."

"Oh no," he protested, raising his hands. "I've had enough digging for a lifetime."

"Then what are you doing here at an archaeology conference? It looks like you might be stepping back in."

"I was meeting someone." Yigael was halfway to a pout, to the amazement of Valentina.

"Meeting who?"

"You," Yigael said.

The two burst into laughter and then Valentina got down to business.

"So let me get this straight," Yigael said forty-five minutes later. He pushed aside the empty ramekin that once contained the heavenly soufflé and picked up his third espresso. "First, you come across an old scroll tag that looks, ah, fishy. You examine the scroll and find a short letter written by a Julia to the pope. You speculate that this Julia could have been a bishop—a female bishop, no less—and then you tie her to Julia Lucinia, mistress of the Herculaneum villa. This Julia has disappeared from all records. You have no idea where she is buried, but you want me to find her. Am I correct?"

"That's about it," Valentina answered.

"And you think that I have not only the interest but the magical powers to do this?"

"I'd say." Valentina nodded.

"Well, isn't this just a pip of an idea," Yigael remarked, pausing for several seconds. A rare wide grin spread across his face. "I like it."

"Thought so." Valentina smiled, glad to have him aboard.

Yigael scrubbed the conference and flew to Rome.

In the short time between leaving Paris and arriving in Rome, IAA had issued papers for Yigael as Deputy Director of the IAA and Senior Excavating and Research Archaeologist. With these in hand, he headed for the Vatican, where he was waved through.

The Vatican libraries, fondly known as the Vat to researchers, is a sprawling complex, recently renovated to equal the finest research libraries in the world. Composed of a disorienting warren of grand halls, subterranean bunkers, spiral staircases, office and reading rooms, high tech laboratories, and glass-tiled data centers, the library represents the entire breadth of the history of Western Civilization.

Separate from the main libraries, the Vatican Secret Archives—a misnomer because nothing there is secret—is located under the Vatican parking lot. These archives contain more than fifty-two miles of bookshelves holding millions of papal missives, documents, and letters. The oldest and most precious of the letters and papers in the archives are stored in climate-controlled lateral files, more than 75,000 of them.

Yigael found Valentina and Erika in their workspace in the underground bunker where the most ancient papyri were preserved in cool, dark, humidity-controlled vaults and specially designed storage units. They both wore sweaters in the cool, dry room.

"Yigael!" Erika jumped up and, much to his consternation, wrapped her arms around him in a warm hug. Then she passed him the scroll, which she had re-housed in its Plexiglas case.

Yigael studied the scribbled-over tag. Then, he sat down and read the ancient Latin. He looked up for a moment and then down at the letter again. He reread it. He did not have to compare the handwriting with that of Julia Lucinia. If Valentina told him they had a match, that was good enough for him.

Prior to his arrival in the archives, Yigael had reviewed a report that Paula Kirkpatrick had sent to Valentina and Erika on what she could find out about Julia. The reference to a Julia in two letters added punch to the idea that she existed. *If so*, Yigael thought, *it's time we find her, for history's sake*. He looked up and locked eyes with Valentina.

"You're on," he said. "I have to make a phone call."

NINE

Professor Jacques Ignatius pushed the classroom door open and rushed through. He had just finished a lecture to students at American University in Paris. The only class he taught, it was sandwiched in between his lengthy research sessions.

Jacques seemed always preoccupied, behind schedule, and a bit bumbling. That's the way his students viewed him, anyway. But that was a cover. While his research into the ancient world was real enough, Jacques was also a valued Mossad operative delivering intelligence from informants he had cultivated over two decades. Far from the bumbler, Jacques organized his days to the letter and always watched his back.

Just as he reached his office, he heard jingles from the mobile phone he had left behind on his desk. Hastening through the door, he reached for his phone and glanced at the caller.

"Hey," he answered. "I've been meaning to get in touch. What's this about your leaving the agency? I never would have thought—"

"How soon can you get to Rome?" Yigael interrupted.

Caught off guard, Jacques said, "What for?"

Ignoring Jacques, Yigael said, "Can you meet me tomorrow in my office?"

"What, no sooner than that?" Jacques replied.

"Jacques, I need you here."

Jacques sighed. "Got it. Yes, I can do it."

"Okay. We'll talk when you get here."

"I'll call when I land."

Yigael and Jacques had history together and many missions in common. Theirs was an easy relationship—as easy as one could get with the cantankerous, demanding Yigael. Their good- natured wrangling was entertaining to those who worked with them and could only have come because the two were alike in many ways. Both were loners, inept at small talk, and stuck in work.

The next morning at eleven, Jacques boarded an Air France Airbus for the two-hour flight to Rome.

After leaving the archives, Yigael took a cab to his office in the old San Lorenzo district of Rome. He had chosen this area, considered drab by many, to get away from the touristy city center. He had an affinity for the large student presence and the bohemian-artsy ambiance. The office had served him during his years with Mossad, and he saw no reason to give it up now.

Yigael's first instinct was to decline hearing what Valentina had to say, but as she began her dissertation about Julia, his interest picked up. Valentina's intensity was like a magnet drawing him into the mystery. And the pursuit was something he couldn't resist. Piecing together history was exhilarating. It made each day one to look forward to. Ignoring the search would be impossible.

Yigael understood the potential risks Valentina would face if her research led her to conclusions that went against Church doctrine. He had no interest in taking down the Church or causing controversy. As a scientist and an archeologist, however, he was driven to find whatever was long buried and bring truth to the surface."

Yigael felt that he could track down this woman by drawing

a chronology of social, political, and religious life of the time and placing Julia within the historical period. From what he already knew about her, he could reasonably discern other things about her life. If he were especially lucky, he would soon know where she was born, where she died, and much of her life in between. *A challenge, though,* he conceded.

Yigael needed Jacques on board from the get-go, since the professor would be in charge of the field search team should they identify Julia's likely burial place.

Valentina prepared a plate of fruit and cheese that she could nibble on in the quiet of her flat as she considered her next steps.

Her cell phone rippled. One look at the display and a smile replaced her look of concentration. "*Ciao, tesoro. Ti manchi.*"

"*Ciao, bella. Anche tu mi manchi.* Any chance you can get free and fly up here this weekend?"

"Not a chance. Yigael's in town, and we've got to have a few strategy sessions. Maybe you can come down next weekend?" Valentina asked hopefully.

"I've got a trade summit in Brussels that weekend. What about...no, I suppose you're going to be tied up for a while in Rome."

"I promise we'll make up for it when this is over. We need a month on a desert island."

"With nothing but naked beaches," Luca said with humor.

Valentina laughed. "Perfect."

"So, do you have Yigael hard at it?" Luca asked.

"You know him. I'm relieved he signed on because I don't know who else I could have turned to." Valentina balanced a half-glass of Pinot Grigio on her plate and headed for the sofa setting her snack on an end table. "He's drawing up a plan and I have to do the scary part."

"And what's that?" Luca said.

"The funding. I've been debating how I'm going to get Cardinal Ricci to pay for a search for a female bishop. He's not likely to cotton to that." She laughed at the thought

"How about telling him you've found evidence of a first-century bishop that isn't in the register of bishops? You don't have to say that the bishop might be a woman. He'll be intrigued."

"That's exactly what I was thinking. He'll want to know more, of course, like where we would search. He won't be able to fund without knowing that."

"Well, give Yigael a little time to nail that down."

"Oh, yes. He'll find her. I've never known him not to."

"There's one big question I have. I know you've thought about it," Luca said.

"What question?" Valentina asked.

"You'll have to deceive the cardinal to take this on," Luca said. "I wonder whether you can do it."

"Oh, that," Valentina said. "I have thought about it and it scares me to death. But I will do it."

Luca roared with laughter. *"Che è la mia ragazza."* That's my girl.

After the two rang off, Valentina had a final thought. She knew that she would have to maintain total secrecy so that Cardinal Ricci would not find out what they were really up to. Currently, there were only five people who knew about the discovery in the archives: Erika, Paula, Yigael, herself—and Luca, of course. But as others were brought in on the project, as they would need to be, word might leak.

I must guard against it as best I can, she thought.

Valentina rose to clear away the plates and tidy up the kitchen, but as she considered what lay ahead, she collapsed back down onto her sofa, burdened by the intensity of it all.

"Jacques." Yigael clapped his friend and colleague on the shoulder, which was a reach up Jacques's beanpole frame. "Thanks for coming."

"As if there's a choice when the grandmaster rings." Jacques's eyes gleamed as he smiled.

"Hey, hey, none of that. I thought you'd be delighted get out of your drab little lab and into the world," Yigael said. "Come." He gestured toward a black leather armchair. "Espresso?"

"Not yet." Jacques wanted to hear what Yigael had on his mind.

"I'll have some," Yigael interrupted. He kept a second high-priced espresso machine in his office and headed toward it. Within minutes, his efficient movements had produced perfection. A rich aroma filled the air as he lifted his cup.

"Tell me about the agency," Jacques said to Yigael's back. "You quit?"

"I did. Thank you for asking."

Nothing more would be said. Jacques was sure of that. He knew—they all did—the torture Yigael had suffered in the deaths of his wife and son. No one dared venture into that territory. That door was clearly shut. Apparently, so was the one dealing with the agency.

Yigael carried his cup to a matching black leather chair adjacent to where Jacques sat and got right to it. He divulged the puzzling letter found in the archives by Valentina and Erika and related what little they knew about Julia.

"The mission is to find her," Yigael ended.

"Needle in a haystack," Professor Jacques said as he steepled his fingers in front of his nose. "Where are we staying?"

"Villa San Lorenzo Maria."

"Nice."

TEN

The next morning, Jacques took his laptop out to a wrought iron table in the hotel garden and began his search. He thought his best chance would be Ariadne, an online register of archeological databases. With so few data points, however, the query could take forever. He typed in what little he knew, and started the databases running. In the meantime, he scoured every online research database he had access to, running multiple queries in Lexus-Nexis, WorldCat, Proquest, and every major university library catalogue, hoping to find some mention of Julia. Finding nothing, he kept his computer running and headed toward a handful of administrative offices in Rome that still kept original documents, on the off chance that one of them would mention her. One problem lay in the fact that very few documents that old still existed, and of the few that did, most were fragmentary at best.

In the quiet of his office, Yigael began his own search by assessing Julia's possible background. Creating a chart on poster board, he listed a chronology of events between AD 50 and 110, figuring that Julia had to fit within these years. He noted the years of significant historical events and religious dealings in Rome, and then jotted down all emperors and religious leaders next to their years of rule.

He slid Julia's name into slots he knew as fact. There wasn't much—documents found at the Herculaneum villa signed or written by Julia in the general time frame of AD 64–70, and a Roman court document dated AD 67. Yigael could place Julia in Rome in the general timeframe of AD 85–96, because of her letter to Clement and the two additional documents Paula had come up with.

Then what happened?

Yigael had just finished his timeline when Jacques knocked on his office door.

"Nothing," was all he had to say.

"Valentina came up empty, too." Yigael held up his chart. "So I guess this is it. This is all we've got."

Seated in the leather side chairs, Yigael and Jacques reviewed the chart now leaning against his desk. Yigael reached for a red Sharpie and drew a circle around the date AD 96. "We don't know anything about her after this."

"Well, what happened to her?" Jacques asked.

"Between 96 and 98, Emperor Domitian allegedly began harassing the Jewish and Christian communities, shaking them down for taxes."

"If he did, that would have been the beginning...."

"Yes, but we don't know for sure. We *do* know that he exiled or executed Roman nobles who were believed to be adopting Jewish ways."

"But where does Julia fit in?" Jacques asked.

"If a Roman noble became a Christian, he or she was considered dangerous and became an enemy of the state."

"Dangerous times for our Julia, then."

"Precisely. Especially if Julia were actually a bishop. Living in Rome, she would have been in danger." Yigael rose from his chair and stepped toward the window. He watched a couple of students enter a family pizzeria located in the center of this dreary street.

"That fits with Domitian," Jacques said.

"Well, we don't know if he led a full-scale persecution, but if he did, he came after my people as well."

"The ones who could get away fled to Ostia," Jacques said.

"Yes, the nearest bolt hole was Ostia, no question," Yigael said.

"So. We have Julia. A Roman citizen. A noblewoman. A Church bishop. Too close to Clement, perhaps. She comes to the attention of Rome?" Jacques said.

"And if she does, she's dead," Yigael said.

"But if she escapes," Jacques said, "she flees to Ostia, where she can vanish."

"My people would have hidden her. They certainly hid a number of others."

"So we go to Ostia."

"We do."

Yigael realized that he was operating more on intuition than fact. But he had always depended in equal measure on both, and his intuition had served him well in the past. "She's an old woman at this point. If she gets to Ostia, she never leaves. She dies there."

"There's an ancient synagogue in Ostia Antica. She might be in the necropoli near there. Maybe the Isoli Sacra?" Jacques said. "Excavations have been going on for years."

Yigael rubbed his hands together in anticipation. "We'll organize the search."

Yigael briefed Valentina and Erika by phone. Afterward, he and Jacques began to assemble the search team.

⸻

It never ceased to amaze Valentina how Yigael could so specifically and exactly conceive a master plan for any operation. She did not think to question his strategies, as he was consistently so precise. But perhaps it was not so surprising after all. As a spy, he knew how to make logical yet risky decisions quickly.

Valentina knew that many vied for excavation funding and only plans that were considered sexy—bringing prestige and media attention—would get the limited monies available. Well, her proposal was certainly sexy, but she'd need to find a way to sell it that did not show her hand. One week later, when she felt ready, Valentina coolly picked up the phone.

ELEVEN

"Julia," Marcus said as the two were breaking their fast with porridge, cheese, and honey- sweetened bread. "I'm thinking to create a *contubernium* between Draco and Cassia. They have worked together for nearly half a year. I have seen the interest in his eye. She is a strong girl. They should produce healthy, hardy slaves. Please see to it."

"What?" Julia stammered. "What are you talking about?"

"You heard me."

"But what if Cassia doesn't want to live with Draco? She is only fifteen years of age."

"Julia. Do not protest in this. I will not have it. Just do as I say," Marcus ordered, raising his voice. Marcus had become used to Julia's meddling in his management of certain of their affairs, but he had always won out by ordering his wife to her duty.

Julia was taken aback. Marcus had never before made demands where her personal maid was concerned. She considered such interference off limits.

"Husband, I will talk to Cassia about living with Draco, but that is all I will do for now. We will meet again to speak of this."

With the day's events before him and a reception scheduled

for evening, Marcus reluctantly let Julia have this small victory. Heaven knew he had larger battles to wage.

Changing the subject—he didn't want to dwell on letting Julia have her way—he asked, "Is all in readiness for our guests tonight?"

"Marcus, is not everything always ready for your guests?"

"Yes, actually." Secretly amused by his wife's feistiness as long as it didn't interfere with his own schemes, Marcus rose from the breakfast table and headed for their small household shrine.

As Julia passed by the shrine a few moments later, she smiled secretly at her husband and his religious rites. I've never seen anyone so bound up in his prayers, she thought. He prays to so many gods, you'd think he was the wealthiest, most powerful man in the realm.

Marcus Aquillius was an ambitious man, keen to flatter his superiors while holding in contempt anyone he thought beneath him. Even as a boy in school, he was known to be a bully among his peers, while the masters heaped praise upon his swollen head. He was perfect senatorial material and determined to wear that laurel. For the moment, though, he had to be satisfied with his administrative post as an elected aedile, responsible for maintaining public buildings.

As May turned Rome warm, Julia's marriage chilled, and her idea of romance fizzled. Marcus had been aloof from the start, talking with her only about household affairs. She yearned for affection, but Marcus was cold as stone. Still, he was respectful, and for that, she was grateful.

Tonight would be yet another of Marcus's famous soirées, meant to impress the high and mighty. Julia sighed. *Another party, another four casks of the finest wines and foods! I hate these affairs!*

As an educated woman and inquisitive by nature, the superficial nature of these gatherings left Julia bored silly. Though she did her best to be a charming and gracious hostess, the wives of Marcus's associates were banal creatures, endlessly interested in nothing more than gossip and infighting. Julia managed to make these women feel comfortable while evading their catty rounds of character assassination. Well liked by all, she was becoming sought after as a beautiful and admired guest at their social circles. Julia wondered whether she would ever find women with whom she could enjoy laughter and meaningful conversation.

After her husband left their shrine, Julia made an uninspired trip there. She began her prayers, but soon gave up for lack of interest and a preoccupation with Marcus's instruction about Cassia. While Julia had argued with her husband, she knew she would have to accede to his wishes. She just hoped she could ease her maid into the situation.

After checking on the state of her household and the dinner preparations for the evening party, Julia went to her room with Cassia to fashion her hair and get dressed. As she was slipping on her bracelets and attaching an elegant shoulder broach to her fine silk *stola*, she stated to her maid in a falsely casual tone, "The master wants you to begin, ah, living with Draco, as a couple. We should be making arrangements."

Cassia froze and then drew back. "Please, mistress, n-no." Her voice was a whisper.

"Why not, Cassia? What's wrong? Surely it would be all right."

Cassia gulped. "Please, mistress, do not make me do this, please." A tear appeared.

"Cassia, decorum, please! I married a man I didn't know. You have known Draco for some time now. Do not make me force you to do this. I would be pleased for you to enter into this willingly."

Cassia steadied herself. "I cannot. Never. Do to me what you will, but do not ask this of me." Cassia's voice was chillingly dull.

Julia took her maid's hands and pulled her closer. "Cassia, speak to me. What is it?"

She turned Cassia's hands palms up and glanced down. A small red slash crossed the girl's wrist. Suspicious now, Julia pushed up Cassia's sleeves, and what she saw shocked her. Bruises marred both of Cassia's arms.

Julia locked eyes knowingly with her maid. "Anywhere else?"

Cassia shook her head no. She looked at her feet, ashamed. "The steward has made advances. Every day he corners me when no one is around. I fight him, but he continues. I am afraid of him. I hate him…and," she added with a wail, "I love another."

Oh dear God, Julia thought. She dropped Cassia's hands. "What is this about?"

"It's true," Cassia said, shamefaced.

"Ah." Julia gazed at her maid with a combination of exasperation and compassion. "Someone at the house here?"

"No, mistress."

"Who then?"

"Quintus," Cassia said softly, looking down.

"I see," Julia said, the light dawning. "And this was the reason for your distress when we moved here?"

"Yes, mistress." More tears streamed down Cassia's cheeks.

"But you have managed to see him anyway, haven't you?"

"I see him on my half-day each month."

"And you know that these, ah, visits put you in peril?"

"Yes, mistress," Cassia whispered, a gulping sob escaping her.

Julia walked to her window and stared out. She turned to her maid and said sternly, "Go now. See to your duties. Speak to no one, and *try* to look more cheerful."

Julia felt conflicted. On the one hand, her maid was obliged to follow her mistress's orders. To defy or refuse instruction was unthinkable. On the other hand, Julia herself despised Draco. How could she order her maid, a young girl whom she loved, to submit to this malevolent man? Julia was not surprised that Draco had forced himself on Cassia.

Then there was the matter of the man Cassia loved.

Julia sighed again. *What will I tell Marcus?*

TWELVE

Julia had much to think about, and she wanted to do it alone. The next morning, she left for the marketplace in her lightest linen tunic and *stola*, a blue *palla* covering her head. For the first time in her married life, and quite against custom, she set out unaccompanied. The day had turned unusually hot and steamy for May, and Julia dabbed at the moisture covering her brow.

Visitors to Rome, the heart of the empire, already filled every conceivable space in the city center. The sharp scent of just-picked lemons pierced the air. Freshly baked bread tantalized the senses, while meat searing in cook shops and vegetables arranged in colorful mosaics in open-air stalls drew in crowds.

As Julia maneuvered through the hordes, she was mindless of the noisy haranguing of orators and poets, the shouting of merchants, and the noisy beating of cobblers' hammers. Once, she felt a tug at her arm just as the crowd jostled her, and she almost lost her balance. She looked down to see a small boy scurrying away from her. She would find when she returned home that her copper bracelet was missing.

The party ran into the early hours of the morning, and Julia had not been able to discuss her maid's state of affairs with

Marcus, and for this she was glad. Overnight, she had determined the course she must take, but now she had to determine how to present her case to her husband. Of two things she was sure: To protect Cassia, she would not speak to Marcus of Quintus. But Draco must leave their house, for she would not tolerate violence within it.

Julia was weary when she arrived home from the markets and a bundle of nerves when she reclined to dinner with Marcus that evening. While she had gone head to head with Marcus on many previous occasions, this was the first time she would deliver an ultimatum.

"Marcus," Julia said, settling into her cushions upon the couch in the family's *triclinium minus,* the most intimate of her home's three dining rooms. She kept her voice low and level. "Yesterday I spoke with Cassia, as I said I would, and the result was most revealing."

Marcus frowned and raised his brows just as he was about to take a bite of fish into his mouth. Instead, he let it fall back down onto his plate. "Is that so? Whatever do you mean?"

"Cassia has bruises on her arms," Julia told him calmly. "Dark, angry bruises. And Draco caused them. He's has been assaulting her, harassing, and threatening her since we arrived here. I've only just found out." Julia met his eyes dead on, refusing to act the part of the submissive bride.

"Hah!" Marcus chortled, dabbing his lips with his napkin before tossing it aside. "I knew he had an eye for the girl. All the more reason to pair them up."

"Marcus, how dare you!" Julia jumped up, put her hands on her hips, leaned across her dinner plate, and declared loudly, "I will *not* have my maid battered and bruised by the brute you use to run this house. Never! I demand he be removed immediately."

Marcus had had enough. In a fit of temper, with his face red and his veins pulsing, he leapt to his feet and threw over the small dining table, their dinner and glasses crashing to the floor. He lunged toward his wife but stopped short and backed away.

He had come horribly close to a blow to Julia's face, but in the best households, men did not show violence toward their wives. If he were found out, it would not bode well for his future. "Sit back down and resume your place in this house as my consort and hostess. Your opinions are not important to me, and your demands will not be tolerated." With this, he casually sat back down and picked up his chalice of wine.

With an outward calm she didn't feel inside, Julia took her seat and looked at her husband directly. "Marcus, listen to me carefully, for I mean this: it is either Draco or me. If you refuse me, I will move out of here and take Cassia with me. *And* my dowry. *And* my father's political support."

As soon as she was sure he understood those ramifications, she continued, "Once this becomes known, I will make certain that the Aquillius household will be talked about as one that tolerates the most decadent of behaviors, one that allows its servants to do as they please. Our friends and your colleagues will perceive that you are unable to control your servants, and they will perceive it as a weakness. Think of what that gossip might do to your reputation. It seems that you would want to guard against that." With this, she smiled with a malicious coldness.

Marcus raised his glass as if to toast his wife and then smashed it against a wall.

Julia didn't flinch.

Seeing that she refused to be intimidated, Marcus moved to leave the room but at the last moment had second thoughts. He had no doubt that his headstrong wife would carry out her threat. He could not afford to lose her father's political support.

Marcus turned back, his words taking on a desperate tone. "Why?" he shouted. "Why are you behaving like this?"

"Isn't it obvious?" she said, seated calmly, voice modulated.

"It isn't. Not to me."

"Marcus, even if you do not care that Cassia has been violated, I do. This is my home, and I will not live in a home where young women risk being assaulted, even if they are only serving women."

For all his bravado, Marcus was a weak man. It showed in his petulance when things didn't go his way. "But Draco is the best steward I've had," he whined. "Good ones are hard to come by."

"He may not be as trustworthy as you believe," Julia countered. "Cook has complained to me about wine that has gone missing from the storage cellar. She has accused your precious Draco, since he is the only other one with a key to it." With this, she chose a fig that had remained on a serving platter and took a bite.

Marcus, conceding defeat, made a sarcastic bow toward his wife. *"Domina,* thank you for defending the honor of my household." Then, an ugly sneer returning to his face, he spat out, "But I warn you, do not try my patience again." Marcus rose and stomped out of the room.

Julia took a deep breath and sipped from her water glass. She was shaken. Marcus was within his rights to marry the slaves off however he wished. As a wife, her preference in this was of little import in either law or custom. Cassia, as a slave, had no say whatsoever. And Julia knew in her heart that had Cassia been fortunate enough to have been born in a fine home, with noble parents, and had Julia been born to a commoner...well, it might have been Julia falling into the arms of some brute at some master's command. She shuddered.

THIRTEEN

Rome AD 57

Cassia looked out Julia's bedroom window and saw the sun shining on her mistress. She watched as Julia carried a basket of herbs collected from the garden over to the rose bushes planted near a border hedge.

She turned away from the window and began to put away her mistress's clothes, just delivered by the laundress. Only two days before had Julia confronted her, and Cassia was trying to control her emotions. At the same time, what lay ahead terrified her. A light rap on the door caused her to jump. Then the door opened, and the young slave, Orin, poked his head inside.

"The steward sent me to have you make up the large guest room," he instructed.

"But that is not my station," Cassia protested.

"And that is not my problem," Orin retorted with a grin. "I guess you had better take that up with him." Orin's head disappeared, and the door closed.

Cassia had no illusions as to why Draco had ordered her to another room. Cassia dropped down onto Julia's bed and buried her face in her hands. She felt trapped and helpless.

Without further delay, because she knew that lateness would incur even more wrath, Cassia hurried to the guest bedroom.

63

Relief filled her when she found no one there. However, as she began her tasks, the door swung open and Draco appeared. Moving quickly, he closed the door behind him and stepped toward Cassia. She forced her eyes closed and wished that she were somewhere else.

Draco grabbed her arms and forced her down onto the bed.

Cassia struggled. With all her strength, she freed her arms and struck at Draco, trying to slap him away.

Amazed by her grit and enraged at her impudence, Draco viciously forced Cassia to submit. As he yanked at her skirt and tore at her undergarment, the door cracked open.

Orin immediately took in the scene and, mortified at his break-in, quickly pushed the door closed. His voice squeaked as he passed Marcus's orders through the closed door. "Steward, the master is asking for you. He wants to see you immediately." Orin hustled away.

In a pique, Draco pushed himself off Cassia and stood glaring down at her while he organized his disheveled dress. Cassia turned her eyes upward and avoided Draco's look.

"Next time," Draco snarled at the quivering girl.

Draco was unconcerned that a lower servant had discovered him in a compromising position. Exiting the bedroom and seeing Orin scurrying down the hallway, Draco called out, "Why didn't he come to me himself? I am the steward. He doesn't speak to other servants. He speaks only to me."

Still putting space between himself and the steward, Orin responded, "I know only that he asked for you to see him in his study."

Draco looked wary. He never liked the unexpected. *What could the master want? he wondered. I have tended his home well. I have kept the others in line and punished them when they deserved it. I have been heavy handed sometimes, maybe. He might have found out about the wine. But it's fair compensation, considering all I do. Draco was skilled at self-justification. If that's it, I will blame it on someone else…the new servant, Milo.*

When Draco was gone, Cassia moaned in misery. She faced the wrath of her mistress and the master over Quintus, and she faced further demeaning assaults at the hand of Draco. Feeling dizzy and still trembling, Cassia straightened her clothing and ran weeping back to Julia's room.

Marcus stood at the window in his study and watched his wife cutting roses of *Paestum*, which she would arrange into a centerpiece for their evening meal. The basket of herbs lay at her feet.

It's certainly not shrubbery I'm interested in this morning, he thought as he stood with a jaw clenched over the upset in his household. He didn't like being put on the spot, certainly not by his wife. But now, Marcus was more enraged with the knowledge that his steward had been stealing from him. Now he had an untidy task to perform.

Marcus did not much care about his steward's outside activities as long as they didn't disturb the running of his house. He knew that Draco could be brutal, but Marcus saw that as an acceptable way to keep the other slaves in line. When it came to stealing from him, that was another matter entirely. Draco would pay a heavy price for it.

The curtain separating the atrium from the *tablinum* was open. Draco walked through. "Master, you asked for me?"

Marcus turned from the window and appraised his steward. When Draco saw Marcus's expression, he swallowed hard. He had committed so many offenses within this household that he didn't know which one had surfaced. But Draco was sure from the look on Marcus's face that at least one of them had.

In a barely controlled tone, Marcus said icily, "You are to be transferred immediately to my orange farm in Messina, where you will work the fields as a farmhand."

Dumbfounded yet stoic, Draco protested, "But I have served you well, master. Why?"

"Not *well*, steward, as I have only now learned. You are lucky I am not having your head. You know the price for stealing."

"Stealing?"

"From my wine cellar," Marcus said.

"But, master, that was not me but the new servant, Milo. Pray, I would not—"

"You say you would not. But as my steward, you would neglect to report theft by another?" Marcus challenged.

"Master, I would have, but the new servant threatened—"

Marcus sneered at Draco. "Gather your clothing. You will leave in the morning." With that, he brushed past Draco.

Shaking with anger at the thought of being stripped of his position, Draco waited for a few moments for Marcus to disappear. Then he headed to the workshop. On the way, he bumped into Babudius, his cohort in misconduct.

"What?" Babu asked, seeing the hateful expression on Draco's face. "What has happened?"

"The master, that loathsome miser, Marcus Aquillius is sending me away. He is sending me away to die in the fields."

A look of understanding passed over Babu's face.

"It was the wine," Draco answered in near desperation. "He found out. For all the years of loyal service I've given him—"

"It's not the wine," Babu interrupted. "At least, not all of it."

"What? What do you mean?"

"It's Cassia."

"Cassia. But she would say nothing," Draco blurted out. "That's nothing."

"It was *something* to the mistress," Babu confided.

"What do you know?" Draco pressed.

Babu looked from side to side, making certain that they would not be overheard. Then he leaned in close to Draco's ear. "I overheard a conversation last night at dinner between the master and Julia."

"Of what did they speak?" Draco demanded.

"Shush." Babu raised a hand to stifle Draco. "Of Cassia's injuries. The mistress insisted you be dismissed for causing her harm."

Draco's eyes widened in sudden understanding.

Babu continued, "But you don't know the full story."

"Tell me."

Babu again looked about searching for unwanted listeners. He saw no one. "The master planned to marry you to Cassia, but when the mistress saw her bruises, she demanded otherwise."

The witch. So that's why I'm being sent to the ends of the earth. In a venomous whisper, Draco said, "I will get my revenge."

"Not here you won't," Babu warned.

"I'll kill the *puttana* tonight," Draco said, referring to Cassia.

Babu grabbed hold of Draco's arms and shook them. "You will not get away with it."

"I will be in Ostia by this time tomorrow and on a ship to Messina the day after. They will not catch me," Draco said smugly.

"You put yourself in peril," Babu hissed. "The maid is always close by her mistress. You cannot carry it out without notice. They will catch you before you leave."

Draco considered this. "There must be a way."

"She's a whore," Babu said. "Cassia is screwing one of the Lucinius slaves, Quintus. Expose them, and the master will kill her himself."

Draco looked thunderstruck. He presumed that he knew all things in the Aquillius household. "How do you know this?" he growled.

Babu shrugged. "They meet in the olive orchard outside the Porta Flumentana on the Via Aurelia on the first Sunday." He grinned. "I like to watch."

Draco scrutinized his cohort. "Don't say a word to anyone else. You have one more job to do for me."

FOURTEEN

Rome AD 57

Quintus turned slowly and ceased stacking wood when he heard footsteps approaching. A young man stood before him, a man Quintus didn't know. He was obviously a slave, outfitted as he was in a cheap woolen tunic.

Quintus squinted under the bright afternoon sun. "What can I do for you?"

"I was told to bring you this," the young man answered. He held out a sealed note.

Quintus looked curiously at the man. "And who are you?"

"I am Orin. I come here from the Aquillius...."

At the mention of the Aquillius name, Quintus grabbed the note.

> *Meet me in the grove just after dark tonight.*
> *Cassia*

This was most unusual. Quintus had never received a written message from Cassia before. Indeed, he had no idea what her hand looked like. He looked up and asked, "Who gave you this note?"

"Babudius gave it to me. He said it was urgent," Orin answered.

If the note had come from Draco, Quintus would have been suspicious. He knew very well from Cassia the grotesque assaults she had to bear at the steward's hand. Quintus hated the steward and wished, to no avail, that he could defend Cassia.

"Thank you, Orin. Tell her I'll be in the garden at nightfall."

Orin bowed slightly. Then, realizing with embarrassment that he was standing beside another slave and certainly didn't have to bow, he turned and sped off.

Cassia entered the workshop with her mistress's jewel box in hand. It had a broken hinge and Julia wanted it fixed. Cassia stopped dead in her tracks when she saw the master there with Milo, the new servant. Cassia had never seen Marcus Aquillius in the working quarters before.

"So sorry, master." Cassia turned to leave.

"Wait," Marcus commanded, giving attention to Julia's maid for the first time.

"Yes, master?"

"What do you know of the wine stores?"

"Forgive me, Master. I—"

"Draco has accused this man," he said nodding in Milo's direction, "of filching the wine, and he will say nothing. What do you know?"

"I know that Milo has nothing to do with the wine," Cassia claimed boldly, refusing to look away from her master.

"Oh, yes? How do you know this?"

"I have seen Draco in the cellars and drunk on your wine many times."

"And you have said nothing?"

"Master, my orders are to report to the steward, Draco."

"I see," Marcus considered, recognizing the futility of pursuing that line of questioning.

Marcus gave Milo a long look and, without a word, took his leave.

"You didn't have to," Milo said to Cassia. "I can take care of myself."

"Of course I did," Cassia responded tartly. "*You* weren't doing a very good job of it, were you?"

It was dusk when Quintus arrived where he and Cassia always met. Cassia had not yet appeared, and Quintus sat down, resting his aching back against an olive tree. It was quiet in this place, but not completely dark, as a full moon, with its yellow glow, gave life to the grove. Quintus sensed that even though Cassia had not yet come, he was not alone.

Approaching from behind, Draco stepped stealthily toward Quintus. As Quintus heard a twig snap, he turned sharply. In an instant, he knew he had been duped. Then Draco was upon him, wielding a club with fury, battering Quintus's body until it lay lifeless before him.

The search for Quintus began at dawn. Vesia Lucinia refused to believe that this young slave had simply run away. Quintus was dependable and always eager to please. When Vesia questioned the servants about his dealings on the previous day, she learned that Quintus had left the estate at dusk. For where, they knew not.

Vesia dispatched the entire household to look for the boy and report to her when they had news.

At the same early hour that the search for Quintus began, two guards armed with short swords arrived at the Aquillius home to escort Draco to Ostia. Unseen by anyone, the three men set out for the port city. There, the guards would turn Draco over to a contingent of armed watchers who would see that he was aboard a ship to Messina the following morning.

Marcus Aquillius was in his office at the Forum that afternoon when an aide mentioned to him that a slave had gone missing at the Lucinius estate and had turned up dead in the olive grove. The information sparked Marcus's curiosity, since the incident involved his wife's family.

"Who was it?" Marcus asked his aide.

"A young slave named Quintus," his aide responded. "Well thought of, too, he was. Surprised everyone when he ran off, but now it looks like he didn't. He was murdered, beaten to death."

Details of the incident caused a chain reaction and much commotion in the Aquillius household when Marcus returned home that evening.

When she learned of Quintus's murder from her husband, Julia leaped up from her dining couch and charged out of the room in search of Babudius. Perplexed by his wife's reaction, Marcus followed her.

It hadn't taken Julia two seconds to grasp the implications of the murder. She knew immediately that Draco was responsible. He had wanted Cassia for his own, but he couldn't have her and had been sent away instead. Obviously, he had learned of Cassia's and Quintus's liaison and had taken his revenge first.

Julia grilled Babu when she found him in the kitchen. "What do you know of this? You knew the steward best."

"They were up to something," Cook declared as she removed a

hot pan from the oven. "Seeing their heads together..."

"And just what were you up to?" Julia interrupted, not taking her eyes off her servant. "What do you know of Quintus's death?" she insisted heatedly.

"Julia, just what is going on here?" Marcus demanded, barging into the kitchen and banging his head on one of the overhead pots. "Damn it all," he yowled in pain.

"Be quiet, Marcus. Babudius, you had better be forthcoming this instant."

"Mistress, truly I have no knowledge of this and no part in it."

"We will see about that."

"Julia, what on earth?" Marcus exclaimed, holding the aching bump on his head. "What possible interest could you have in a slave at your parents' house?"

"Be quiet, Marcus," Julia said again.

Orin was unlucky enough to enter the kitchen at this time, and Julia whirled to face him. "Orin, what do you know about the murder of Quintus, a slave at the house of Lucinius?"

Orin's eyes widened and his face turned pale. "Murdered! I saw Quintus only yesterday."

"And how would you have seen this man?" Julia asked bluntly.

All innocence, Orin looked from one to another of those assembled. He cowered slightly when his eyes came to rest on the master.

"A note," he said, returning his eyes to Julia. "I carried a note to him. Babudius gave me a note to take to Quintus. Quintus read the note and said, 'I will be in the garden tonight.'"

Julia whirled around to face Babudius again. "Do you wish to change your story?" she hissed.

Understanding nothing of what was happening in his kitchen but seeing that Babudius was lying to his mistress, Marcus seized control. He would find out what was going on in his own home or else.

"Orin, summon Milo to the kitchen," he ordered. "Julia, wait for me in my study."

By the late evening hours, life had settled down in the Aquillius household. Milo had taken Babudius to quarters and was watching over him in order to prevent escape. Orin had been dismissed for the night, and Cook was fanning herself at the kitchen table, wondering at the alarming events disturbing her world. She had just finished mixing vinegar and water together into a vessel, but now her *posca* failed to interest her and sat untouched at her elbow.

In their chambers, Marcus listened closely to Julia's litany of events with surprising calm.

When she finished, he said, "Wife, just why did you not consult me when you found out about Cassia's liaison with Quintus?"

"Marcus, she is my maid. She came with me from my family home. She is under my control and my protection. I will see to her."

Marcus sighed. He had enough on his plate and was glad to hand off punishment of the maid to Julia. "Be sure to handle her well."

"Yes, Marcus," Julia said contritely, relieved that a battle over this issue was one she would not have to wage.

The next morning, Marcus issued an order for the arrest of Draco. He sent for the Vigiles Urbani, the watchmen tasked with guarding the city and capturing runaway slaves. Three officers, centurions all, were dispatched to Ostia to hunt down Draco and drag him back to Rome. They found him wandering the ports, seeking a ship to make his escape.

Marcus didn't spend much time deciding what to do with the offending slaves. Because their crime had been visited only upon a lowly servant, Marcus decided to be done with it—a trial would be vexing and take up too much time. He would simply send them both away with a more severe punishment.

Upon Draco's return, Marcus ordered him and Babu branded. The two would be sent to Messina to work as chain laborers. Milo was appointed their escort, and by the time the two boarded their ship, Draco was grimacing and gripping two fingers he would never quite be able to use again.

~~~

The night before, Cassia had been putting away jewelry in the now-repaired jewel box, unaware of the household goings-on. It fell to Julia to give her maid the distressing details about the death of her lover, Quintus. When she did so that morning, her maid bore it stoically.

Cassia had expected death for the both of them. For Quintus, it had happened—not as she had anticipated, but it didn't matter. He was gone. Her fate was still to be decided, and Cassia predicted, even hoped, that she would die, too.

Julia looked into the contorted face of her maid. There was much she wanted to say, but she would leave it for later, when Cassia's grief had subsided and she might pay attention. Julia refused to insult her maid by plying her with empty platitudes.

"Cassia, I do not pretend to know what you feel. I have never suffered a loss such as yours. But there are two matters I must address. First is your terrible loss. Second is your disregard for the rules of the house. I have considered these things and have come to a decision. I hope it is the right one."

Cassia looked at her mistress respectfully but without interest.

"I am sending you home to your family. I expect you to work hard there, to help your mother and father, and to guide and teach your younger sisters and brothers. You will immerse yourself in their lives and be comforted in their presence. In three months' time, you will return here, and no word will be spoken again of this matter. But know this: no further infractions will be borne. Now, pack your things. You leave in the morning. Milo will see you home."

FIFTEEN

Father Orio Rinaldi stuffed a bag of chocolates into the bottom drawer of his desk, flicked the wrappers of those he had eaten into the trash, and hoisted his hefty girth out of his chair. He rapped on the door of Cardinal Antonio Ricci's dark, wood-paneled office and poked his head inside.

"Your Eminence, Valentina Vella wants to meet with you before her next regular appointment," the cardinal's secretary informed his boss. "Something about a new discovery and funding for a search."

Cardinal Ricci raised his eyebrows. *What?* "Schedule her in." *What the devil could she have found?*

Cardinal Antonio Ricci had always been a man of ambition. He'd set his sights on the top spot from the first day he'd served as an altar boy, and since that time he'd schemed to stay ahead of those who were just as ambitious as he was. Ricci had muscled his way onto the pontiff's ridiculous Study Commission on Women's Ordination and managed to take the lead as coordinator and research director. As a staunch defender of Church doctrine, the idea of female priests was abhorrent to him, and he intended to shut down debate on the subject once and for all, and without having his bias questioned.

Hiring Valentina and Erika had been a masterstroke. The two women were tops in their field and reputed to be to be utterly apolitical. Erika was unknown to him, but he knew Valentina to be a child of Church parents. The fact that he'd hired two women for this work would set to rest any arguments regarding his bias against women.

In fact, Ricci liked women very much, and Valentina in particular. He'd followed her work with interest and had finally met her when the two found themselves on a panel discussing the tricky and varying ownership laws among nations pertaining to new archaeological finds. Ricci was not immune to Valentina's beauty, nor was he impervious to her intellect. He'd had the opportunity of meeting with her on several occasions and sought out her company whenever the opportunity presented itself.

At a dinner reception in London, the two found themselves at the same table and he'd had a marvelous time. Drinking too much wine and enjoying the company of a beautiful woman, he initiated a heated and friendly debate about certain Church restrictions and found himself confessing doubts about its strictures regarding sexual chastity in the priesthood. He'd made a fool of himself, but Valentina had taken it lightly. He was forever grateful to her that his words had never come back to him. She had kept them to herself.

While she waited to be escorted into the cardinal's office, Valentina mulled over how she had deliberately set the stage for the cardinal with the teaser about a search. She wanted the seeds planted before she approached him so that he wouldn't be taken off guard. These old men rarely responded well to surprises.

Valentina looked up as Father Rinaldi appeared from behind Ricci's office door and beckoned her forward. Rinaldi was always amusing to look at. *Like a gnome,* Valentina thought. He was a round little man with a bald pate and a bulging midsection that pushed against his cassock. *I don't like him,* she thought. *When he is not surly and rude, he is toadying up to someone.*

Cardinal Ricci gazed at Valentina and, without rising, motioned for her to sit down. As she walked toward a chair adjacent to his, Valentina had to curb a smile at the striking differences in appearance between Father Rinaldi and his boss. She wondered how they could get along, even if appearances weren't everything. The cardinal was tall and lean, with a long neck on very narrow shoulders. He kept his salt-and-pepper hair slicked straight back. High cheekbones and fine, narrow brows might have dictated an aquiline nose for a nearly perfect visage, but instead Cardinal Ricci had been endowed with a short snub nose, which made him look slightly ridiculous.

Between them sat a small table laden with tea and pastries. "If you would prefer coffee," Ricci began.

"No, this is fine. Thank you, Cardinal."

Father Rinaldi poured the tea and then gestured toward the lemon and sugar.

"Both please, Father, but just a little," Valentina said.

Rinaldi added a bit of sugar and set a lemon wedge on the side of the tea saucer.

Cardinal Ricci exchanged pleasantries only until the door closed behind Father Rinaldi, and then he got right to the point. "You've found something."

"We have."

"Let's have it." Ricci straightened against his chair back.

"Well, it's quite off subject of what we were hired to find, yet I felt we could not ignore it."

Ricci breathed a sigh of relief, a smile warming his face. "So, tell me." He leaned forward.

"Cardinal, we found a letter bearing the signature of a Church bishop that we've never heard of before."

"What?" Cardinal Ricci shook his head slightly. "You what?"

"We can't be sure yet, but it appears to be a letter to Clement."

"An unknown Bishop! Good God. What is his name? How did he sign the letter you refer to?"

"A tag on the letter refers to a Julius," Valentina hurried on, "and we have clearly identified the document as from the first century." She knew the hook was set. "We've done a bit of research and know where our new bishop may be buried."

"All that in so short a time?" Cardinal Ricci looked astounded.

"Yes, Cardinal. We believe our bishop may have been martyred. The timeline points to the persecutions under Domitian and coincides roughly with the martyrdom of Clement. That trail leads us to the port of Ostia." With this, Valentina went silent and simply waited.

Ricci calculated. This had nothing to do with why he'd hired these women, but by Jove! The discovery of a martyred bishop would draw attention away from any women and bolster his reputation. *This will provide testament to the men who had died to found the Holy Mother Church. This discovery couldn't be better for me.*

"Who would lead the search?" He was in.

Valentina hesitated. "Yigael Dorian."

Ricci groaned. "Is there no one else?"

"He's the best."

"He is. I'll grant you that," Ricci admitted. However, he was uncomfortable with this Israeli agent. The relationship between the Vatican and the Israeli state was often uncomfortable, for myriad reasons. "Where is Yigael now?"

"He's here in Rome, assembling the field team."

"Anyone I know?"

"You know them all—that is, all but the volunteers. They haven't been selected yet."

"You are quite presumptuous," Ricci remarked, giving Valentina a sly look while repressing a smile.

"Eminence, I hope you'll forgive me, but I felt confident that you would want to proceed, and that beginning to organize quickly would serve you well." Valentina gave Ricci a glance from underneath her lashes and handed him the necessary grant application documents, all t's crossed and i's dotted.

She's making me forget who's boss here. I need to run to confession every time I spend time with her. "This will need to go through the proper channels before we can attain funding. It's not up to me alone." He frowned, his voice brusque as he waived the sheaf of documents at her.

Valentina bit her tongue. This was not something Ricci would want his name on in the end, but she could not refuse him. She hesitated before agreeing. "Of course, Cardinal."

To Valentina's surprise and delight, Ricci pushed the grant through in record time, with the Pontifical Academy of Science approving the funds within three weeks.

SIXTEEN

Rome

The last member of Yigael's field team to arrive in Rome for a meeting was Anna-Marie Mannes. Since she was taking the hour-long train ride from Orvieto, where she'd been on a short holiday and because Yigael was staying close by the Stazione Roma Tiburtina, he decided that they would meet at the Hotel Delle Provence, a ten-minute walk from the depot.

Valentina was early and the first to arrive. She allowed herself a tiny rush of excitement that this undercover scheme was kicking off. She felt a little like a spy and was smiling secretly to herself as Erika strolled in.

Within a half-hour, the seven colleagues had assembled. The best of the best, they had all worked together on one adventure or another.

The field team leaders consisted of Jacques and three seasoned experts, drawn from several different disciplines, ranging from history, art history, and geology, to archaeology. All were knowledgeable archaeological investigators. Yigael had worked with them in his various travels. They were tough, smart, and flexible, and he could call on them in a moment's notice. Anna-Marie Mannes, Philippe Gaston, and Carol Connors would each lead a group of volunteers. Jacques would oversee as on-site supervisor.

As they all enthusiastically greeted one another, Yigael scurried around the edges like an impatient kindergarten teacher waiting for his class to settle down. Yigael rearranged the chairs and guided his flock toward them. Valentina and Erika were well aware of Yigael's obsessive perfectionism, and they shot each other knowing glances.

Edgy as ever, Yigael got to the point quickly. He had already briefed Anna-Marie, Philippe, and Carol about whom they were seeking in Ostia's old burial ground, and he didn't need to repeat himself. He reiterated that they must maintain absolute discretion. The volunteers, all graduate students, would be told nothing, except that this was an Ostian dig in ancient burial grounds.

"Any questions so far?" Yigael asked.

The team leaders gave each other a brief glance before shaking their heads.

"We're good," Philippe said.

"Okay then," Yigael responded. "Let's get to it."

Before detailing the search itself, Yigael showed his group the encryption software that would keep their email secure. He distributed to each a new Android smartphone, which would keep their data and phone conversations protected.

He then handed each team leader a list of their student volunteers, explaining that he intended to remain in the background. Next, he handed them an aerial-view rendering of the Ostia Antica and then instructed, "We have five necropoli associated with Ostia. The Porta Romana has already been played out, so we can skip it. One team goes to the Isola Sacra site, and another team goes out on the Pianabella. Take the largest team there, because most of that site hasn't been excavated yet. Keep an eye out for anything that might be an isolated tomb site. There are a few in this region. Divide your grids into square-foot segments, and assign two volunteers to each zone."

Then Jacques took over, coordinating the groundwork. "Philippe, you'll take care of ordering the equipment. Carol, I need you to buy work boots and clothing. Get pants and shorts, because the weather is changeable right now. Get sizes from the volunteers."

Jacques assigned Anna-Marie the personal items for the crew: cameras, thermos flasks, large-brimmed hats, waterproof gear, sunscreen, pocket notebooks, and pens.

Normally, Jacques would arrange for the needed permits for their activities, but Cardinal Ricci had used his influence with the mayor of Ostia to fast-track them. He had arranged for everyone to bunk in at the castle of Julius the Second, located next to the archeological site.

The old medieval castle, originally built for defending the coast, had been turned into a papal residence. Over the years, it had served as a barn, a prison, and now an exposition space and tourist attraction, with a section set aside as a dormitory for Vatican guests, students, and visiting scholars. The rooms were stark, almost bleak, but mindful of his budget, Ricci determined that these would suffice.

A big plus in staying at the castle was that they could walk to the search site. The drawback was that there was no one there to provide meals. Jacques told Philippe to hire a cook for breakfast and dinner at the castle and to put together box lunches for the field.

"We'll work Monday through Saturday, seven to six," Jacques added. "Sunday is yours."

"Okay," Yigael said, "have we missed anything?"

"As if," Erika mumbled to Valentina.

Hearing no questions, Yigael said, "Let's go."

"Yes, let's go—to lunch," Valentina called out. "Follow me."

All seven rose. Six of them followed Valentina out of the meeting room and onto the streets, where she led them on a short walk to the Trattoria Monti.

Yigael took off in the other direction. He would check out of his hotel and return to Jerusalem. One never knew how long a search would last, and he preferred to wait it out at home.

SEVENTEEN

Rome, AD 58

Julia had hoped that the birth of their first child would bring her and Marcus closer together, but it was not to be. Marcus wanted a son and blamed Julia for failing to give him one, which was outrageous as all knew that it was the father who planted the seed. The mother was only the soil. He was disenchanted with Livia Marca, the new baby girl, and paid her no attention. Marcus's hopes were revived, though, when his wife became pregnant again early the next year. Surely, he had succeeded in planting a son this time.

Until the birth of her baby daughter, Julia had continued to live in the shuttered, narrow world of the ruling class, but this new arrival gave her respite from the cold indifference of people in that class. She became immediately captivated with Livia and refused to relinquish care of her to a wet-nurse. Livia became Julia's reason for being, and through her daughter, the new mother began to feel rejuvenated. In spite of this, she was still lonely for adult companionship, for connections that spoke to her soul and her intellect. Her wish for a true friend and companion was answered in a most unexpected manner, and the bond was to become deep and profound.

Milo sat in a quiet corner of the workshop, repairing a filigreed dish. Though large and muscular, he was good with his hands, equally competent in repairing the most delicate object or in re-roofing an entire villa. He figured that was why he had been transferred from the Aquillius villa in Herculaneum to the house in Rome. Always something to fix.

It hadn't taken long for Milo to make a name for himself at the house in Rome. Marcus had sensed qualities of leadership and loyalty in Milo and had promoted him quickly to be the new steward. On the surface, Milo was a mild-mannered, soft-spoken slave. Underneath, unseen by all, was a core of steel with a resolve that would never waver. He vowed one day to be free.

As he worked on the fragile dish, Milo let his mind wander, as it often did, to his idyllic upbringing in a small Gallic village. His peaceful life had changed when the Romans marched in, pillaging, raping, and murdering the villagers.

"Milo, whatever are you thinking about? You look miles away." Cassia stood at the workshop door. "Never mind, come quickly. The mistress needs you."

Milo glanced up at Cassia, gave her a smile, and rose up from the table where he'd been working. He was heartened to see that Cassia seemed quite her old self. Perhaps she'd put the past behind her.

Milo found Julia in the dining room with a monthly calendar spread before her. "We have some scheduling to do," she said to her steward. "Come and sit."

Just as Milo was taking a place opposite his mistress, Julia changed her mind. "It's stuffy in here. Let's go to the garden for a bit."

"Yes, mistress," Milo responded. "Perhaps I should return to—"

"No, no, I want some company. Come along." Julia hoisted herself up from the heavy chair, her protruding belly limiting her flexibility.

Milo followed his mistress out into the courtyard. The spring sun burned brightly.

Julia beckoned Milo to a bench adjacent to her. She considered the house steward for a moment, this man with whom she felt growing harmony. Yet she knew so little about him. "Milo, we've worked together all these months. Tell me, how did you come to us? And do you like it here?"

Milo averted his eyes. "It is not my place to like it or not like it, mistress. I have no say. I do what I'm told."

Julia knew very well the truth of her servants' lives. But that truth had never been said straight out to her, and she felt taken aback by Milo's blunt reply.

"Yes, well," she said with a far-off look. "But tell me, how is it you're here? You are from another land. I hear it in your speech, though not too much."

"I came here from Gaul as a boy," he answered. "I learned your language and have been speaking it ever since."

Julia kept her eyes on Milo. "What of your mother and father? What brought them to Rome?"

"They never came to Rome, mistress. Only I did."

Julia asked curiously, "But why?"

"When I was fifteen," Milo said, "my mother and sister died beneath the hooves of Roman soldiers, and my father and brother were speared. I was rounded up with other boys and marched to the sea. It took many days and many died of starvation along the way. When those of us who survived arrived at a port, we were thrown onto a barge loaded with cattle. And then we were sold off as slaves. I ended up in Herculaneum."

Julia breathed deeply. A haunted look darkened her face. "I had no idea," she said, her discomfort palpable.

Though Julia knew that warm relationships between masters and servants were in no way out of the ordinary, something troubled Julia about her relationship with Milo. There was wrongness about any person owning this man. He was becoming her friend, and she simply could not consider him to be her property.

With Milo as her house steward, he and Julia formed a

formidable team in the household. With his administrative skills and her meticulous planning, the house of Aquillius now operated with military precision.

For the many evening banquets she hosted that summer to further her husband's career, Julia set down new rules. Gone were the nights of drunken debauchery. Only orderly, dignified behavior would be tolerated. If guests found these peculiar restrictions confounding, they said little, preferring instead to accept them as it meant mingling with the great upper crust. At first alarmed by his wife's idiosyncrasies, Marcus's misgivings gave way to grudging admiration as he watched political leaders and military giants queue up to be in her presence.

If Marcus's social life was on high, his political career seemed to stall. For three years, he had put his time into a position that was well beneath his station, yet no one had seen to his emergence onto a larger stage. He blamed Julia and, as his frustration grew, his sniping was dished out to all members of his household. Increasingly, he spent his nights drinking, gambling, and whoring. While his time in office hadn't been deemed noteworthy, his indiscretions won him the attention he'd been seeking. Within a year, he'd received a promotion—far away from Rome.

EIGHTEEN

Ostia, AD 59

"Marcus, I am eight months pregnant. You cannot expect me to travel in this condition," Julia said as Marcus gave his wife news of his rise to proconsul and governor of a Roman province in Asia.

"And why ever not? You seem to be able to do everything else you set your mind to."

"Marcus, it will be most difficult, and Livia—she is just a year old. Surely you can see that we cannot travel at this time."

"Why oh why did I marry such a contentious creature?" Marcus said with a sigh. "Other wives would not dare to protest their husbands' orders," he added with a bit more venom.

"I am not other wives, Marcus."

"Indeed not. But I have no intention of refusing this post, and I will take my family with me," he said, forestalling her next objection. "Make haste. We leave in a fortnight."

Resigned, Julia turned away, thinking about the plans she must make.

On a hot August morning, Julia and Marcus, followed by Milo and Cassia, who held the bundled up toddler, Livia, in her arms, boarded a cargo ship in Ostia for the trip to Ephesus. Milo and Cassia were the only servants going along. The others would stay in Rome. Marcus planned to find additional help in the Asian slave market.

As the craft left port, the skies cleared and the sun shone brightly on the sparkling sea. Nevertheless, the Mediterranean could be unpredictable, and in two days' time, a storm came upon the vessel, bobbing it about like a cork.

Motion sickness took its toll on all of them, but Julia fared the worst.

"I don't think I can take much more of this," she complained to Cassia at the end of their second day at sea. Julia was keeping to her bed in the cabin assigned to her and Marcus.

Cassia bathed her face with a cool cloth. "It will be all right. This is the worst of it. It'll be over soon. You'll see."

But Cassia, for once, had got it wrong. Within a few hours, Julia's contractions began. Cassia told Milo, who summoned Marcus.

"Damn and blast," Marcus cried out upon observing his wife, pale and in pain. "This had to happen here?" Mindful, though, that Julia was about to give birth to his hoped-for son, he rushed out to scour the ship for help. He found no success locating a doctor or midwife. He had to settle for a heavyset, gray-haired passenger named Placidia who boasted that she'd given birth multiple times and knew all about it.

"Nothing to it," Placidia claimed to those who had gathered when they'd heard that a woman on board was in labor.

With no other choice, Marcus pulled her into the cabin. "See to it," he ordered before departing.

Julia had expected to deliver her baby in Ephesus, which, as the second-largest city in the empire, boasted the finest physicians. She knew that giving birth in these conditions would be risky. She shuddered. "What's to become of me and the baby?"

"Now, never you mind," Placidia said as she bustled about the tiny cabin. She ordered Cassia to see the captain for olive oil, sea sponges, and woolen cloths for swaddling the baby. "I suppose it's too much to hope that there's a birthing stool on board, but ask." As Cassia turned to leave, Placidia added, "Get some herbs, too, the stinky ones."

Placidia called on the deity Juno Lucina to preside over the delivery, and as she did, as was the custom, she let her hair down and loosened her clothing, a reverse binding ritual to induce labor. Julia, too, unbound her hair and clothing in order to relax.

Placidia patted her own ample stomach, intending to be reassuring. "Seven, all told, came from right here." Placidia's enthusiasm was peaking. She rolled up her sleeves, pushed Julia's knees up, and parted her thighs.

Julia grimaced.

With Marcus on deck and Milo minding Livia, Placidia and Cassia tended Julia for an excruciating eleven hours. When finally the baby appeared, Marcus entered and was the first to notice that his second child was not the boy he had hoped for. With a clenched jaw and saying nothing, he departed the cabin and spent the remainder of the voyage on deck.

The slightly premature baby, Flavia Marca, got on surprisingly well, but Julia did not. Afflicted with a fever, she plunged into a fitful sleep from which she could not be roused. When the ship reached harbor, Marcus dispatched Milo for help. Julia was transferred to a temple, where a doctor tended her and others offered prayers, hoping to save her life. Several days later, the doctor determined that Julia would survive but would never again bear children. It was well into the next year before Julia felt well enough to venture into her new surroundings.

When she began to explore Ephesus, Julia found it to be a thriving, prosperous, multicultural port city. Ephesus was a melting pot filled with people from all over the region: Greeks, Romans, Egyptians, and Jews, Nubians and Nomads, and others the likes of which she had never seen before. There were shrines to every god or goddess imaginable, with the most exquisite honoring the goddess Artemis. With not much else to do, Julia visited them all. With Marcus preoccupied and distant, she began to socialize with the women of her station, but became bored with their frivolous gossip and soon bowed out of their gatherings. Milo, who could distract and comfort Julia, seemed to have turned his attention elsewhere—she had no idea where. In time, she became depressed and began keeping to her room, leaving the care of her girls to Cassia and the wet-nurse.

After a few weeks, Milo knocked on Julia's door. He found her gazing out a window at the unfamiliar landscape. "My lady?"

"What is it?" Julia asked irritably. "You have certainly made yourself scarce lately."

Understanding that his mistress was troubled, Milo said in his quiet way, "Mistress, would you accompany me to a place you might find interesting?"

"Where?" Julia inquired listlessly.

Milo smiled mysteriously but said only, "This evening at seven."

In the wealthy section of Ephesus, private gatherings were being held that the Romans deemed subversive. The members were being watched, and some of them had even been arrested.

Milo was blind to the risk he was taking by attending the gatherings, because what he was getting was far more important to him than what he was risking. For the first time in his life, he had friends he could be himself with and share his dreams with—particularly his dream of freedom.

He hadn't known when he'd first walked into this home that he was becoming part of a budding sect. They called themselves "followers of the way." Others labeled them heretics, subversives, even atheists. Some called them Christians or Nazarenes. He didn't care what they were called. He knew only that his life was becoming something to be valued. Through the camaraderie he enjoyed there, he was coming to understand that freedom from slavery was one thing, but freedom existed in more than one sense. It was also a state of mind, wherein one's thoughts and daily behaviors could become indicators of a fulfilled life. Milo was beginning to see that he might even be able to attain happiness.

Milo had a particular affinity with the woman who seemed somehow in charge. Her name was Prisca. She was educated and worldly, but these things seemed unimportant to her, as she demonstrated a straightforward friendliness with all around her. Milo sensed a particular wisdom in Prisca, and he thought that Julia might benefit from it.

"Where are we going?" Julia asked. She and Milo had walked into an upper-class neighborhood where she noted the presence of soldiers in the shadows. "I don't like it."

"There's no trouble here," Milo assured her. They approached a large home. Milo rapped on the front door with the bronze knocker. Julia put the thought of the soldiers out of her mind as the wooden door opened and a smiling woman of just about her own height peered out.

"Milo, come in." She turned to Julia. "I'm Prisca. Welcome."

Julia gave a start and flashed back to Adrianne, her adored older sister who had died when Julia was only six. *This woman is so like her,* she thought. *Her eyes, their shape, they are Adrianne's.* She brought herself back to the moment. "Hello Prisca. I am Julia."

"Please, come in." Prisca then turned and hurried away, seemingly intent on something that needed dealing with right away.

Milo and Julia entered the house through a passageway leading to the dining room, where a group of twenty was gathered. Milo introduced Julia. They sat quietly and listened to the light banter of the others before being served a meal.

"Who is that?" Julia whispered to Milo, referring to a bald-headed little man with a pointed beard sitting at the far end from her. He seemed odd to her.

"You'll see," Milo replied. Julia looked at Milo curiously.

After the meal, everyone rose and filed into the reception room.

Prisca stood before the group and waved forward the man whom Julia had noticed earlier. Upon closer inspection, Julia could see that the dark-skinned man was short and slender with bushy eyebrows. *He is far from attractive,* she thought. *Yet there is something about him. Yes, he is appealing in an odd way.*

Prisca clapped her hands once. "Glad you're all here to welcome Paul. We don't often see our Paul anymore. His travels take him far from Ephesus these days, and so it is my pleasure to present the man who has, more than any other, brought the word of Yeshua here and to the world."

Whatever is this? Julia gave Milo a surprised, slightly scathing glance. Julia had heard of this growing movement, but she knew nothing about it. She was sure, though, that she was in no trouble. Milo would never subject her to danger.

As Paul spoke, his words shocked Julia. They ran counter to everything she had been brought up to believe. Julia had entered this home with a fixed set of principles she had never questioned. Her world was one of many gods, magic, and sorcery. Men dominated with absolute authority and wielded their power unyieldingly and brutally. Julia had accepted her way of life and thought about it very little. But Paul was presenting a creed altogether different.

He talks of one God, like the Jews do, Julia thought. And he speaks that everyone is equal in this one God's eyes, whether fine man or slave. He honors women as well as men, seats masters and slaves together without respect to their rank. How can they claim to worship with no temple? No god would ever take this seriously!

Paul hurried out after his talk.

"Where's he going in such a rush?" Julia asked haughtily.

"He's always on the run," Milo said. "I brought you here to get acquainted with the hostess. She's someone I think you'll like."

"No, I don't think so," Julia said. She watched as Prisca busied herself with the others. "I want to leave."

With reluctance, Milo stood to go home. Julia followed him out, but gave a backward glance toward Prisca. She felt vaguely drawn to the woman and didn't know why. At the same time, she felt suspicious of this group, and when she saw the soldiers still watching as she turned toward home, she shivered and told Milo not to bring her back.

NINETEEN

Ephesus, AD 59

When Marcus summoned Julia to his study the following morning, she wondered what was on his mind. He rarely sought her out anymore because of his displeasure that she would produce for him no sons. *Perhaps he'll be complaining about the rotten oysters last night.* She sighed.

Julia found Marcus at his writing table, fingering a document that, by his sour expression, portended no good news. Marcus looked up at his wife and, unusually for him, flashed an empathetic look before remembering himself and returning to his usual stone-cold countenance.

"Your mother is dead," he stated flatly.

"What?" Julia looked stricken. "How?" She gripped Marcus's desk to steady herself.

"She was taken ill some time back. She died a fortnight ago."

Julia moved to an adjacent chair and sat down heavily. "I must go to my—"

"The funeral is done," Marcus interrupted. "No need for you to go. Your father has interred your mother's remains in your ancestors' mausoleum." Marcus shoved the document to one side and picked up another, an apparent signal for her to depart so that he could get on with other matters.

"I must go to my father," Julia said in a low voice. She rose and left the room hurriedly before Marcus could respond.

Julia went straight to her bedchamber, distraught that she would never see her beloved mother again. With trembling hands, she tried to think through her next step, but her mind was muddled. Finally, all she could do was sob over her loss. She kept to her room through the rest of the day and at last fell asleep, exhausted. When she woke in the morning, she sought out Milo and gave him instructions for her travel. Then Julia faced Marcus over breakfast.

"I'm going to Rome," she said. "My father will need me."

"There is nothing you can do there." Marcus's tone was cold. "You will remain here."

"But, Marcus, I have not seen my father in a year's time. I must insist on this trip," she argued forcefully. "I have made plans to go."

A horrible stillness overcame Marcus. His face turned red and puffy. He looked as if he would explode in anger, but he kept his tone low and level. "You are no longer subject to your parents' authority. You are under my command, and I refuse to allow you to leave."

Julia was not in the slightest afraid of her husband. "Marcus, I am not interested in the law of which you speak. You cannot stop me from seeing my father. He needs me. I have reserved passage for myself and the children—and Cassia, too. We leave tomorrow. Milo has made the arrangements. He will stay behind to run the house."

"Is that so?" a steely-eyed Marcus said coldly. "Not only are you disobeying my command, but you have taken it upon yourself to order the rest of the servants to do your bidding. This is mutinous in the extreme, and I will not have it." Seething now, Marcus's tone turned low and dark. "I will decide who leaves Ephesus and who does not. And you will not. If you even think of defying me, I will post an order at the harbor with the ships' captains. You will be prevented from boarding."

Facing defeat but unwilling to give in just yet, Julia pleaded once more with her husband. "Marcus, my mother's death is a terrible blow. Please, allow me this. My father will be bereft, and we have always been close." She paused, and a new idea surfaced. "What if I were to go alone? Please. You would not miss me, and Milo will see to—"

"There will be no further discussion," Marcus said. He rose and walked out.

In the weeks that followed, Marcus came to regret refusing his wife a visit to her father. Julia did not forgive her husband, and her resentment did not diminish. She avoided his presence, only partaking of meals with him—in silence, since she refused to engage in conversation. Julia was no longer the charming, vivacious wife Marcus could show off. Instead, she had turned sullen and indifferent.

Marcus's refusal to allow her to travel back to Rome laid bare for Julia the reality of her life. She was no more free than her slaves. She was as much Marcus's property as they were. She had no control over her own life. She was simply playing a role as if on stage, with her actions choreographed by the director, her husband. She found herself living somewhere between the independent spirit she knew herself to be and the domineering husband who would crush her. Julia dwelt on this depressing dilemma and yearned for a way out. Meanwhile, she would have to bide her time, and though still indifferent to her husband, she determined, for the good of her household, that she would return to some level of cordiality.

If there was one note of cheer in Julia's life, it came from the liaison she perceived developing between the quiet Milo and Cassia, who had returned slowly to her natural exuberance after the upheaval of Quintus's murder.

After arriving in Ephesus and settling in, Julia noted Milo's and Cassia's daily silent communication as their eyes met and their shoulders nearly touched when they stood side by side, receiving instruction from their mistress.

Unhappy in her own loveless marriage, Julia decided to live a little vicariously. *I must further this match,* she thought.

Certain of her intuitive abilities, Julia sought out her husband and played him when he made an unusual appearance at lunch the following day.

"Marcus," she said casually, abandoning her moodiness, "do you remember your desire to pair Cassia with Draco?"

Marcus gave a start at hearing his wife's voice for the first time in weeks and wondered what she was up to. Then he frowned. "Don't remind me," he grumbled.

"But the idea was a good one. Perhaps not with Draco...."

Marcus displayed curiosity but also suspicion. "What are you suggesting?"

"Milo and Cassia. They seem to get along. They have no one else here, and wouldn't it suit your purpose for the, ah, *production* of more slaves?"

"What makes you think a man such as my steward would want anything to do with that weak-minded slut? She's already sent two men to their ruin," Marcus said forcefully.

"Marcus, Cassia has grown up. I believe this alliance could serve you."

"You're interested in having me 'served' after your intolerable brooding of the past weeks?"

"Marcus, are you wishing another war between us?"

"Far from it," Marcus groused. "All right. Talk to her. But I don't want another mess like the one we had last time."

Julia did not answer her husband but reclined and, with a straight face, finished her lunch. Inside, she was smiling.

Marcus's mind raced ahead to several appealing possibilities with the union of his two slaves. First was the probability of adding more slaves to the fold, slaves he would not have to purchase. Second was the fact that the union of these two would bind them more securely to the Aquillius estate. As a couple, they would be less likely to run off, a vexing conundrum for many Roman landowners.

This might very well work, Marcus thought as a satisfied expression spread across his face.

TWENTY

Ephesus AD 59

"Cassia, I know of your feelings for Milo." Cassia dropped the tunic she had just picked up from the floor. "No, no, mistress. We have done nothing. You must believe me."

"I do believe you," Julia said as she took Cassia's hand. "I know there has been nothing explicit between you. However...."

Cassia looked at her mistress with a mixture of curiosity and fear.

"You needn't deny it. It's plain to see."

"Oh, mistress, I am sorry."

"What if I told you not to be sorry?"

"Not sorry?"

"What would you think of a marriage between you and Milo?" Julia offered.

"Oh, mistress, I don't know what to say. Milo...I don't know what he feels. I don't speak much with him, only about our work."

"I venture to say that Milo will not complain about such an alliance," Julia chuckled.

"The master," Cassia stammered.

"The master is of no concern."

"Oh!" Cassia dropped down on her mistress's bed with a thump. Julia smiled.

Milo and Cassia were married a fortnight later. In a break with Roman practice, Marcus and Julia witnessed the rite. The newlyweds were given quarters off the kitchen.

In a rare moment of joviality, and in an attempt to appease Julia, Marcus granted Milo status as a freeman. However, it was not quite a moment of great munificence, because he did not grant the same to Cassia, and neither would be free to leave their patron's employ. Milo would still be tied to serving the Aquillius household, and well he knew it.

The new alliance did bring some happiness to Julia, and that helped the time to go by quickly. However, she still longed to return to Rome and her aging father.

~~~~~~~~~~~~~~

If Marcus had learned anything after conveying bad news to his wife the first time, it certainly didn't show when, four months later, he once again summoned her to his office.

"Your father is dead," he said bluntly.

"How?" she asked.

"No cause was determined."

He died of a broken heart! And I could not be there to comfort him.

Ignoring her tears, Marcus continued, "I will send agents to oversee the properties immediately. The revenues will go a long way to securing my position."

Julia glared at him. *His first thoughts are always to his own interests. These are my properties, my inheritance, yet he will take and use and ruin them as he sees fit!*

For the first time, Julia's thoughts went to leaving the cold, unfeeling man she called her husband. *But I have nothing to take with me, except for my dowry. And if I go, he'll take the only thing that matters to me—my girls.* Knowing the power he had over her, she tried her best to push these rebellious thoughts from her mind.

"You may go," Marcus said.

Julia retreated to her room, refusing to see anyone, declining to eat. She was inconsolable.

Cassia confided to Milo, "I don't know what to do. She won't even let me in to see her."

Milo responded, "I'll go to her."

"Come with me first." Cassia went to the kitchen and pulled a small tray down from a shelf. She assembled a vessel of wine, a bowl of hot broth, and a chunk of bread. She placed them on the tray. "Take this."

Milo knocked at Julia's door, and then simply opened it and walked in. He offered Julia the tray. She turned away from Milo, indicating she had no interest in what he had brought. Milo set the tray on her dresser.

Staring into space, Julia spoke in a dull monotone. "My parents are gone. My sister is gone. I have no one."

"But it isn't so," Milo said. "You have a family, your daughters, others who care about you."

"Did you ever get over the loss of your family?" Julia asked.

Julia's question told Milo that his mistress might be willing to make her way back to the world. "In ways, I think I have never got over the pain I felt that day. I still feel it. But I knew I must get on. I had no choice. It was that or die myself."

"I cannot do it. I cannot bear the pain I feel now," Julia replied.

She needs the friendship and comfort of another woman, one with her background, one who can empathize and show her the way out of her troubles. Milo thought for a moment. *Prisca.*

Noting Milo's faraway look, Julia asked, "What is it?"

"Nothing, my lady. Here, please, some broth?" he coaxed.

Some weeks later, a courier arrived at the Aquillius home with a letter for Julia from the Lucinius family solicitor. As she read it, tears splashed onto the ink-filled page before a slight smile crossed her lips. She took the letter to her bedroom, where she hid it in a box of valuables.

TWENTY-ONE

On the Road between Rome and Ostia
Present Day

Professor Jacques Ignatius left Rome on a mild Saturday morning in May and headed west in a rented green Fiat. Three minivans, each filled with a team leader, four volunteers, and an extensive amount of gear, followed. Within forty-five minutes, they would be passing through modern Ostia and checking in at the old castle. They would lunch at the cafeteria next to the museum, and then spend the afternoon tromping about the ancient ruins of Ostia before being briefed Sunday and beginning their work early Monday morning.

"You'll want to watch out for black scorpions and snakes," Jacques warned, blinking twice as the group of sixteen dined al-fresco on pizza and cold drinks. "The scorpions aren't particularly dangerous, but the asps are deadly."

The volunteers exchanged anxious glances.

"But don't worry," Jacques said reassuringly. "If you don't bother them, they won't bother you. Your team leaders all have anti-venom in their first aid kits." He heard a few chuckles, but received even more nervous looks.

Jacques was in his element, on his feet lecturing before a group of naïve students.

"This is really a magical site," he continued. "You'll actually see much more here than in Pompeii. And the first thing you'll see is a cemetery." He went on to explain that Romans were not allowed to bury their dead within the city, but since they wanted their departed ones close by, they placed their tombs along the main roads, as close to the town walls as possible.

After describing the many sites they would be viewing, he amused his small audience by telling them, "Be sure to notice the twenty-four-seater public—very public—toilets near the temple. You won't see any walls or doors separating these seats for privacy. No, the ancient Romans simply sat side by side, doing their business and planning their evening entertainments at the same time."

On Sunday morning, the volunteers entered a chilly, bare meeting room at the castle and arranged themselves in a semi-circle on metal chairs. Jacques faced them, while the team leaders stood behind their charges.

"You twelve volunteers are the foundation of our search," Jacques began. "Without you, we will find nothing and therefore know nothing. We have an opportunity to learn untold things about the people who once lived here and the lives they led."

Jacques explained that this exploration would not be a dig in the conventional sense. "Rather than excavating for artifacts, you will be combing the necropoli and examining each and every burial site. Look for plaques, inscriptions, even graffiti." He paused before going on. "The purpose is to study early Roman funerary inscriptions for a better understanding of ancient languages and, therefore, Roman life."

He then told the students they were to document each site by photographing it and noting by hand its location and distinctive elements. "The graves are often shared, with centuries of remains heaped on top of each other. The inscriptions, where there are any, may be covered over. You'll need to clean off the debris, layer by layer without destroying anything," he warned. Jacques held up a kit filled with handpicks, brushes, charcoal, and paper for rubbing the inscriptions. "The team leaders will be on-site to answer any questions you might have, and they'll collect your data each day.

Three weeks later, as the warmth of May turned to the heat of June, excitement had faded. The student volunteers and the team leaders were hot and cranky. Jacques was frustrated. Cardinal Ricci was incensed, and Valentina was distraught.

For the students, it had been one long, exhausting day after another. Even though they hadn't known the true purpose of the search, they had expected a big find of some sort to brag about to their family and friends when they got home. The boredom and tedium were adding up.

Bothered by the waning energy of the students, the team leaders found themselves irritable as well.

Jacques had tired of trying to keep his team together and was ready to chalk this project up as hopeless.

Cardinal Ricci had lost patience. His calls to Valentina were now daily occurrences. He wanted some answers in return for his money, and he wanted the answers he expected.

Valentina was a wreck. No matter that she had discussed with Ricci the fact that a find couldn't be guaranteed. All of that had gone out the window. Ricci wanted his bishop, and she didn't know what to do next.

Only Yigael remained calm. He had pulled the rabbit out of a hat on many occasions, and he didn't see this time as any different. The obvious had failed, so Yigael began to look elsewhere.

Just south of Ostia lay the Porta Laurentina necropolis. It was of the first century, and excavating had already begun on it. Yigael dispatched Jacques and the teams to that site.

For Jacques, this meant starting over. He would have to get new permits and scope out the new site, and this would take time. Mindful that everyone needed a break, he called off all work for a couple of days and sent the volunteers, along with the team leaders, off on their own. Nearly everyone wanted to explore Rome, and the next morning, they set out in two of the vans to do just that.

One of the team leaders, Anna-Marie, stayed behind.

TWENTY-TWO

Ostia

Giuseppe Benoni had watched over the ruins of the old synagogue at Ostia Antica for fifteen years. After so many thousands of years, the gold, jewels, and most precious artifacts had been lost to grave robbers or removed to one museum or another. Tourists were another matter. On the lookout for souvenirs, they posed a constant threat to these ancient remains. It was Giuseppe's job to maintain the premises and keep an eye out. If he saw any untoward activity, he was to call authorities.

Giuseppe lived in the residential area of modern Ostia, three houses from a corner not far from the old castle. His home was a cottage left to him by his mother, and it featured a small, lovely garden in back that his mother had planted and Giuseppe meticulously maintained.

At an early age, Giuseppe had been diagnosed as developmentally disabled. When he was born, the doctors and nurses shook their heads sadly. His eyes were almond shaped, his head was too small for his body, and his facial features were undersized and flat. However, his heart was strong. Learning for him had been fraught with fits and starts, a frustration for his impatient teacher and weary mother. Yet in the end, he exceeded expectation. And Giuseppe had a gift, one that would surface later on.

Giuseppe's parents had worked together from the front room of their small house—he a tailor, she a seamstress. When mother and son returned home from the public market one morning, they found Giuseppe's father slumped over his sewing machine, dead of an aneurism. Giuseppe was only eight.

He grew into a shy and retiring adult. Under five-and-one-half feet tall, Giuseppe appeared even shorter by walking with a slight stoop, head bowed, eyes cast down.

Recognizing that he would not have an easy time after she was gone, his mother persuaded her brother, a government worker, to provide a simple job for her son. With that and her cottage, he should be able to take care of himself. For Giuseppe, this was a good arrangement. After his mother's death, he settled right in and for years had rarely come to the notice of anyone else.

No one except Anna-Marie. She wondered about this lonely soul, and feeling sorry for him, began to greet him each day. During her breaks, their paths sometimes crossed, and they would sit together under the shade of an umbrella pine, Giuseppe entertaining Anna-Marie with stories of the old ruins. Anna-Marie came to realize there was much more to this introverted young man than met the eye. While recognizing his limitations, she was amazed at Giuseppe's memory for detail. She was not much surprised, then, when he told her he could name almost every stone, home, monument, and temple in Ostia Antica.

Anna-Marie was grateful for some free time. She had been unable to catch up on her personal tasks, so, as the others left for Rome, she spent the morning washing her dirty clothes in the castle cellars and hanging them to dry in the courtyard of the dormitories. Then, she left the musty basement to catch some fresh air and set out, reversing her usual direction and heading away from the ruins toward modern Ostia. Giuseppe was emerging from his cottage as she turned onto his street, and when he spotted her, he immediately waved her over.

"Do you want to come in?" Giuseppe asked his new friend.

"Sure." Anna-Marie entered a spotless little home furnished with the heavy, dark, wooden furniture popular with grandmothers all over Italy. The front door opened into a small living room outfitted with a dark brown lounger, a small sofa, and an ancient television. In a corner was an old sewing machine with a foot pedal. An ironing board hung on a wall, and four pictures in walnut frames sat on the shelf over the old mantelpiece. They all showed Giuseppe in the loving arms of his parents.

Giuseppe led Anna-Marie through a doorway into a kitchen large enough only for a tiny table and two chairs. "Why are you on this street?" he inquired. "Do you want to sit down?"

"We have some time off. We're going to explore another burial ground in a few days." Anna-Marie took a seat on one of the kitchen chairs.

"Why?" Giuseppe cocked his head and looked straight down at Anna-Marie.

"We've searched the two nearest necropoli and didn't find what we want," Anna-Marie explained.

"Do you want some tea?" Giuseppe turned toward the sink.

"That would be very nice."

"Okay. I will fix some tea. What do you want?"

"Oh, whatever you're going to have." Anna-Marie gazed out the kitchen window. A sudden gust whipped up a few leaves under the tree in Giuseppe's garden.

"I only have one kind of tea," Giuseppe said, turning to face her. "What are you looking for in the old bone cities?"

"Oh, well…." Anna-Marie laughed at her misunderstanding. She said simply, "We're looking for a Christian woman."

"A Christian lady," Giuseppe repeated. He thought for a moment and then said, "Well, maybe you didn't look everywhere. Maybe she isn't where you think she is." He turned toward the small stove, took the kettle off, and filled it with water. Then he set it onto a burner and lit the fire.

"We looked everywhere we knew to look, Giuseppe," Anna-Marie said.

While the water was heating, Giuseppe took a tin of biscuits from a shelf, placed six on a white plate, and took the plate to the table. He then returned to the stove, took the kettle off, filled two cups with boiling water, and carried them to the table. He returned to the stove, opened a cupboard next to it, and withdrew a box of tea bags. He carried the box to the table. Then he went to the countertop for a jar of white sugar, carried that to the table, and sat down.

"Do you want sugar?" he asked.

"No, this is fine. Thank you." Anna-Marie gazed distractedly around the cottage.

"You think you looked everywhere, but you didn't," Giuseppe insisted.

Anna-Marie looked back at him, surprised. "What? How do you know?"

"Did you find any Christians?" Giuseppe asked.

"Some, but not the right one," Anna-Marie said.

"Was she someone important?"

"Well, we think so. Otherwise we wouldn't be looking for her."

"There's another one," Giuseppe said.

"Another what?"

"Another Christian."

Anna-Marie banged her head with her palm.

"I just told you. You didn't look everywhere. You're looking where everyone already knows everything," Giuseppe said yet again. "You missed a place. I've been watching."

"So…do you think you know where our Christian lady is?"

Giuseppe smiled and nodded.

Anna Marie dipped her chin, raised her brows, and looked directly into Giuseppe's eyes. "Well?"

Giuseppe took the hint. "By the old synagogue just outside of the wall, there's an old tomb. I don't know if there is a lady there, but there is a Christian there." Giuseppe gave Anna-Marie a crooked half-smile.

Anna-Marie looked at him seriously. "No one knows of any

tombs by the synagogue. Jewish people don't like burying their dead too near their synagogues," she said.

"Oh, well, it's not too close. It's outside the wall that goes around the synagogue."

"Well, I haven't seen a wall around the synagogue or a tomb, either. How could we have missed it?" Anna-Marie asked.

"Oh, well, that's easy. You can't see it."

"Right," Anna-Marie said, disbelieving and averting her eyes. "And why would that be?"

"It's buried under the ground."

Anna-Marie groaned. "Geez, Giuseppe, quit teasing me."

"Okay, if you don't want to know...."

"Well, how do you know there's anything there if it's underground? Wouldn't that be kind of hard to see?"

"Oh, no, not at all. It wasn't always under the ground. It used to be on top."

"Ah. Giuseppe, do you think you could start at the beginning and tell me what you know or think you know?"

"Okay. Well, first, I know there's a Christian there because of the cross."

"The cross?"

"Yeah, sure. The cross," Giuseppe said with a wave of his hand.

Anna-Marie's ears began to burn. "Are you sure?"

"Of course I'm sure. I know what a cross is," Giuseppe said while fingering the shape of a cross on the tabletop. "And that's what's on the stone."

"The stone...." Anna-Marie looked closely at Giuseppe, imploring for more information.

"Yeah, the cross is on a stone. The kind that has writing on it."

"Writing?"

"Yes."

"Writing and a cross on a stone."

"Yes."

"What is the writing?" Anna-Marie spoke carefully, wanting to encourage but not offend Giuseppe.

"I don't know. I can't read it. It's not that I can't read. It's just that I can't read what's on the stone. It looks all gobbledygook to me." He sat back and looked away.

"I understand, Giuseppe. I see a lot of words that don't make sense to me, too. Now where is this grave that you think is under the ground?" Anna-Marie asked.

"Over by the synagogue, like I said."

"And you think you saw it once?"

"Oh, for sure. I saw it more than once."

"And if you saw it above ground, how did it get below ground?" For a moment, Anna-Marie thought she was losing her mind with this conversation.

"The earthquake."

Anna-Marie sighed. "The earthquake…."

"Yes, there was an earthquake. That's how it got covered up."

"I see." Anna-Marie considered Giuseppe through half-closed eyes. "Do you think you could show me where this is?"

"Sure."

"Let's go." Anna-Marie stood up.

TWENTY-THREE

Ostia

Anna-Marie and Giuseppe left the cottage behind and set out on foot along the Viale dei Romagnoli in the direction of the ruins. They passed by open fields until they reached an intersection called Via Guido Calza. Then, they turned right and came straight to the entrance.

Giuseppe quickened his pace. He felt excited to be showing Anna-Marie what lay ahead, though worried that she might be disappointed. Giuseppe liked pleasing people.

Anna-Marie was excited, too, and apprehensive. She wondered whether Giuseppe's revelation could mean the end of their search. Or would it be yet another exercise in futility? She felt caught between wanting the best and expecting the worst.

Giuseppe slowed just before entering the ruins and turned to make sure Anna-Marie was right behind him. When he saw that she was, he stepped onto a marble paving stone. All that was left of the synagogue were a few columns and marble blocks.

"See?" Giuseppe said. "This is where the building ends." He stepped down and took about two dozen steps. "And this is where the wall used to be." With this, Giuseppe stepped over an imaginary wall, turned, and pointed at the earth. "This is where the Christian lady is. Or at least, some Christian person is. Right here."

Anna-Marie looked down and saw a tumble of old stones and weeds mixed with pieces of broken-up marble. But as she looked up and then beyond to where Giuseppe was pointing, she saw that the hardened earth backed up to a perfectly lovely park-like setting—a grassy terrain filled with oak trees, poplars, cypress, and umbrella pines.

Anna-Marie looked up at Giuseppe. If he hadn't looked so guileless, she might have thought he was playing a trick on her. But his smile of elation told her that this was no trick. As Giuseppe watched her expectantly, his face fell. It was clear to him that she was disappointed.

Not knowing what to say, Anna-Marie returned her look to the rubble at her feet.

"I said you couldn't see it," Giuseppe insisted. "It's right here."

"I don't think so. Let's go back."

"I'm telling you there's a Christian buried there."

Anna-Marie sighed, frustrated at yet another false hope coming to nothing. It wasn't the boy's fault. She gazed sympathetically at her friend, who was looking quite morose. "Okay, Giuseppe, tell me again what you think is there, from the beginning."

Giuseppe took a deep breath. He told Anna-Marie how he had come to work at the site in the first place. At that time, archeologists who were excavating the old settlement had run out of funds and work had stopped. But recognizing the site to be of importance, the Italian Ministry of Cultural Heritage had decided to upgrade the security for this section of the park.

And that's why Giuseppe had been hired, to watch over the synagogue and its surrounds. He felt proud to have been entrusted with the job, and he took it seriously. He knew each feature of the ruins.

Anna-Marie listened as Giuseppe took the long way around, trying his best to explain. From what she could understand, heavy rains followed by a fast, hard drought had caused the ground to become unstable. Then an earthquake had opened a sinkhole right where Giuseppe had been pointing. The opening in the earth had revealed a partially exposed wall of brick and an engraved stone. He had seen the cross and some words that he couldn't read.

"That's when I knew there was a Christian buried here," he summed up.

But Anna-Marie was not going to get her hopes up so easily. "So, where is it, Giuseppe?"

"Okay. Well, last year," he continued, "we had another earthquake. It was a big one. My window broke, and my pots fell off the shelves. I cleaned everything up, and then I came here and looked around. The hole was all covered up. I couldn't see the cross anymore. But I know it's there." Giuseppe dropped his head to his chest. "I'm sorry if you don't believe me."

"Oh, Giuseppe, it isn't that I don't believe you. I just…I was hoping I'd be able to see it for myself."

Giuseppe still looked downhearted, not quite mollified by her words.

As they left the site, Anna-Marie was thinking hard about what he had said. Floods, droughts, earthquakes were always swallowing up archaeological treasures. Was Julia under there, or was that too much to hope for?

As they neared his cottage, Giuseppe was withdrawn. Anna-Marie touched his shoulder. "Giuseppe, I don't know if this is what we were looking for or not, but you are right. We didn't think to look here."

Giuseppe glanced at her skeptically. He was used to people treating him as if he were stupid, but he'd thought Anna-Marie was his friend.

She tried again. "I'm going to tell my boss about this. I'm sure he's going to want to check it out. And I'd like for you to show me around some more. Okay?" Anna-Marie said and gave Giuseppe a smile.

Giuseppe looked at his feet and simply walked to his front door.

TWENTY-FOUR

Ostia

Anna-Marie didn't look back as she walked the short distance from Giuseppe's cottage to the castle. It wasn't only the afternoon sun that was causing her to sweat. This information could be everything, or it could be yet another dead end. In any case, she would need to inform Jacques of this possible lone Christian. Ultimately, the decision was his to make.

Back at the castle, Anna-Marie put away her fresh clothes and then walked over to the cafeteria for dinner. Not feeling very hungry, she picked at a salad before leaving it and heading back to her room. Then a headache took hold, and she swallowed two Paracetamol. It was too early to go to bed, so she decided to read.

She picked up the *Biblical Archeological Review*, a publication she had subscribed to for several years. She could get lost in articles and photographs of other excavations. By the time Anna-Marie put down the magazine, she was feeling a lot more optimistic. After all, so far, they'd come up with nothing. They had nothing left to lose. If they found something, even if it wasn't a bishop, it would at least be a new discovery. *I'll call Jacques first thing in the morning.*

That decision made, Anna-Marie fell asleep. Upon waking, she fumbled for her cell phone and punched in Jacques's number.

"Hey," Jacques said after seeing Anna-Marie's name on the display. "Where are you? Rome?"

"No, I had some things to do."

"Oh, I thought you'd be with the others. You okay?"

"Yeah, fine, but I think I might have found something, and I need to tell you about it." Anna-Marie sounded intense.

"Okay, I'm at the cafeteria, just finishing breakfast. Come on over."

"On my way," Anna-Marie said.

She entered a bustling cafeteria full of tourists about to make their way to the ruins. She weaved her way to the bar, ordered a double cappuccino and then found Jacques ensconced at a table in the corner. He had pushed his breakfast plate to one side and was working on a cup of espresso.

"Morning," Jacques said.

"Hi. Look, this might be nothing. I don't want to get your hopes up, but…." Anna-Marie's voice trailed off as she searched for words.

"Go on," Jacques said.

Anna-Marie struggled to modulate her voice. She had to raise it a little to counter the din but keep it low enough not to be overheard. "Yesterday, I stopped by Giuseppe's house. You know, the caretaker? He lives near here and he invited me in for a chat, telling me he knew about a tomb site outside of the necropoli that no one had come across yet—he's been watching us, I guess. I didn't really pay much attention to him at first because, well, I don't know."

Jacques nodded. "Go on," he said again.

Anna-Marie recounted the walk in the ruins, the story of the earthquake, and the Christian grave that didn't seem to be there. "But he described a cross carved onto a stone marker."

Jacques sat quietly and considered Anna-Marie's words, his excitement rising. He chastised himself. It was arrogant of him not to have spoken to the caretaker himself. How often had he thought that their best information came from locals? Abruptly, without a word, Jacques rose and walked away. He returned a few moments later with a fresh shot of espresso.

As if he had never left the table, Anna-Marie continued, "If there really is a marker there with a cross on it, I'm figuring that a Christian must be buried there—someone important, right? Otherwise, they'd be in the necropolis or just cremated and stuck in one of the columbaria?" Her voice trailed off.

Jacques gazed at Anna-Marie with an unreadable expression.

The cafeteria was emptying out, and the tourists were going on their way.

"What do you think?" Anna-Marie took a sip of her coffee.

"Did Giuseppe say anything else about the stone marker?" Jacques said, hoping for more.

"No, he just recognized the cross." Anna-Marie shrugged.

"Do you know if he has told anyone else about this?" Jacques questioned, looking around at the now-empty cafeteria.

"No, I don't know that," Anna-Marie answered. "But I doubt he has."

"All right. Let's look into it." Two blinks. "I'm jammed up for the rest of today with officials and permits, but I'd like to meet with Giuseppe in the morning. Could you arrange it?"

"Of course. I think he'll be thrilled. He was hurt because he thought I didn't believe him."

"Well, set it up. We'll go over to Giuseppe's together. I'll meet you in the chapel at eight."

With that, Jacques rose and walked toward the door.

Lord, he is an odd one, Anna-Marie thought as she watched Jacques walk out. *Nice enough, but no social skills.*

At noon, Anna-Marie set out for Giuseppe's house with hope that he would be home.

"Hi, Anna-Marie." Giuseppe opened his front door just a crack. "Are you still mad at me?"

"Of course not, Giuseppe. I never was mad at you." She smiled at him. "In fact," she went on, "my boss wants to speak with you about the gravesite we visited yesterday."

"Am I in trouble?" A frightened-looking Giuseppe started to inch the door closed.

"Not at all. No, of course not," Anna-Marie said in her most reassuring tone. "My boss just wants to know more. His name is Jacques. He is very nice. Would you be willing to speak with him?"

"I guess so, if you're sure I'm not in trouble."

"I am sure you are not in trouble."

Giuseppe wasn't so sure, but he said, "Okay." Then, mindful of the manners his mother had so dutifully taught him, he opened the door wide and asked Anna-Marie in.

The next morning, the three met on Giuseppe's back terrace. Anna-Marie took the porch swing, Giuseppe and Jacques settled on metal lawn chairs. The sun was shining, and the warmth of the day was calming.

Anna-Marie noticed that Giuseppe relaxed after introductions were out of the way. Jacques had a gentle way about him, and it eased Giuseppe, who admitted to a sleepless night, anxious about what he feared might be an interrogation.

"Giuseppe, how long have you lived here?" Jacques asked.

"Well, I've never lived anywhere else," Giuseppe answered.

"I see. Then you must know all about Ostia," Jacques said.

"I know a lot. I'm not sure I know everything."

Jacques smiled and asked Giuseppe to tell him exactly what he had seen near the synagogue ruins.

Giuseppe repeated the same story he had told Anna-Marie, stopping his tale only to consider some questions carefully crafted by Jacques. The professor was particularly interested in details regarding the stone tablet, and he asked several questions about it. Giuseppe couldn't answer all of them, but he remained certain about the cross.

Jacques then asked the caretaker to show him the site.

Giuseppe jumped up like a child eager to show off his new bike, and they all set out for the ruins. When they got there, the caretaker pointed down to the same spot he had shown Anna-Marie.

Jacques stooped down for a better look. He noticed that the rubble was several feet wide. He couldn't estimate how deep. "I think we need to look."

Anna-Marie's heart thumped hard.

"Everyone's back from Rome," Jacques said. "Tonight, tell the volunteers working under you and Philippe that they'll be assigned to Carol at Porta Laurentina tomorrow. I want you and Philippe to start digging here. And let's keep this quiet. We haven't been cleared for this site, but I would rather be asking for forgiveness than permission."

Jacques turned to Giuseppe. "Would you be Anna-Marie's assistant tomorrow? Do you think you could do that?"

Giuseppe's face lit up. He smiled a big smile and nodded. "I already work here, so I would still be doing my job. Yes."

Jacques said, "I'm going to the city offices, and I'll at least get the permit requests filed before we start. That'll give us some cover. See you later."

TWENTY-FIVE

Ephesus, AD 60

"Cassia, the girls need new garments," Julia called out to her maid, who was down the hall in Livia's room. "They have outgrown nearly everything. I'm going to the market in the morning. Please tell Milo. I want him to accompany me."

"Thank heavens," Cassia murmured out of Julia's hearing. "Right away, mistress." *She'll* finally *be getting out of the house. Open air and people in the marketplace...it'll be a good diversion for her.* She ran out of the bedroom to find her husband.

When she found him and told him about the morning outing, he had an idea, and in the early evening, he set out for Prisca's house.

Julia was far from enthusiastic about her venture into the marketplace, but she felt that if she didn't get out soon, she would go crazy. She was still exhausted and red-eyed, still overcome with the grief at losing both her parents, and when she went outside, the sun nearly blinded her.

Arriving at a shop where she would select fabrics and order tunics and cloaks to be made to measure, she felt her spirits lift slightly as she thought of her girls' flair for fashion, even at such young ages. They both had definite ideas about color and style, and their tastes often clashed.

As Milo bartered with the shopkeeper, Julia heard her name called. Turning, she saw Prisca hurrying toward her.

"It's good to see you again." Prisca greeted Julia breathlessly, taking her hand. "I was hoping to run into you. We barely had the chance to speak when first we met." Noting Milo with the shopkeeper, she gave a brief wave.

Julia was again taken aback by Prisca's resemblance to her sister Adrianne. Embarrassed by her rudeness during their previous encounter, Julia reached for words. "Yes, I am so sorry I had to leave so abruptly. Forgive me. I'd meant to call again, but it's been a busy time."

"Lovely fabrics," Prisca rattled on, looking at the ones Julia held.

"Yes, for the girls. They've outgrown everything." Julia was relieved at the change of topic. "And what brings you here?"

Prisca ignored Julia's question. "I know what you mean about being busy. With so many new people wanting to attend our gatherings, Aquila and I are quite inundated."

"Yes, of course. I'd expect no less." Julia was all-politeness, wary again.

Prisca knew from Milo exactly the domestic situation in the Aquillius household. Figuring she had played her game long enough, Prisca dispensed with the pleasantries. "What is it, Julia? Forgive me, but you're pale and thin. You're wasting away. What's wrong?"

Prisca's compassion broke Julia, and her need for companionship overcame her wariness. She needed a friend. "Do you have a little time?" she asked, her voice quaking.

"Of course, my dear. Come."

Julia handed the fabrics to Milo and asked him to finish up with the shopkeeper. "I'll return in a while."

Milo nodded knowingly.

Prisca guided Julia to an herbal shop where they could sit on a bench and sample the teas. Noting their fine clothes, the proprietor eagerly encouraged the two women to take their time in the hope that he might win some hefty sales from passersby who noticed his wealthy customers.

Over the next hour, Julia unburdened herself. She told Prisca everything that had happened since her marriage and shared with her all the details of her broken heart.

Prisca listened to every word and observed Julia with deepest compassion. As Julia wiped a tear away from her cheek, Prisca took Julia's hands in her own and smiled. "I can see you've had a very difficult time. It's hard to lose those you love, and terrible to feel so alone. I know a way to ease your suffering. Would you come to my house tomorrow evening?"

Julia looked at the woman, so similar to her own dear sister Adrianne, and swallowed her tears. "Yes, I would like that very much."

"Good! Come early, before our meeting starts. We'll talk."

Julia and Prisca rose. They purchased none of the disappointed shopkeeper's fine teas, but thanked him and departed.

Julia was eager to speak further with Prisca, and to find a way to mend her pain. It had been so long since she'd had anyone to talk to. She had no interest in this new cult, but she was tired of being alone, with only servants for company. She and Milo arrived early the next day, as instructed. Prisca ushered Julia into a small private study and invited her to sit. Julia expected Prisca to perhaps give her a tea or a tincture or an amulet that would ease her burden. After a moment, Prisca began to speak.

"I went out early this morning," she said, "and saw some disturbing sights at the markets."

Julia wondered what this had to do with her. "Oh? What were those?"

"A slave being beaten by his master. Then a family so poor they had to scavenge the trash heaps for food."

Julia raised her eyebrows. "That's terrible, but those are not so uncommon. Are you surprised?"

"No, I'm not," Prisca answered.

Julia was confused. She'd come to Prisca to unburden herself, to find answers to her own heartache, and here she was, talking slaves and the sweepings of the street. "This has nothing to do with me," she said. "The law is the law, and we cannot change it! Prisca, I came to you for help. My heart is broken in a million pieces and you speak to me of slaves and beggars…." Julia began to cry.

Prisca handed her a cloth for her eyes and spoke gently. "I am telling you how to heal your heart, Julia. Notice others who bear heavy burdens. Give to them what you can, even if it's simply a smile. Give to them, and expect nothing in return."

"I don't understand." Julia sat bewildered.

Prisca said, "Do as I say, and you will see." Then, she rose and went to answer a knock on the door.

Julia learned that Prisca and her husband, Aquila, ran a thriving business as leather merchants and had joined with the Christians some years back. When the couple met Paul, they had immediately welcomed him into their home. They supported him financially as he evangelized, opened new meeting places for worship, and traveled to other cities.

Julia began attending the evening meetings regularly because of her affinity with Prisca. She still considered the new cult far out of the mainstream and therefore unacceptable, but she liked the people she met. They had an ease about them, and she felt their warmth as she engaged in small talk and exchanged laughter. *Dear God, how long has it been since I laughed?* she wondered on the first night.

When Prisca was particularly busy, Julia began to substitute for her at the front door, greeting and welcoming newcomers. It was not lost on Julia that her cares seemed to float away when she was here in the company of Yeshua's followers. In a way, that worried her. *Why can't I feel like this at home?*

When Paul's trips got longer and farther away, Prisca began to help by leading new groups in nearby villages. The gatherings were growing so fast, though, that others were needed to speak at the evening meetings. At first, Julia agreed to organize and set up various meetings. When she was asked to speak, she resisted. But eventually, she got swept along with the tide and, with Milo by her side, did her best to repeat the stories and teachings told by Paul.

TWENTY-SIX

Laodicea, Asia, AD 62

"I can't imagine why I ever agreed to this," Julia complained to Milo as they bumped along in a horse-drawn cart to a distant outpost.

Paul had convinced Julia to take the three-day trip, and she was sorry she had agreed to do it because it had been extremely strenuous. They had endured dirty water, spoiled food, and dingy inns infested with cutthroats, drunks, and all manner of bugs and vermin.

What have I got into? I'm only in this spot because I have a husband who doesn't care about me, she mused bitterly. Julia certainly didn't have to worry about Marcus objecting to this trip. Her husband was rarely home anymore. He took little interest in the household, the girls, and especially in her. Funny, he doesn't object to my journeying throughout the Eastern Empire, but wouldn't let me return home to my father.

The thought fed her resentment, not only toward her husband but toward an entire society where women were viewed as little more than chattel. Her resentment left her cranky and moody.

"We're almost there," Milo said.

"About time, too. Never again, Milo."

"At least we'll be more comfortable tonight staying at a family home," Milo said.

"Thank heaven," Julia said with relief.

Laodicea sat on a hill between the narrow valleys of two small rivers that emptied into the larger Lycus River. It was a flourishing commercial city and one of the chief seats of Christianity. Paul had, yet again, run afoul of the Roman authorities and was cooling his heels in prison for his own protection. His followers had got word to him about infighting among the followers in Colossia and nearby Laodicea. Prisca and Aquila had managed to dispatch his epistle to Colossia, but it fell to Julia to spread Paul's word to the house churches in nearby Laodicea.

As Julia and Milo pulled onto the main road toward Laodicea, they were eager for some good food and restful sleep. Their hostess, Nympha, to whom Paul had directed them, greeted the two with enthusiasm. While they took their evening meal, Nympha filled them in on the hostilities plaguing the local Christians. Not only were they operating in opposition to the local government, but they had become divided among themselves, and she was losing control.

In the morning, the faithful met at Nympha's home. They arrived in disparate groups, and the divisions among them were visible at a glance: wealthy, well-dressed Grecian men and women bedecked in jewels were accompanied by their slaves. Jewish adherents, who came from a different direction, were followed at a respectable distance by veiled wives and daughters.

As they assembled in Nympha's great hall, the tension was palpable. The crowd may have been silent, but they may as well have been beating each other with cudgels, so unmistakable was the hatred they bore one another.

Julia made her way to the front of the group. All eyes were on her, and all seemed filled with suspicion and hostility. Milo stood nearby, and at her nod, handed over the scroll so carefully and diplomatically penned by Paul from his prison cell.

Julia swallowed nervously and then began.

"This letter was dictated by Paul, to both you and your brethren in Colossae. Paul writes—"

"Who are you to be speaking for Paul!" exclaimed a man in the back of the room.

"Why didn't he come himself?" another screamed.

Julia shouted back at them, angrily. "Paul is in prison." At this, the room broke into a cacophony of heated shouts, with some yelling, "Let her speak!"

Others objected to Julia even more loudly, saying that Paul had slighted them by sending a Roman woman rather than a man of their own people. "Why didn't he send Timothy, or at least Epaphras?" someone wanted to know.

"We don't know where Epaphras is," Julia shouted. "We think he was arrested."

Rebuked, the crowd quieted for a moment.

Julia seized the moment. "Please, listen to what Paul says," she pleaded. Then she read, "'Let me tell you how hard I have worked for you and for the people in Laodicea. Do not let anyone deceive you with false arguments, no matter how good they seem to be. See to it, then, that no one enslaves you by means of the worthless deceit of human wisdom, which comes from the teachings handed down by human beings and from the ruling spirits of the universe, and not from Yeshua.'"

As Julia spoke these words, those assembled to her left—Grecian merchants, landlords, and nobility—became increasingly agitated, speaking among themselves loudly, angrily.

She pushed on, her voice rising to be heard over theirs. "'In union with Yeshua, you were circumcised, not with the circumcision that is made by human beings, but with the circumcision made by Yeshua, which consists of being freed from the power of this sinful self.'"

The mention of circumcision silenced the men's voices in the crowd. This subject was a particularly sensitive point for both groups. Neither gentiles nor Jewish followers quite understood what Paul was saying.

Julia was able to stop shouting over the quieter crowd and continued, "'Let no one make rules about what you eat or drink or about holy days or the New Moon Festival or the Sabbath.'"

At this statement, those who'd converted from Judaism began to voice their objections.

"Paul is a Jew! How *dare* he!" a woman yelled.

Another woman on the opposite side of the room shouted, "He cannot take our culture from us! Without the festivals, our crops will die in the fields!"

And again, the room broke into a free-for-all, each side shouting at Julia and at the other.

Julia persisted, struggling to be heard over the roiling crowd. "'But now you must get rid of all these things: anger, passion, and hateful feelings. No insults or obscene talk must ever come from your lips. There is no longer any distinction between Gentiles and Jews, circumcised and uncircumcised, barbarians, savages, slaves, and free, but Yeshua is all, Yeshua is in all.'"

The few who were still listening erupted at this last. They had no intention of abandoning their separate identities, their class distinctions, their biases and prejudices. The idea of uniting under Yeshua was anathema to all they stood for.

Julia recognized utter defeat. She embraced Nympha, pressed the letter into her hands, and fled.

By the time she and Milo reached Ephesus, Julia's mood had shifted. Indignant now, she decided to drop her involvement with the new sect and get on with life as she had always known it. Obviously, this new cult was exactly what people were saying: nothing but a nest of subversives and peasants.

Julia sent a note to Prisca telling her that she wanted to discontinue her association with the Christians, but hoped to maintain a friendship with her.

It would be a long time before Julia would see Prisca again. Later that week, a courier arrived. Marcus had been called back to Rome.

TWENTY-SEVEN

Ostia
Present Day

Anna-Marie and Philippe, with Giuseppe trailing behind, left the castle in the cool of the morning and walked toward the site of the old synagogue, carrying shovels and a milk crate full of tools.

Philippe couldn't help needling Anna-Marie. "So, you think we're going to find something based on what this caretaker says?"

"Hey," Anna-Marie replied, "Giuseppe isn't stupid, and he knows more about these grounds than we'll ever hope to know. So knock it off."

"Okay, okay, sorry," Philippe said.

When they reached the synagogue, they waited for Giuseppe to catch up. When he did, he pointed to the gravesite once again. "It's hard for me to say exactly because it's all covered up now, but I think it's over there."

Anna-Marie and Philippe stepped from the synagogue into a slight depression, and then hiked about ten yards to where Giuseppe had pointed. He followed them.

"Okay, let's get at it," Philippe said.

A shadow covered the site. Anna-Marie and Philippe dropped the milk crate and began digging with shovels. Giuseppe stood by, watching.

Philippe positioned himself at one end of the dig area, Anna-Marie at the other, and the two gradually cut into the earth a few inches at a time, carefully tossing dirt to one side.

They worked through the morning. At noon, they broke for a short lunch of sandwiches and fruit—a box lunch had been packed for Giuseppe as well—and then they began again. As the afternoon wore on, Anna-Marie's shovel struck something solid. The noisy clang caused the pair to stop.

"Probably a large rock," Anna-Marie said.

Philippe's shovel caused another noisy clang. Anna-Marie yelled for Giuseppe to toss over a trowel. She caught it and began carefully lifting earth away from an object buried there.

Philippe joined her, and the two dug carefully a few inches at a time, moving toward each other and throwing dirt to the side.

As they got further along and closed in on each other, Anna-Marie said, "We've got something here...."

"Yeah, maybe. Need to get more debris off," Philippe said.

"That's it, that's it." Giuseppe waved his arms and then pointed. "You've found it."

"What is it, Giuseppe?" Anna-Marie asked.

"It's the top," Giuseppe said. "The top."

"Of the grave?" Anna-Marie stopped work and looked up at him through squinty eyes.

"Yes, the top. But you have to keep going," Giuseppe said.

As Anna-Marie and Philippe continued their work, a six-foot-long slab revealed itself.

"Geez, would you look at that," Anna-Marie said in amazement. "It's marble, I think."

"I suppose it's too much to hope that this is the top of a sarcophagus?" Philippe said.

Giuseppe didn't know that word. This was his find, too. "What's that?"

"Like a big stone coffin?" Philippe answered.

"No, no, no. It's not," Giuseppe insisted. "You have to go down more."

It wasn't easy digging. The earth was unyielding, and exhaustion was setting in, but the two excavators took a deep breath and shoveled some more. It wasn't long before a few bricks came into view beneath the marble slab.

"That's the front," Giuseppe said excitedly.

"So it is," Philippe said.

Anna-Marie thought this might look familiar to Giuseppe, and knew it for sure when she looked up at him.

"That's it. That is what I saw," Giuseppe exclaimed. "Keep going. The cross is down farther."

Giuseppe's excitement was contagious. Anna-Marie and Philippe renewed their digging with gusto.

Another foot down and something glittered at the center. Anna-Marie moved toward it. She took a small hand shovel and, with Philippe's help, dug closer in. Scraping ever more gently now, she moved still more debris. Finally, she reached a rough stone caked with mud. More scraping revealed the carved writing on it: *Familiae Ben-hadad.*

Philippe and Anna-Marie froze.

And then they looked at each other in bewilderment.

Philippe spoke under his breath, "This is no simple gravesite. This is a mausoleum, a family crypt. A family by the name of Ben-hadad is buried here."

"Oh no," Anna-Marie said.

They both sank to the ground. Anna-Marie put her head in her hands. She felt about to cry. "We've got nothing," she said, raising her head to look at Philippe.

"Well, we've got *something*," Philippe said. "It's just not what we are looking for."

"What's wrong?" Giuseppe said sensing the darkening mood.

"Nothing is wrong." Anna-Marie wanted very much for Giuseppe not to see disappointment. She held her eyes on Philippe as she said to Giuseppe in an upbeat tone, "Gosh, but I'm tired. I think we'd better wrap it up for today."

Catching the meaning of her look, he said, "Yes, right, enough for today. Thanks, Giuseppe, for the help."

Giuseppe furrowed his brow. Something was wrong, but he didn't know what.

"So, let me get this again," Jacques said to Anna-Marie and Philippe as they took a late dinner at the castle. You got down to a marble slab, six feet long, and then directly underneath, you found a stone attached to bricks, probably a brick wall, and a family name carved on it.

"Yes," Philippe said.

"So, nothing," Anna-Marie said.

"It's hardly nothing," Jacques remarked. "An undiscovered crypt. But that's not our mission. I'll report it in, and then we can pack up and get out of here, first thing tomorrow. Someone is going to have a great time discovering what's there."

"They will," Anna-Marie said. "I think that mausoleum is built into the hillside because on one side—it would be the back side—it's solid ground with a bunch of healthy trees growing there, but on the other side—the front, apparently—it's just dirt and debris."

"It could be a really big crypt, but of course, we don't know," Philippe said.

"Nuts," Jacques said, his most inflammatory response to any snag.

As the three departed the cold, clammy castle dining room, they came face-to-face with Giuseppe standing just outside.

TWENTY-EIGHT

Ostia

"Here we go again," Philippe said to Anna-Marie as the two exited the castle and joined up with Giuseppe for a second day at the site of the Ben-hadad family crypt.

When Giuseppe left the site the day before, he had worried that Anna-Marie and Philippe didn't believe him anymore because they hadn't found the cross. So that evening, he decided to set things straight. When he found Jacques, Anna-Marie, and Philippe together, he made his case to the three of them.

"I know you think I'm not very smart," he said, "but I know there is a cross there and a Christian, but you have to keep digging."

Jacques put his arm around the clearly agitated younger man. "Giuseppe, we trust you, and not only that, we're counting on you to make sure Anna-Marie and Philippe are digging exactly at the spot where you think the cross is. Okay?"

Giuseppe nodded, a look of determination replacing the one of desperation.

Under Giuseppe's self-assured supervision, Anna-Marie and Philippe dug down into the dry soil, and finally they hit pay dirt. Their shovels found the edge of something. Scraping downward, the outline of a marble slab came into view.

143

As Anna-Marie worked the edges of the slab, Philippe dug with his gloved fingers and a spade, freeing up flat red brick, a few inches thick and nearly a foot long.

"Look at this, Anna-Marie—it's got a legion stamp. This is definitely Empire era." He set the brick carefully aside and started digging more carefully, freeing and stacking more and more bricks.

Anna-Marie stopped and went suddenly quiet.

Giuseppe had fallen asleep under a tree.

"You've got something?" Philippe asked.

"Maybe. Hang on."

Anna-Marie did have something. She bent down, clearing away debris, and held her breath. *Geez*, she thought. She had come to a stone plaque and had reached the top of some engraving.

Philippe scrambled over to see why Anna-Marie was so quiet. "What have you got?" He wiped sweat from his brow.

"Look at this," she exclaimed.

Philippe took one look and started scraping downward. In silence and side-by-side, the two continued removing dirt until a symbol appeared.

"This is unbelievable," Anna-Marie whispered, in awe of what she was looking at. *Giuseppe was right*, she thought with a combination of relief and gratitude.

Jacques recognized the symbol. "This is the Chi-Rho."

"The ancient monogram of Christ." Anna-Marie fought back tears.

Anna-Marie was amazed that Giuseppe had correctly recognized the symbol. "Giuseppe, how did you recognize that this was a cross?" Anna-Marie asked the now-awake caretaker.

"My mamma said that used to be how we made crosses," Giuseppe said.

"My God," Philippe said. "Let's keep going."

Another hour's work and the whole tablet appeared. Beneath the Chi Rho symbol were lines of letters.

"Must be an epitaph," Jacques said quietly.

"Oh my God, would you look at that?" she said so loudly that Giuseppe jumped to his feet and pointed.

"Yes, that's it. I told you." Giuseppe could not contain his excitement and started to jump around.

Εδώ βρίσκεται η Τζούλια επίσκοπος
Εκείνη κοιμήθηκε ειρηνικά
για την εικοστή πρώτη
του μήνα Ιανουάριο κατά το
έκτο έτος του Τραϊανού

"I can't read it," Anna-Marie said.

"Neither can I." Philippe's lips turned down.

Anna-Marie felt her heart pounding so hard that she thought it would burst. As blood rushed to her head, she became dizzy and began to fall backward. Philippe caught her and set her upright.

Looking frightened, Giuseppe stopped dancing. "Are you all right, Anna-Marie?"

Anna-Marie gave him a thumbs-up. Then, she put her fingers to her temples. "We need Jacques right away."

"Yes, I would say so," Philippe responded. "Call him."

She dug into her pocket and grabbed her phone. With shaky fingers, she punched in Jacques's number. When he answered, she quickly asked, "Do you read Greek?"

"What? Yes, of course."

Yes, of course. What doesn't he do? Anna-Marie thought in amusement. "Well, you'd better get over here right away."

Silence for several seconds. "Explain, please?"

"We've come to the cross that Giuseppe talked about. It's a Chi Rho. There are some letters under it, Greek, I presume. It looks like an epitaph, but neither Philippe nor I can translate it."

"You don't mean it." The professor's voice was surprisingly calm under the circumstances.

"I do."

"Leaving now."

Anna-Marie could barely contain herself, and in her excitement, she threw her arms around Giuseppe. "Whatever would we have done without you?"

Giuseppe blushed crimson, blinking rapidly. He had for so long been passed over for any human touch that he felt overcome.

A little embarrassed, Anna-Marie relaxed her embrace and looked at Giuseppe for a moment. She couldn't help thinking that if all these sophisticated, experienced archeologists had simply asked an unpretentious local caretaker what he knew, they could have saved hundreds of hours of needless work. She was, of course, assuming the best.

⁓

Jacques bent over to examine what Anna-Marie and Philippe had uncovered. He noted that the tablet was about two feet by three feet and mortared to the brick wall. He read the words to himself and then turned his head and gazed back up at Anna-Marie.

Never effusive, the professor said, "Not bad. Nice work."

Philippe rolled his eyes.

An exasperated Anna-Marie said, "Is that all you can say? Read it to us, Jacques, for God's sake."

"Yes, yes, of course." First his habitual two blinks. Then he read aloud,

HERE LIES JULIA EPISCOPA.
SHE FELL ASLEEP IN PEACE
ON THE TWENTY-FIRST OF JANUARY
IN THE SIXTH YEAR OF TRAJAN.'

Great job, you two," he added.

"Well, it hasn't been just us, you know." Anna-Marie nodded toward Giuseppe. "He gets most of the credit here."

Giuseppe stared down at his shoes.

Seeing how uncomfortable the young caretaker seemed to be, Jacques approached him and put a hand on his shoulder. "Good job, mate. Thank you." He turned toward Philippe and Anna-Marie. "Gather your tools." Then, he jogged a few feet away while reaching for his phone.

"You what? Where?" a startled Yigael said.

"Near the periphery of the synagogue."

Yigael had been napping and hadn't yet come to. "Wait a minute."

He dropped the phone, squinted, and rubbed his eyes. Then he sat up on the edge of his bed, ran thick fingers over his bald pate, and picked up the phone again. Abra had vacated her place on the pillow beside Yigael and taken a position beside him.

"Okay, Jacques, let me have that one more time." He gave Abra's head a rub.

"We found her, Yigael. Julia. We found her over at the old synagogue, next to it. We got to the epitaph. That tells us she's there."

"Details?"

"Fill you in later. Meantime, I'm waiting for your orders. I know how much you like it when I go off on my own." Jacques grinned to himself. He still loved to badger the always-tense Yigael.

"Never mind, you yokel," Yigael snapped. He still felt foggy. Sometimes, these days he felt as if his whole system needed an oil change. "Okay, when did you find her?"

"Philippe and Anna-Marie located her just minutes ago." Jacques ran through the details of the discovery for Yigael.

"Good, good. That's good." The fog was clearing. "Okay, I'm up. I'll get a plane out of here. First, I have to make some calls." Then he yelled into the receiver, "Secure the site."

"Done," Jacques responded. "And your room is ready," he added.

Yigael scowled and hung up.

Jacques jogged back to the site. "Giuseppe, do you think you could stay and keep an eye out here for the next hour or two? Until security gets here? It would be a big help to me."

"Yes, I think I could," Giuseppe answered, his enthusiasm undimmed.

"Don't let anyone come close. And do not tell anyone what's here. Okay?"

"Yes, okay."

"Good, we're counting on you." Jacques gave Giuseppe another shoulder pat.

He looked at his watch and turned to Philippe and Anna-Marie. "It's nearly five. I want the volunteers to finish out the day, leave the site, and return to the castle as they usually do. Anna-Marie, call Carol and tell her to stay on-site. We'll pick her up."

By the time Anna-Marie and Philippe finished gathering their tools, Jacques had double checked with the overseer regarding security and was waving Anna-Marie and Philippe over to the car.

"Okay you two, in you go," he said.

As Anna-Marie stepped in, she gave a backward glance to Giuseppe, who smiled and waved.

After picking up Carol, the four of them headed for the cafeteria. They seated themselves at a small corner table, each with a cup of tea. Jacques cautioned them, "The volunteers must suspect nothing."

"Of course," Anna-Marie said.

He turned to Carol. "As soon as we finish here, I want you to post a notice on the castle bulletin board announcing a meeting this evening in the chapel right after dinner."

He continued, "I'll tell the volunteers that the search has ended because we've run out of funds and that they need to return to their rooms, pack their belongings, and be ready to leave for home in the morning."

Jacques turned to Carol once more. "Make all the plane reservations and print boarding passes out of Rome. And be sure they're all accounted for tomorrow morning and that they're all on the bus out of Ostia."

"Got it," Carol said.

"Now. Yigael and Valentina will soon be arriving. Who else, I'm not sure. So, Philippe, get rooms ready and see to a new meal schedule with the cook. And order some better wine. I'm sick of drinking this vinegar they sell to the tourists.

"Thank heaven," Philippe mumbled under his breath.

"What do you want me to do?" Anna-Marie asked.

"You need to keep an eye on Giuseppe," he said. "Make sure he doesn't get yap-happy."

TWENTY-NINE

Rome

Valentina dug through her bag, scrambling to find the secured cell phone Yigael had given her. The team was calling. Maybe they'd found something. She pressed the green button. "*Si, pronto.*" Hello. She sat down suddenly at her desk.

"When?" she asked, waving a hand for Erika to sit down.

Valentina and Erika had stopped off at their office before wrapping up their day and heading for home.

"Just a little while ago," Yigael answered. "Jacques just called."

"Truly? You mean it?" Valentina put a hand to her face, astonished.

"I would hardly joke about it," Yigael said.

"No, of course not. It's just that I was beginning to lose hope." Valentina had been fielding ever-increasing phone calls from an impatient Cardinal Ricci, who persistently questioned her about "the holdup" on finding the old bishop. She, in turn, had become more and more panicky as time went on and nothing was found.

"Well, never mind that," Yigael said.

"Look," Valentina glanced up. "Erika's here, too. I'm going to put you on speaker." She punched the speaker button. "Okay, what else can you tell me?"

151

Yigael continued, "They found the grave site in an unexpected place, most unexpected."

"Not in the necropoli? Then where?" Valentina asked.

"In a private family crypt near the synagogue. A family by the name of Ben-hadad. They're not inside yet, of course, just on the outside, but they uncovered a plaque with an early Christian cross on it, and there is an epitaph for Julia Episcopa."

"When are you planning on opening it up to see if she's in there?" Valentina asked.

"From what Jacques told me, we'll need to dig down, shore up the edges of the site. A few days at most," Yigael said.

"Ye gods, I'll have to tell the cardinal," Valentina said. A look of dread came over her face. "Is there anything more you can tell me before I speak with him?"

"At the moment, that's pretty much what we have. When are you coming?" Yigael wanted to know.

"Right away. I'll toss a few things together and leave first thing in the morning."

"I'm flying to Rome at noon tomorrow. I'll catch the train to Ostia," Yigael said. "Oh, and one more thing."

"What's that?" Valentina asked.

"When you speak with Ricci…" Yigael started to say.

"Yes?" Valentina responded curiously.

"See if you can't get him to do something about the accommodations. I'll be damned if I'm going to stay in that musty, cold castle of his."

Valentina smiled to herself. "I'll see what I can do."

"Strange," Erika said, sitting on the edge of her seat. "But why would she be buried near the Jewish synagogue in someone else's family crypt? There aren't even supposed to be crypts there! And if she was a bishop…I mean, wouldn't the Church have made an arrangement for her? That makes no sense."

"I don't know," Valentina said.

"Wow, I really didn't expect we would find her," Erika confessed.

"Nor did I, but now I've got a huge hurdle to leap over."

Valentina gave Erika a pained expression. "What am I going to say to Cardinal Ricci?"

"Just tell him you found a bishop. I don't think you can let on that this bishop is a woman, can you?" Erika said. "Besides, we won't *really* know it's a woman until we examine the bones."

Valentina poured two glasses of water from a carage tht sat at the corner of her desk and gave one to Erika. "I hate deceiving him. It's not ethical. But if I don't, he'll stop the money and use his pull to revoke the permits."

"I'm sure he would, definitely," Erika agreed.

"I'll think of something," Valentina said. Changing the subject, she asked, "You coming?"

"Let me think about it. I could stay working here while you're there."

"What's the matter? Don't want to get your hands dirty?"

Erika gave her good friend a playfully scornful look.

Valentina sped to the Vatican and once again found herself outside Cardinal Ricci's office, facing his secretary.

Father Rinaldi was seated at his wood desk, an open carton of what looked like a half-eaten cannoli on top of it. As Valentina turned her back and headed for a chair to wait, Rinaldi quickly captured the cannoli carton in the crook of his arm and pulled it into the top drawer, hoping that Valentina wouldn't see him do it. When Valentina turned and sat down, she noticed the pinched expression on Rinaldi's face.

My God, she thought, *if he gets any rounder....*

Rinaldi rudely turned his back on his guest and noisily opened a file cabinet behind him. "He'll only be a moment, *Dottoressa.*"

"Thank you, Father," Valentina responded as politely as she could.

Turning around to face her, Father Rinaldi brought up why Valentina was there, hoping that she would take the cue and give him fodder for gossip. "The cardinal has been very interested in this project of yours." He sniffed. Father Rinaldi knew little about what was afoot in Ostia, but he was keen to know more and pass it on.

"Truly," Valentina responded with a secretive smile. *What a gossip mill this place is,* she thought. *A bunch of bored old biddies in bright red dresses.* She had not spoken to anyone about the nature of her request for a meeting, and she certainly wasn't going to give anything away to this rotund underling.

Father Rinaldi saw a tiny green light flash next to his desk drawer. Looking disappointed, he said, "I think the cardinal is ready for you now. You can go on in."

Valentina rose, walked toward the cardinal's entrance door, and rapped softly. Then, she turned the knob and opened it.

"Come, come." Cardinal Ricci beckoned from behind his desk. "Please sit."

He sat back on his thickly-cushioned leather chair while he motioned Valentina toward the carved wood chair in front of him.

Valentina sensed the cardinal was in a foul mood.

"So, Valentina, are we finished with your wild goose chase, so that you can get back to the work I'm paying you for?" Ricci snapped at her.

"Cardinal, I have—"

Ricci interrupted her "By my count, you'll be out of funding next week. You led me to believe that you knew there was a bishop and that you knew where he was. You misled me. You used this Holy Office, and you used my influence in order go on this wild goose chase. How dare you! Furthermore, you are making a fool out of—"

It was Valentina's turn to interrupt. "Cardinal, we found the bishop." She gave him her most winning smile.

Walking into his office, Valentina had had moral qualms about misleading the cardinal. He had relieved her of her guilt with his petulant ranting.

Caught off guard, Ricci fell silent. Valentina watched his

expression turn from sullen anger, to greed, to quiet calculation, and then back to his usual stony self-control. "Have you?"

"Indeed, we have."

Seemingly overcome, Ricci slumped back in his heavy chair.

Valentina went on. "I will caution you that we don't know much yet, because the discovery was made only in the past few hours. However, we believe this is the bishop we were looking for. We found an inscribed tablet with a cross above it. The inscription indicates that the person buried in this place was a bishop and that this bishop died during the reign of the Emperor Trajan. That would calculate to AD 104, give or take a year or two."

"By God, this is better than I expected," the cardinal said smugly as he pondered the accolades that were sure to come his way.

"Keep in mind that we haven't opened the tomb yet. We've only found the inscription on the outside of a crypt. You know how these things go. We might find nothing. But Jacques is applying for the permits we need to get more equipment to the site. We'll need to excavate further than we've got permission for, and we'll need to stabilize the tomb before we can open it." Then Valentina coyly remarked, "I'm sure we could proceed much more swiftly if Your Eminence were to intercede on our behalf."

"Yes, of course. Consider it done. And get on with it."

"Thank you, Cardinal. Oh, and one more thing?"

The cardinal narrowed his brows. "Yes, what is it?"

"The student volunteers have been let go. That leaves just the professionals. We no longer need the dormitory rooms that the castle provided. Frankly, the castle isn't all that comfortable," she added. "No offense." Valentina looked down, pursed her lips, smoothed her skirt, and dared herself to look back up.

Cardinal Ricci was staring at her legs.

Valentina cleared her throat. "Eminence, I understand that your nephew presides over the church there. Could you arrange to have the staff put up in the chapter house?" she asked boldly. "We'll need five rooms. We could make it work with four if two of the men share." Valentina knew all too well that many rectories had rooms to spare. At one time, it would have been filled with Augustine brothers, but those days had long gone.

"Of course," Cardinal Ricci said. *Anything she wants.* "I'll call Francesco."

"Thank you, Cardinal."

"You just be sure to keep me up to speed on the excavation."

"Yes, of course, Cardinal."

That woman, Cardinal Ricci thought after Valentina departed. *If only I weren't sworn to God....*

He summoned his secretary and instructed him to call his nephew, Father Francesco Ricci, and arrange for rooms at the Basilica Santa Aurea. He also ordered Rinaldi to notify the overseer at the castle that the remaining guests would be moving out.

Father Rinaldi was irked that his boss wasn't letting him in on what was going on out there in Ostia. He wasn't surprised, though, because the cardinal often kept things close to the vest, to the irritation of his nosy secretary.

Valentina departed the Vatican feeling victorious about garnering better living quarters for her colleagues and smug about deceiving the cardinal. But as she stepped outside Vatican borders that afternoon on her way home to prepare for Ostia, she thought more apprehensively, *The day of reckoning is going to come.*

THIRTY

Rome

Valentina tossed her beloved overalls into a weekend travel bag and added a sun hat and a few toiletries. She exited her apartment for Ostia wearing jeans, a T-shirt, and a pair of hiking boots. She wanted to be prepared in case they scoped out the site before digging.

Valentina had long maintained that archeologists belonged in the ruins rather than the classroom, but it had been a long time since she had got her hands into the earth. She loved fieldwork. She found satisfaction in digging and brushing, in shoveling particles into sifters and then waiting for the surprises. It was like magic to her. She also loved trading the stiff boardroom attire she usually wore for her ancient bibbed overalls that were broken in just right.

Valentina's excitement was building. She parked alongside the beautiful Basilica Santa Aurea, standing directly across from the old *castello*, walked across the courtyard to the priory where the priest lived, and pressed the doorbell. A middle-aged man opened the door and greeted her. He was dressed in a long, black-hooded cassock tied at the waist and a short cape that covered his shoulders. It was Franciscan garb, but this church was Augustinian, a similar mendicant order founded in the thirteenth century. Their mission, to educate and help the poor.

"You must be the cardinal's nephew. Father Ricci?" Valentina said.

"Yes. And you must be *Dottoressa* Vella," the priest said warmly, kissing her on both cheeks. "And please, call me Father Francesco."

"And I'm Valentina." She beamed. "This is a beautiful place."

"Yes, it is."

Valentina sensed the kindheartedness of this man and warmed to him immediately. *He seems nothing like his Uncle Antonio,* she thought.

"Please, come in," Father Francesco said as he welcomed her into his office. "And please sit down."

"Thank you, Father. Are the others here?" she asked as she took a seat.

"Not yet. I'm told they're still at the castle, packing up. I understand you're not staying over?"

"That's right. I'll go home at night."

"Even so, I have a small extra bedroom, a cell, really, but it's adequate. We've far more room than we need these days. You can use it to change, freshen up, and rest when you want to."

"You're very kind, Father. Thank you."

Valentina noted that Father Francesco *looked* nothing like his ascetic-appearing uncle, either. The priest was late thirtyish, of average height, with a fringe of graying hair circling a bald spot at the crown. His weather-beaten olive complexion provided the perfect setting for a large Roman nose and big brown eyes with curiously long lashes.

Father Francesco had just opened his mouth to speak when there was a clatter outside on the stone steps. Anna-Marie, Philippe, and Carol, and their several bags, had arrived. Valentina greeted them and then introduced the three to their host.

"Welcome to our little chapter house," Father Francesco said. "We're glad to have you. Now, let me show you around before I take you to your rooms."

Father Francesco passed through the high arched doorway and went directly to the refectory, with its high beamed ceiling and its pale, stuccoed walls. Along one wall, one could just make out a faded fresco of the Madonna, upon another hung a large, wood crucifix. At the center of the room stood a long, heavy, and battered wooden table where generation upon generation of holy brothers had taken their meals. A similarly rustic old sideboard held stacks of stoneware plates, silverware, and serving pieces, as well as a large bowl filled with apples, oranges, and bananas. Light streamed in through large windows, opened wide to reveal a center courtyard filled with herbs and flowers.

"This is where we take our evening meal," Father Francesco said, then escorted them next into the kitchen where they could smell the aroma of something tempting being prepared.

"Our cook, Concetta, will prepare lunches for you to eat in the field. For breakfast, you're on your own, but there is plenty of food available here—muesli and fruit, prosciutto, cheese, yogurt, and Concetta's homemade bread."

Exiting the kitchen and heading for the stairs, Father Francesco said, "This house is yours to come and go as you wish, but we lock up at ten. If you intend to be out after that, you need to let someone know, so that we can make arrangements to let you back in. There are always a few brothers about, though not so many as there once were."

"I doubt anyone will be going out after dinner, Father," Valentina said. *We'll all be exhausted,* she thought.

Father Francesco led the group to the top of the stairs and assigned each a room. Jacques and Philippe would share. Anna-Marie and Carol would each have her own room. Yigael would also be on his own, in a room next to the cell Valentina would be using.

"Please, take your time settling in. Dinner will be served in the dining room at seven, right after Vespers," Father Francesco said. "Of course, you are always welcome to join us for evening prayer," he added hopefully.

Yigael arrived within the hour, and he and Valentina couldn't wait to visit the dig site. When they saw the plaque, Valentina felt her heart flip. "Oh wow. I feel almost dizzy. Can this be real? Could Julia really be here?"

"I think we're onto something," Yigael said, trying to contain his zeal.

"You think?" Valentina laughed. She saw right through her friend. The sparkle in Yigael's eyes was a dead giveaway, and it warmed her to see his enthusiasm coming through.

"In the morning, then," Yigael had said.

The two felt almost giddy as they returned to the priory.

The team had not been together since the day at the train station, and their conversation around the dinner table was animated.

Concetta carried out of the kitchen a steaming dish of penne pasta dressed simply with fresh herbs, olive oil, and a local *pecorino romano,* then a huge tray of *veal meatballs* smothered in a layer of her secret Sicilian sauce, and all talk stopped, replaced by sighs of bliss. The cook was not done, bringing crusty warm bread and an olive, fennel, and blood orange salad to finish the meal. Jacques and Philippe were happy to see that two liters of Chianti had also made their way to the table.

"I see why you like it here, Father," Yigael said, taking in the heavenly aromas from Concetta's delicious creations.

After weeks of dubious castle and cafeteria food, the team deeply appreciated the homemade feast of their welcoming hosts.

As they dined mostly in silence, Father Francesco wondered about his visitors. *They haven't said a word about why they're here,* he thought.

The team knew that with Father Francesco, the cook, and a housekeeper creeping about, they had to stay silent.

THIRTY-ONE

Ostia

It took four excruciating days to stabilize the site, during which time Valentina might have continued her work in Rome. But feeling too impatient to concentrate on old documents, she handled her nervous energy by driving back and forth from Rome to Ostia to see how the work was progressing. Finally, when the all clear came and the dig started, she felt too excited to return home, so she stayed overnight in the cell provided by Father Francesco.

Antsy to get out to the site, she woke before dawn. But finding no one else up, ventured outside where she crossed paths with Anna-Marie, who had just completed an early morning run.

"You must have been over the moon when you uncovered that plaque," Valentina said.

"I was," Anna-Marie said. "I nearly fainted."

"We still know so little about her," Valentina said.

"I guess we'll have to see what her bones tell us about who she is," Anna-Marie responded.

"If she's there," Valentina said.

"There's that," Anna-Marie said.

The two women walked toward the basilica and stepped inside. They stopped in the nave of the fifteenth-century structure and gazed up with admiration at the magnificent rose window.

"And to think that a caretaker led you to her," Valentina said. "We got lucky."

"Yes," Valentina said. "And Giuseppe, such a sweet fellow." She had talked to him several times during her trips to Rome and back.

Valentina and Anna-Marie walked slowly toward the apse that featured sixteenth-century frescoes before moving on to view the painting by Pietro da Cortona called the *Ecstasy of Saint Monica*.

"So, Erika isn't joining us?" Anna-Marie asked.

"Her specialty is textual archaeology. She hasn't worked in the field for quite a while," Valentina answered. "But aside from that she's staying there to field Cardinal Ricci's never-ending calls," she laughed, "trying to keep him happy."

Anna-Marie smiled. "Think we'd better get back?" She headed for the door.

"Yes, Yigael will be chomping at the bit. He thinks he's hiding his impatience, but I know him all too well," Valentina said. "And I'm also champing at the bit." She laughed again.

"Yes, of course, Holy Father." Father Francesco Ricci all of a sudden got taller in his chair. It wasn't every day a poor parish priest received a call from Il Papa. "My uncle told me nothing. He just asked if I would host them. And they've said nothing, which is odd. Usually, archaeologists talk our ears off because they're so excited about their work."

"Find out what you can, Francesco. Your uncle has always been a bit too sly for his own good. He wouldn't send a team there if he wasn't up to something interesting."

"Of course, Holy Father. And thank you for cueing me to Uncle Antonio's bronchitis. I wouldn't know otherwise. Glad he's feeling better."

"Take care of yourself, Francesco."

Father Francesco heard the click as Pope Augustine ended the call.

It had been an unlikely alliance—a simple parish priest and the supreme leader of the Church—but their friendship had come about quite naturally.

Pope Augustine and Antonio Ricci had served together as cardinals. When Ricci's nephew, Francesco, decided to follow his uncle into the priesthood, Cardinal Ricci had been pleased. But when Francesco had decided to join a mendicant order rather than follow in his uncle's footsteps and ascend the Church hierarchy, Cardinal Ricci became furious. Francesco, passionately absorbed in serving the Church and its parishioners, viewed ecclesiastical careerism to be in opposition to Yeshua's call to serve the poor. Cardinal Ricci's disappointment in his nephew's apparent deficiencies—and his damnable spiritual purity—had turned to bitterness, and he dismissed his nephew.

Pope Augustine, then known as Cardinal Zembala Mozombe, had entertained a different opinion of the young novitiate. He saw a unique appeal in the young cleric that the older one lacked. Francesco had inborn warmth that drew in followers. It was a rare charm, an invaluable asset, one that Cardinal Mozombe wanted to nurture. He became a mentor to the young man, and when Mozombe was elected pope, the first black pope in Church history, their friendship endured. However, their conversations weren't as frequent as once they had been.

Father Francesco was mulling things over. His uncle had been unusually guarded in his request for accommodations. Giuseppe had been tagging along with one of the women in this interesting group, and in fact, they all seemed more than a little interested in Giuseppe. *I must have a talk with him,* Father Francesco thought.

⁓

Anna-Marie and Carol met in the kitchen to collect lunches for the team. Concetta had put sliced mortadella, salami, cheeses, olives, and several slabs of homemade focaccia into individual boxes and filled a cooler with bottled drinks.

They piled into two vans and headed toward the site. Their excitement was unmistakable.

When they arrived, Giuseppe was waiting for them. As a courtesy, Jacques had invited the curious little man to join them.

"*Ciao*, Giuseppe," Valentina said. "I'm glad you're here with us today."

Giuseppe smiled and then glanced around nervously at the tightly-wound Yigael, whom he had not met before. He edged backward. "I won't be in your way. I'll just watch."

The entire group stood silently at the edge of the site and gazed at the engraved stone tablet that Giuseppe had alerted them to, each having separate thoughts about what would come of their discovery.

Valentina was most moved by the sight, even though she had seen it in the days before. She felt her heart race a little, reading what the stone announced was behind it—potentially. She wondered whether the grave had been plundered. To find intact a two-thousand-year-old crypt was a rarity.

Yigael plotted out the area for excavation and ordered a trench dug and covered with a geo-synthetic fabric. He instructed the team to dig down in one-foot increments and widen the trench a foot at each level. This would allow them a natural, convenient step down while making for a large enough area at the base to work in. While digging, Philippe would take digital photographs, and Anna-Marie would draw sketches and keep detailed notes.

They moved into action as one. Philippe put on safety glasses and lowered himself into the trench. Anna-Marie did the same, while Carol and Jacques lugged over a divided milk crate holding hand shovels, trowels, brushes, and hoes. Soon, they were all at work, except for Yigael, who chose to scope out the ruins of the synagogue and roam through the grounds. As he returned from his survey of the park, everyone else was happily talking, sharing gossip and catching up on mutual friends and acquaintances.

"Hey, you all working here or just jawing?" Yigael asked returning from his mini-walk.

"Put a lid on it," Philippe grumbled. "We're working. Why don't you jump in here and get yourself dirty?" he added with a grin.

The serious Jacques had been his usual, quiet self. He wondered at the lives of this crew. Now in his mid-forties, he felt he didn't have much of a life. He had poured himself into research analysis, which had earned him respect but also a divorce. No one ever seemed to notice or ask about him. Perhaps this was a sign he ought to, well, get a life.

"What are you up to, Anna-Marie? We haven't heard much from you lately," Carol asked as she stood up, put a hand to the small of her back, and stretched.

"Oh, you don't want to hear, truly. Been in love twice, broke up twice, had two jobs, and now I'm here," she said in rapid-fire fashion.

Giuseppe was rapt. He hadn't heard so much conversation in years. These people were surprisingly entertaining.

After the first foot, the earth became softer and more pliable, and their pace quickened. They dug through the morning, and then broke for lunch.

The afternoon brought some answers. First, they came to a corner of the tomb and then another corner, both unbroken, evidence that this was an undisturbed burial ground. Second, they reached the tomb's fascia.

When the top of a doorway appeared just below the Ben-hadad family stone tablet, work stopped, and they all fell silent.

Yigael broke the silence. "Well, here we are. This is something." He took a deep breath, awestruck. No matter what he uncovered and discovered in his lifetime of work in the field, he never ever failed to exhibit a reverence for each discovery. They never failed to move him.

"Okay, careful now," he said. Yigael jumped into the trench, picked up a mini mattock, and began scraping around and in front of the door. Down about a foot, he could see that the top of the doorway was arched and accented with smooth stones.

The workday had been long, and the sun was setting. Their

anticipation building, Philippe and Anna-Marie began to clear the way to break through. Carol and Valentina chiseled around the edges. Then they all got quiet and focused on what lay ahead. They would have to wait until morning, though, to enter whatever lay within.

THIRTY-TWO

Ostia

M orning brought overcast skies and a gentle cooling as the team found itself once more in front of a doorway that would lead them inside an ancient tomb.

Anna-Marie looked over her shoulder and caught sight of Giuseppe hurrying across the landscape to catch up. *What's he been up to?* she wondered. *Well, I can't watch him every second. Unlike him to be late, though.*

"Yes, Holy Father." Father Francesco was seated at his desk, phone to his ear. "I've just spoken with Giuseppe. He wasn't keen to talk about the gravesite because he said they were his friends, and he promised not to talk about it, but Giuseppe is a good boy, and since I am his priest, well, he has never kept secrets from me."

It was early afternoon. All eyes were on the door. It was a solid block of stone, about four feet high and two feet wide. As

Philippe looked around it to where there might be a soft spot to break through, Valentina noticed hinges on the right side, barely visible because of encrustation.

Valentina tugged at the door, but it was stubbornly immovable.

Yigael scanned around it. "Philippe, get some picks over here. The mud in the cracks around this door is too hard to break through. But be careful. Try not to damage those hinges. Come on, people! Let's go!"

It took another two hours of backbreaking work before Valentina tried the door again. This time, it jerked open just a crack.

Valentina looked again at Yigael, who nodded and gestured for her to continue.

She pulled again, and the door creaked open further, allowing just enough room for someone to slip through.

"You first," Yigael indicated to Valentina.

Valentina hesitated, took a deep breath, ducked down, and walked through the doorway, Yigael right behind her. The only light came from the slightly-open doorway. Yigael retreated and asked Jacques to bring in the portable lamps.

The others knew not to intrude. Protocol required them to stand back. Their turn would come when the first in command— Yigael—invited them in.

Yigael and Valentina entered the burial chamber again and turned on the battery-powered lamps.

"Oh, my." Valentina exhaled.

Yigael wasn't listening to her. "Look how the ceiling is curved and arched. It was designed to withstand earthquakes," Yigael commented. "Even that long ago...." His voice trailed away while his eyes fixed on a menorah painted on a wall. "This is a Jewish burial crypt. Look at the menorah and the ossuaries set into these niches. He counted. "Five of them."

Valentina's eyes were riveted elsewhere. "Yigael...." The tone of her voice caught his attention. "Look." Her voice was a whisper. Her attention was trained on a small side chamber and the human remains lying atop a foot-high slab. "I think we found her."

Yigael turned and saw what she was looking at.

"Holy God. Could it be?" Valentina said.

She and Yigael noted the shredded cloth scattered among the bones. Looking carefully at every detail on the slab, Valentina spotted a ring. She recognized its significance, but she didn't touch it.

"This is the symbol of the bishop rank," Valentina said to Yigael. "And look at this." She pointed to a stone set against the wall at the base of the bones. A message had been scratched onto it. Valentina moved closer to the stone and read,

HERE LIES JULIA LUCINIA EPISCOPA,
FOLLOWER OF YESHUA, LEADER OF CHRISTIANS.
TODAY IN DEEP SORROW,
I BURY MY BELOVED MOTHER,
A WOMAN WHO SUFFERED MUCH
BUT INSPIRED MANY.
MAY SHE REST IN PEACE,
AND MAY HER STORY BE THE TRUE TESTAMENT
TO THE LIFE SHE LIVED.
LIVIA MARCA AQUILLEIA

"It's Julia," Valentina said in a whisper. "We've found her." Tears gushed, and before she could curtail them, a sob erupted.

"I know," Yigael said putting a hand on her arm.

Valentina read the parchment again. "Her story?" she said.

"Look there," Yigael said.

Then she saw it. A tasseled scroll, wrapped in decayed oiled leather hidden under a piece of frayed cloth to the left of the bones.

"What can this be?" she said.

"You'll know soon enough," Yigael said. He looked down to where a cedar box sat at the side of the alcove. The box was about the size of a file cabinet. He noticed leather hinges that seemed to hold the lid in place. He carefully lifted the lid just a notch to see what was inside. The old scroll box was filled with fine white sand, with a few remnants of cloth peeking out.

Yigael lowered the lid back down. Then he looked up and saw a single cup set among rags on a tiny shelf. *An old drinking vessel,* he thought.

When the two gathered themselves Yigael stepped back outside and yelled, "Philippe, the cameras."

All procedures, every act from this point on would take place like a choreographed ballet, with all involved working smoothly in unison.

Yigael entered the burial chamber once again, this time with Philippe and Anna-Marie.

Philippe pulled out his digital camera and began shooting every inch of the crypt, while Anna-Marie took copious notes on all that was there.

Philippe began in the far-left corner, shooting from high to low. When Yigael was satisfied that Philippe had snapped every inch of the small room and Anna-Marie had documented everything, they all exited.

In an extreme show of courtesy, Yigael invited Giuseppe to enter next, even though etiquette called for Jacques, as the field supervisor and next in command, to go ahead of anyone else.

After each had taken a turn, they all gathered under a tree for a break before going on.

Anna-Marie came up with a question still unanswered and on the minds of all. "Why was she buried in a Jewish family crypt?"

"We don't know. We might never know," Yigael answered.

They were all silent, pondering this mysterious question. Then Giuseppe, who had been listening to these worldly scholars, said very simply, "My mama told me that Joseph of Arimathea put Yeshua in his family tomb, because they were friends. And he was a Jew and Yeshua was a Christian. Maybe she was like Yeshua and didn't have a place to go, so they put her here with them." It all made good sense to him.

"That very well may be it," Valentina said.

Yigael arranged for removal of the tomb's contents. He sent Carol back to the priory to gather storage containers. The team would tag each item for forensic investigation and then cushion it before placing it in an airtight container. Julia's bones would be packed and sent to a lab where osteoarchaeologists would X-ray and run DNA tests to determine age and sex. The scrolls near Julia's bones would be lifted ever so carefully by the gloved hands of Valentina—she prayed they wouldn't disintegrate—and placed onto a soft protective foam cushion before being quickly placed in a polycarbonate packing box. All of these would be hauled to Valeri, Valentina's and Erika's lab.

One task remained before leaving the site. Valentina must notify Cardinal Ricci. She was unsure how much to reveal and sought out Yigael.

"You have a lot of work ahead of you, weeks and weeks of it," Yigael said. "You don't really know everything you have, so how much can you tell? Tell him the minimum. You have broken through and found the bones, along with some documents and artifacts. He'll be satisfied. He knows there's not much to be said until you finish your work."

Valentina placed the call and got Father Rinaldi.

"I'll put you through," Father Rinaldi said officiously.

"Valentina, what news?" Cardinal Ricci asked, his fingers pressed tightly to his forehead.

"Wonderful news, Cardinal. We've entered the crypt. We discovered the bones and found artifacts and scrolls. They're ready for transport, and as you know, Erika and I will have our work cut out for us."

"Good work, Valentina." Ricci relaxed. "Get to it," he ordered.

"Of course, Cardinal."

Thank heaven. This couldn't be better, Ricci thought jubilantly. The cardinal was normally a circumspect leader, cautious about what he would reveal at any given time, especially these days when trouble seemed to lurk around every corner.

He knew better than to move too quickly on any find, but in this case, he found it impossible to wait. It was a breach of protocol to circumvent the Vatican press office, but Ricci wanted to make sure that he received the credit for this discovery. *I'll issue a press release today announcing a news conference tomorrow. I'll say simply that the Vatican has a revelation of worldwide significance. The press will show up. They always do.*

Cardinal Ricci pressed a button on his intercom. "Father Rinaldi, get in here."

THIRTY-THREE

Rome, AD 64

It was the year of the great fire in Rome, the fire that raged for more than six days. When the smoke cleared, much of the city of two million lay in ruins. Many blamed Nero for the fire. It was known that he wanted the land cleared so that he could construct extravagant new palaces, but he had been denied permits that would have torn down most of Rome. Nero, in turn, blamed the Christians. Vexed by their growing influence, he used the fire as an excuse to exterminate them. He arrested, tortured, and crucified Christians by the hundreds.

The Aquillii returned to Rome only to find their home on the Capitoline Hill burnt to ashes. Just as Nero was building Domus Aurea, his new palace in the burned-out center of Rome, Marcus bought one of the homes still standing near the Forum, and then he went to work as a new elected magistrate.

Raising Livia and Flavia and managing the house kept Julia busy, but she no longer played hostess to the political leaders Marcus had previously tried to impress, largely because he was out night after night as the coveted guest at others' banquets, and he never invited his wife along. Of course, as a magistrate's wife, she was invited to ladies' banquets and luncheons, but found that the company of Roman matrons bored her silly. They talked incessantly of nothing other than men, children, and the latest hairstyles.

Though she had distanced herself from the Christian communities and their endless quarrels after Laodicia, she found herself missing the company of people who discussed ideas and concerned themselves with more than idle gossip and the frivolities of noble life. Making subtle inquires, she began to cultivate new friends among the followers of the way.

"Peter is speaking tonight," Milo whispered, finding Julia in the kitchen, conferring with Cook about devising some simpler meals, what with Marcus out all the time.

"We don't need so much rich food," she was saying before turning around and seeing Milo.

"He's just arrived in Rome," Milo said.

"Who?" Julia wiped her hands dry with a towel after putting some vegetables into a terra-cotta bowl.

"Peter. Yeshua's apostle."

"Indeed," Julia said.

"Yes. And people are flocking to hear him. Would you like to go?"

Julia thought for a moment. "Yes. I would like to."

Milo was surprised because, while Julia was making new friends among the followers, she had kept her distance from discussions of doctrine or the Jewish notion of one God. Moreover, she still maintained her family shrine to Janus and Vesta, as all Roman homes must.

However, she loved these people for their imaginings of a new world, where all stood in spiritual equality, where the poor were as beloved as the wealthy, and where the central command of their faith was that they were to love one another.

At sunset, as Julia stepped out with Milo and neared the house where the meeting would take place, they found a crowd waiting outside. Milo scanned the gathering, looking for Roman soldiers. Surely, with so many people gathered, they would be on guard, but he was surprised to find none there. *A blessing,* he thought. *With so many people here.* He guided Julia forward toward the front door so as to keep her safe should trouble arise with soldiers making an appearance. They could escape through the front door and out the back.

A couple stepped out of the house—the homeowners, presumably—followed by an old, worn-out-looking man. The old man stopped and surveyed the crowd. His eyes came to rest on Julia. Perhaps it was her finery that set her apart. He gazed at her for several seconds, and then looked away. The younger man of the house shouted, "Follow us."

They led the visitors around the house and into a large walled garden that could accommodate the crowd.

When it was clear to Julia that the old man was Peter, she wondered what in the world he could have to say that drew so many to hear him. But when he began to speak, he became impassioned. His face lit up, his voice warmed. The love with which he spoke of his Master and his Master's message was writ in every line of his face. He spoke of his days with Yeshua, of healing the sick, of serving the poor, and of his own terrible betrayal, running to safety while Yeshua faced his awful execution at Roman hands for the crime of disturbing the Pax Romana, the Roman Peace. When he was done, Peter retreated into silence.

A heavy burden to bear, Julia thought as she looked at Peter's stooped frame.

Because the Christians needed a larger space for their meetings, Julia offered her home. Nero's rage and persecutions seemed to have subsided, but Julia knew she nonetheless needed to be circumspect and do her best not to attract attention of the authorities. However, she was fairly certain that Nero's soldiers wouldn't dare to come after the wife of a judge. As for Marcus, he ignored Julia so completely that he didn't notice his wife's new activities.

After that first night, Julia found that she loved more and more listening to Peter's oratory. He was mesmerizing, but try as she did, she never got to know him and never could call him a friend, though she wanted to. *He is wounded,* she thought. *Those stories about his personal demons must be true. There is something morose about him.*

175

Sometime after Peter began speaking at Julia's home, Milo picked up awful news and hurried home to tell her. "Peter has been arrested. They picked him up on the street."

"Oh, no." Julia said. "It can't be. He was here only last night."

Milo understood the implications of this arrest. "Will you go to him?"

Julia stared into the distance, eyes filling with tears. She recalled Peter's lifelong shame at having abandoned his own teacher.

"I think I must."

When Julia arrived at the *tullianum,* the prison on the northeastern slope of the Capitoline Hill, she learned that Peter had been charged with treason and sedition. Nero had ordered him publicly executed. Julia had been mistaken in thinking that Nero's passions had cooled. She and her friends were clearly in more danger than she had realized. The jailers allowed Julia into Peter's prison cell, but ordered Milo to stay back.

Julia found Peter inexplicably calm. "I don't know what to say." She reached out to him, but he drew back.

"You need say nothing. My fate is set, and I am ready to die."

"But—"

"I'm glad you came," Peter interrupted. "Hear me now. You must."

"What is it?" Julia scanned Peter's deeply lined, bearded face. He seemed to her to be burning with intent.

"I have worked with a scribe for a number of years. He has written some precious documents and will be in danger very soon. I ask that you take him in. I can ask this only of a person of means and position."

"Where is he, and how will I know him?" Julia asked.

"The scribe will find you." In a wholly uncharacteristic gesture, Peter grasped Julia's wrists. "He must be protected and his works kept safe. Promise me."

Julia didn't hesitate. "I do promise, Peter."

"Go now. I must be alone." He released his grip on Julia.

Knowing she would never again see this man, tears streamed down as Julia turned toward the cell door.

Despite her horror about Peter's fate, Julia headed for the markets the next morning. She had placed herself in enough danger visiting Peter in the first place. To appear openly concerned with the matter would place her in greater danger still. As they finished shopping and gathered their bundles together, Julia had the odd feeling she was being watched. Once they came to one of the busier intersections, Julia relaxed, but just as she did, a man, slightly stooped, crossed in front of her, causing her to stop so that she wouldn't bump into him. Julia nodded faintly and moved to step around him, but he blocked her.

"Please," the man said.

"You be on your way," Milo said. "Leave the lady alone."

"I mean no harm. I need to speak to her."

Julia looked the man over and noted that he was quite gaunt. She watched as the man quickly examined his clothing, suddenly realizing, it seemed to her, how dirty and tattered he looked—a beggar in the street approaching a noblewoman.

"We search for peace in our homes," he said.

Julia recognized the words as a code among Christians.

A family of four mingled for a moment with the little group, but Julia ignored them. When they were a few away, Julia whispered so that no one else could hear, "Ah, you are the scribe...the scribe Peter spoke of. You are the one."

The scribe nodded.

Julia scrutinized the man. "My name is Julia. Come with me. I daresay I have been expecting you."

THIRTY-FOUR

Rome AD 64

Julia indicated one of the benches in the *tablinum*. "Do sit."

A servant entered and offered the scribe a cup of warm spiced wine, which he gratefully accepted, wrapping his fingers around the cup.

After the servant left the room, Julia studied the scribe for a moment. His dark skin was remarkably unlined, but the gray in his beard, along with his hunched back, gave away that he was no longer young. He was filthy, tattered, and exhausted.

"How came you to be in such a state?" she asked.

The scribe looked down at the cup as steam rose from the flush of hot liquid. "I am in danger here in Rome. I've been living with Peter. When he was arrested, I ran and have been hiding in the streets."

"But surely they were after Peter. Why would you be in danger?"

"I have a library of scrolls. They're a record of Yeshua's words."

If Julia hadn't become so enthralled listening to Peter speak of Yeshua and his teachings, the scribe's news might have run right past her. But since she had, her mouth dropped open and she sat up in shock. "You have what?"

"Yeshua's words. I was with him, too. I wrote them down."

"The actual words of Yeshua?" Julia was nonplussed.

"Yes."

"By gods! Where are they?" Julia jumped out of her seat.

"They're in our lodgings. Where I stayed with Peter. I'm afraid to go back there. The soldiers will be looking for where Peter lived. It's only a matter of time before they find our place. If they find me there, or the scrolls...."

"Oh gods," Julia said again. "Yes. These scrolls—Peter told me they must be protected. *You* must be protected." Julia's mind darted about in all directions. *I must find Milo.* "When did you see Peter?"

"Early this morning. The soldiers didn't see me as a threat and let me in. Peter cautioned me about the danger and said I must seek safety with you."

"Yes, yes. We must get you settled." Then Julia noticed how exhausted the man was, pain evident in his demeanor. "But first we have to get those scrolls. Milo," she yelled.

At the same time that Milo was hoisting the scribe onto the cart for a trip to his apartment, Roman soldiers were interrogating merchants in the neighborhood where Peter had been arrested. They had orders to bring in anyone associated with Peter and confiscate the "subversive writings" he had been spreading about.

After using strong-arm tactics on the local shopkeepers, the soldiers learned that Peter lived in a six-floor apartment building nearby, but they had been unable to determine which apartment had been his. That meant that they would have to knock on many doors until they found the right one. Two soldiers began on the street level in a row of shops. Two more took the stairs to the second level. The soldiers had reached level four when the Aquillius cart pulled up and stopped on a side street.

Julia, Milo, and the scribe hopped out.

Julia had raced out of her home at the last minute, dressed in Cassia's work clothes and a head covering and, despite Milo's protests about her going along, had jumped up on the cart.

"I may be able to get us out of a bind if need be," she said. "Let's go."

When they arrived in the scribe's neighborhood, Milo scanned the area for signs of trouble. Julia looked around noting that she fit right in with this working-class neighborhood. People on the street paid them no notice, but still not wanting to call attention to anything they were doing, the trio, carrying cloth sacks rolled up as small as they could make them, stepped into a side entrance and began climbing the stairs. Arriving at a landing on level four, Milo glimpsed two soldiers, their backs turned to him.

"They're here," he whispered. "The soldiers, they're here." He motioned the scribe and Julia behind him as he ducked behind a post.

The scribe quivered. He had no resources left to deal with trouble. The soldiers disappeared into an apartment.

"Come on," Milo said, leading the way. "Hurry." The three crept up two more flights. Floor six.

As they hurried along the hallway toward the scribe's apartment, a small boy with huge, dark eyes and outsized ears burst out of another unit. He was holding a ball. "Hey, I haven't seen you here before. Who are you?" He looked ready for a nice long chat.

I've got to get rid of him, Milo thought. Thinking quickly, he reached down and tousled the boy's hair. "How good are you with that ball?"

"Pretty good."

"Let's see about that. Here, let me toss it to you. Run to the stairwell."

The boy raced to the stairs and reached them as Milo tossed the ball. The boy caught it, raising a victory fist in the air.

"You go on out and play," Milo said. "I think I saw a group of boys just down the street. Hurry now."

The boy rounded the post and disappeared.

"Thank God," Milo muttered. "Now, where?" he said to the scribe, pointing to several units.

"Here." The scribe shook as his fingers fumbled with a key. Inside, they breathed a sigh, but only for a moment.

"Where are your things?" Milo looked around, dismayed at the abundance of documents in disarray. "Let's get to it."

They heard a loud voice and a banging from down the hall.

"Okay. We don't have much time," Milo said, "and it's going to be tricky getting out of here."

They loaded up the scrolls and the scribe's tools and writing supplies, along with his personal effects.

Just as the last papyrus had been recovered, a loud banging shook the door, and a soldier shouted, "Open up in the name of the emperor!"

Julia hissed, "Get into the other room. I'll handle this."

Milo opened his mouth to protest.

"Go! I'll be fine."

Milo felt caught between his need to protect his mistress and his duty to follow her orders. But he knew that if the soldiers saw him and the scribe, they were all done for. One look from Julia sent them both, along with the sacks of belongings, into a bedroom.

Julia opened the door a crack. "Yes?"

"Stand aside, woman. We're coming in."

"Oh, you'll not be wanting to come in here." Julia addressed the soldiers in a singsong voice.

"Out of the way." One of the soldiers raised his elbows to push through the door.

"Oh, no. You'll not be wanting to come in." Julia exaggerated her singsong.

The soldiers hesitated and looked at each other. "And just why is that?"

"It's my moon time. Oh, no. You'll not want to come in."

The soldiers took two sharp steps back. Indeed they wouldn't be going in. No Roman man, even the bravest, would get any-where near a woman during her menstrual cycle. The soldiers hustled away.

Julia sagged with relief. Milo and the scribe emerged from the back room, anxiety written all over the scribe's face.

Milo pressed his ear to the door, listening for sounds coming from the hallway. Hearing nothing, he opened the door for a peek out. No one there. "We were seen by that boy. We need to get out of here before he comes back."

The trio flew down the long corridor. To Milo's relief, the scribe was surprisingly quick on his feet.

Reaching the stairs, Milo issued a warning. "We're not out of the woods yet. They can see us on any of the floor landings. Watch me and take my cue." He led the way.

On floor five, Milo spotted a soldier entering an apartment. He held back until the soldier was fully inside. Then, they scrambled all the way down and exited through the same door they had entered. They stashed the scribe's scrolls under a floorboard in the cart, and Milo and the scribe hopped onto it. Milo gave Julia a hand up, and away they went.

Once home, the scribe found that Cassia had prepared a bath for the scribe and laid out a fresh tunic. She'd prepared a room for him on the front side of the house. It had a window and a cushioned bed. Worn out, he washed, put on fresh clothing, and then collapsed onto the bed.

When called to dinner, Julia, her daughters, and the scribe settled onto couches to dine. If Livia and Flavia had any questions about the man sitting before them, they didn't ask. Both girls had become accustomed to all kinds of strangers filing into and out of their home. But neither Julia nor the scribe could eat a thing, and they left the girls to finish their meal while they retired to an outer room.

THIRTY-FIVE

Rome AD 64

If Julia was horrified by Peter's ugly death, the scribe was inconsolable. In that, they bonded, but they chose to speak of other things. Although she had heard vaguely of this scribe, Julia had never before met him. And oddly, Peter, who had worked with him so closely, had never mentioned him.

Julia asked the scribe why this was so.

"My presence was kept quiet because the documents I was producing were a threat and had to be kept hidden. If Nero or his henchmen got wind of them, they would be confiscated and destroyed, and everyone who had anything to do with them would be executed. The fewer people who knew about me, the better."

"What are you called?" Julia asked him. "What is your name?"

"I left my name the day my master was murdered. Now, I am only the scribe."

They were quiet for a moment. Julia's mind returned to a conversation with Marcus that had taken place only weeks before. He was finally paying attention to her involvement with these Christians, because more and more of his peers had learned of it. They openly criticized Marcus for allowing his wife to be involved with them. It was creating a rift in his public life and threatening his status. He had demanded that Julia cease her association with these people under threat of divorce. He even hinted that he would publically denounce her.

Marcus was not simply being hysterical. As Peter's murder had made clear, Nero's vendetta against the Christians was not over. They were all in danger. She made her decision.

"I know I have just taken you in, but it's too dangerous here. We need to go."

"If my presence causes you danger—"

"No," Julia said. "You are part of this household now."

The scribe looked relieved. "Where would we go?"

"My husband has a villa in Herculaneum. We'll take refuge there."

The scribe looked at Julia thoughtfully. "I must continue my work somewhere."

Julia described the country villa, high on a bluff overlooking the Tyrrhenian Sea. "I think we will be safe there. It's remote and quiet enough that few will be interested in what we do." *And I will be away from my husband's threats.*

"I long for a quieter place." For the aging man, the clatter in Rome, the throngs of people in the streets, and the constant sight of marching soldiers had proved too much.

On the spot, Julia summoned Milo and explained her decision to move. "Please make arrangements for the move. The scribe and I will go first, because I think we need to get him out of Rome quickly. You and Cassia can follow with the girls later, in a few days."

Julia confronted Marcus the following morning at the breakfast table. She did not intend to confide the whole story to him.

"Marcus, the girls and I are going to Herculaneum for a while. Our stay may be lengthy."

Marcus arched a brow. "As you wish. You may take your maid."

"I'll be taking Milo, too."

Marcus narrowed his eyes to slits. In a forceful voice, he said, "Be damned. I won't have that. Milo stays here."

"Milo will want to be with his wife. And he is free to do as he wishes, as you know."

"He is not...." Marcus stopped, realizing the truth of Julia's words. He couldn't fight it. He didn't have an argument. He had freed Milo. "Then Cassia will stay here, too. You can go on your own."

Julia sighed. She was unafraid of her husband and knew she had him with this battle. "Oh, really? You would send your wife on a long journey without protection?" She failed to mention that Milo would not be traveling with her. "How do you think that will reflect on your good name?"

Marcus threw down his napkin and stomped out, turning back to say, "Good riddance to you, then."

"The road between Rome and Herculaneum can be dangerous as we pass through some of the more remote places," Julia remarked to the scribe as they reclined in the dining hall for the last meal Julia might ever enjoy in this house. "But we will join with a caravan of traders and other travelers. That will keep any would-be robbers away."

The scribe said, "My fate is in God's hands. I am not afraid."

For this last meal, Julia had insisted it be a celebration. Marcus was out for the evening. She lit candles, and the dining room became ablaze with their flickering. The meal was splendid: turtledove boiled in its feathers, sea urchins cooked in egg sauces, and Jericho dates roasted in honey. Julia was pleased to see the scribe finding pleasure in it. For the final course, they had cakes dipped in wine. For this sweet, the scribe offered his own cup for the dipping.

"This cup is my most cherished possession. It seems such a little thing, but...." the scribe broke off mid-sentence. "Not tonight. Tonight, we must be of good cheer."

Well before dawn the next morning, Milo hitched two horses to the covered family cart. He loaded food and the scrolls onto it, and then carefully covered the contents with wool. He looked anxious as his mistress prepared to depart.

Julia gave him a reassuring look and his forearm a light squeeze. "We will see you soon."

Heading into the city along the Via Claudia, they found the narrow streets still quiet. Within the hour, as the sun broke the horizon, they would be crowded with wagons veering back and forth as they delivered their wares to eager merchants.

At the Roman gates, a guard stopped them. He looked surprised to see a woman steering the horses, but Julia was no stranger to such dealings. When she was just a child, her father, wanting her to be adept at many things, had taught her to ride and manage their horses.

The guard gazed at Julia and the scruffy man seated next to her. His manner gruff, the guard yanked on the reins. "Where are you going in such a hurry under cover of darkness?"

Julia's boldness took over. "I am Julia Lucinia. My husband is the magistrate, Marcus Aquillius. I am delivering legal documents to his offices in Herculaneum. Please pass me through."

Intimidated by the mention of the magistrate's name, the guard nonetheless demanded to know more and jerked his chin up. "Who is he?"

"Excuse me? I am the *domina* of the house of Aquillius, and he is a slave." Julia pretended outrage. "Do you dare to disparage my honor? Let me through, or I swear to all the gods on high that my husband will hear of this, and he will see you sent to the furthest outposts of Germania for this insult!"

The guard blanched white, face pale, and cheeks flushed. "No, mistress, apologies. We are to check for Jewish heretics and troublemakers...."

Julia straightened her back and raised her eyebrows.

The man began to stutter under her glare. "Oh course, *Domina*, I mean no insult...." Stopping while he was ahead, he simply waived Julia through.

As they passed through the gates, Julia breathed deeply, then turned to the scribe and found him shaking. "What is it?" she asked.

"I am remembering back. When I was just a boy finishing my

schooling, I went to Nazareth looking for the man they called Yeshua. On my way home to Sepphoris, two soldiers stopped me. They robbed me of my coins and water, and then they ordered me to walk between them all the way home. They taunted me the whole way, and I was never sure that they would not kill me before I reached my family. It was terrifying, and every time I see Roman soldiers close by, my fear returns."

Julia and the scribe met with no further troubles getting out of the city, and the scribe, relaxing some after being confronted by the guard, noted, "Here I am on the road again. How strange and yet so familiar."

The sky was becoming the color of stone. Soon it would be morning, another new day. An icy drizzle was subsiding. They turned and looked behind them. The gates had disappeared from view. Julia looked at the vast expanse of open road before them. They had three days' journey ahead.

THIRTY-SIX

The Vatican
Present Day

Cardinal Ricci faced nearly fifty members of the news media from the center of a long, ebony table in the Vatican pressroom. He was flanked by four colleagues to whom he had given news about the newly discovered bishop.

The Vatican press director stood near the door, fuming that Ricci would bypass the press office and call a presser on his own. Such rare events nearly always created a calamity of factual errors that he and his secretary had to clean up. This time, by the time the press office had gotten wind of Ricci's intention to hold his own press conference, it was already a *fait accompli*. He sighed and glanced at his secretary, who was distributing an updated press release.

"Before informing you of the reason for your visit here today, let me state that the knowledge we have right now is limited," the cardinal stated. "Further information will be available some weeks from now after we arrive at all the facts."

Impatient for the cardinal to get on with it, reporters shifted in their chairs.

Cardinal Ricci cleared his throat and looked around the room. He immediately spotted Michael Levin of *La Carta* in the first row, and he frowned. Levin was an American expat and a thorn in Ricci's side.

An aggressive reporter, Levin consistently turned up dirt the Vatican would prefer to keep swept under the fine wool carpets.

Ricci straightened and began. As was the expected protocol for these events, the first five minutes were spent with Ricci thanking his superiors, his underlings, his predecessors, and every department head in attendance.

A snore rattled out from the back of the room.

Ricci cleared his throat. "Under my direct supervision, a team of the finest archaeologists at my disposal were directed to search for a new, unknown tomb in the nearby diocese of Ostia. Under my direction, my researchers found a clue to the existence of an unknown first-century bishop. Of course, as a man of science, I knew that this clue had to be followed. It wouldn't do to leave one of our earliest Church fathers lost to history." Ricci looked up at the reporters expectantly. A few were taking notes; the rest looked politely bored.

"This finding is of great historical significance," Ricci went on. "We believe this bishop to be Julius Episcopus, an unknown father of earliest times. Moreover, not only were his remains found, but we have uncovered artifacts and ancient scrolls, seemingly intact."

A few more of the reporters picked up their notepads and started scribbling. Scrolls and ancient texts were good research bait. Readers loved them.

"We believe that after a forensic study has been completed, this man will reveal to us more about the establishment of the Holy Mother Church and will illuminate our most ancient sacred traditions. Unfortunately, I am not at liberty to reveal much more, and the investigation is ongoing. However, I will do the best I can to answer your questions." Ricci looked around for raised hands. "Mr. Levin."

Michael Levin rose. "Thank you, Cardinal."

Just minutes before Levin took off for the news conference, he had spotted a new email with an attachment. He read it hurriedly and then printed the attachment, which he now used in his query to the cardinal. "I have information ahead of your presser that the first-century bishop they found in Ostia is a woman. Would you like to address this?"

The sleepy room suddenly woke up.

"Ridiculous," the cardinal interrupted. Then he chuckled and said, "Of course the bishop was male."

Levin remained standing and plowed ahead. "A source close to the excavation claims that a plaque over the tomb reads Julia Episcopa, not Julius Episcopus. Julia, of course, is a woman's name. The word *episcopa* would be the female form for *bishop*, I believe. How do you explain—"

"I know what *episcopa* means," Ricci snapped. "It's simply an honorary title, perhaps for the mother of a bishop. I would suggest that you check the facts before bringing such 'observations' before us. Our find is a bishop, not his mother."

"I would like to, Cardinal, but it seems that the area has been cordoned off."

"Quite," the cardinal said, looking self-satisfied.

"However," Levin continued, reaching into his coat pocket, "I received this photograph just this morning. I believe it's as good a look at the site as we might get. It's a picture of the plaque in Ostia. Of course, the etching on the stone is in ancient Greek. My source tells me the translation reads 'Julia Episcopa.' Would you take a look at it?"

Levin offered up the photo. The press director strode over, taking the photo for the handoff. He glanced at it and handed it to Ricci, smugness written all over his face.

Ricci bent over the photo for a long moment. "Where did you get this?"

"I'm sorry, Your Eminence," Levin said, "but I cannot...."

As Levin's colleagues all looked at each other in bemusement and then at Cardinal Ricci, he rose, mumbling, "No more questions."

"I don't see how we can keep it from Cardinal Ricci any longer." Valentina and Erika had returned to their office with their treasures.

"Yigael doesn't think it's necessary yet to reveal what we have," she continued, "but I think I'm going to have to trust my instincts on this."

"I don't envy you," Erika said. "Are you going to own up to the fact that you've known all along?"

Valentina gave Erika a beleaguered look. "I don't know. But he'll probably figure it out at some point."

"Oh boy, I don't want to be around for that." Erika laughed. "Sorry," she said, still chuckling.

Valentina brought her hands up to her face and cupped her head in them. "Oh, me."

Erika said, "Look, I've got something cooking in the lab…." And off she went.

Valentina's cell phone pinged, and her face turned pale when she saw the display.

"Yes, Your Eminence?"

"*Dottoressa* Vella, what is the meaning of this?" Cardinal Ricci's soft, low voice disguised the rage boiling just below the surface.

Valentina's stomach lurched at his question, especially since he called her *dottoressa* and not Valentina, as he always had. But she brought calm to her voice. "I'm not sure I take your meaning, Cardinal."

"No? Well, I thought you might be expecting a call from me by this time," he went on.

"Might I ask why that is, Your Eminence?" Valentina's heart began to thump.

"And just how long have you known we had no Julius Episcopus entombed in Ostia, but instead have a Julia Episcopa buried there?" Ricci's voice rose in indignation.

"Oh," Valentina said in a tiny voice before slowly sitting down.

"And that I had to find out through a member of the press, no less?" he continued furiously.

"Oh?" Valentina said in surprise. Word of the press conference had not yet reached the archeologist.

"And soon the entire world will know about this blunder," he shouted, "and at my expense." If there was one thing the cardinal could not abide, it was looking the fool in front of others. He had taken great care in his life to avoid just such mishaps. "Perhaps you can explain your duplicity to me?"

"Oh, I meant to tell you. The time just...."

"The time just," Ricci echoed. "The time just...*what?*" he bellowed.

"Well, Erika and I were talking just this morning," Valentina blabbered in near-comic desperation. She hoped to shift the focus until she could gather herself.

"No, no, no, no, no. How dare you," Ricci scolded. "You deliberately kept facts from me. I wonder whether you misled me from the very beginning."

Valentina was silent for a moment, and then she came to herself and spoke in a calm, even tone. "Cardinal, may I ask why on earth you would speak to the press before finding out the entirety of what we have here? We cannot be certain of anything right now. We haven't even begun our work. Whether this bishop was a man or a woman...why, we have only bits and pieces of information as of yet, and certainly nothing definitive. It will be months, maybe years, before we can ascertain with certainty anything we found. There is an entire, complex story here, and it is for us to put the pieces together and understand it."

Valentina was hedging, and she knew it. Nonetheless she forged on. "I'm surprised at you, Cardinal Ricci," she admonished, amazed at her own boldness and wondering what would happen next.

There was only silence from the cardinal. *What could he possibly be thinking?* Valentina had no idea.

"Cardinal?" Valentina ventured after several seconds of wondering whether he was still on the line.

"*Dottoressa* Vella, you have put me in an untenable position," Ricci continued, ignoring Valentina's outburst. "And you are going to get me out of it. Do you understand?"

Valentina's mouth felt filled with cotton candy. *Here it comes,* she thought.

"I want to know who leaked this. Find out."

"I don't know, Cardinal. I didn't even know about the—"

"Find out. I want this person," Ricci said in a mock-soothing tone. "And now, you are going to set the record straight. You will call that damnable reporter from *La Carta,* Michael Levin, and this is what you will say...."

"Where are you, *caro?*" It hadn't taken Valentina but two minutes to get Luca on the phone.

"Bruges, a trade thing. What happened? Are you okay?"

"No. Nothing is okay."

"Just breathe. Take a second, breathe." Luca was alarmed. Valentina wasn't a woman to panic. He heard her take a few deep breaths, and as her breathing slowed, he said, "Okay, Valentina. Tell me what's going on."

Valentina told Luca the long and short of Ricci's news conference, the leak, and his orders to her to talk to the press. As she told him the story, she began to feel steadier and more in control.

"He wants blood, and I cannot say that I blame him," Valentina said of Cardinal Ricci. "He wants me to bring the source of the leak to him. I have no idea who did this, Luca, but if I find out, I'll kill them first, and then I'll hand them over and let Ricci kill them too!" Valentina said.

"I don't blame you," Luca said. "I don't get it, though. Your security was airtight. You need to talk to Yigael and find out what happened."

"He's my next call," Valentina said. "And then, I need to do that interview and see if I can fix this."

"What are you going to say?"

"The truth, more or less. We know nothing, there has been no forensic testing done yet. It's just another Ostian dig. I'm going to bore *La Carta* to death, and hope they lose interest."

Cardinal Ricci sat in front of his fireplace that night, rationalizing that Valentina might be right. Who knew who lay in that crypt in Ostia? And how many news stories turned out dead wrong? He would hold out hope. He had to. He didn't want his dream for the top spot shattered.

THIRTY-SEVEN

Rome

LaCarta | The Vatican

Does the Cardinal Have All the Facts?

di Michael Levin
June 17th, 2018

Vatican City — Cardinal Antonio Ricci stormed out of a press conference yesterday when his announcement of a new discovery backfired. Ricci called reporters to the Vatican to announce that an ancient tomb containing the remains of a bishop have been discovered near the ruins of the synagogue in Ostia Antica. Ricci told reporters that this bishop has been identified as Julius Episcopus, a first century church 'father'.

According to sources, the press conference was called outside of normal press office protocol, and unfortunately for the cardinal, he seems to have been misled. A photo of a plaque at the site indicates that a Julia Episcopa—a woman—is buried there. If this is the case, it seems that the bishop is a bishopess.

Valentina Vella, PhD, a leading archeologist and a central

figure in the excavation at Ostia, claims that it is much too early to say whether the remains of a first-century bishop will turn out to be a man or woman. According to *Dottoressa* Vella, whether this figure was a leader or even a member of the early Church is also too early to tell.

"It will take months, perhaps even years, to decipher what we have," *Dottoressa* Vella told *La Carta*. "We must study everything found there and put the pieces of this life together in a logical, methodical fashion before any claims can be made."

This discovery could have interesting implications within the Vatican hierarchy, considering its current battle regarding the role of women within the Church. While Pope Augustine has recently entertained the notion of an expanded role for women, including allowing females in the deaconate, he has stopped short of endorsing them for full priestly ordination. Even so, he has faced harsh criticism from forces within the Holy Office for even the small steps he has taken for inclusion, and some in more conservative quarters have gone so far as to accuse him of heresy.

The beleaguered Holy Father has already been waging war with the conservative factions within the Holy Office because of his seeming openness regarding the rules surrounding marriage, divorce, and homosexuality. If this bishop turns out to be a woman? Be prepared for heads to roll.

Regardless of the gender of our new bishop, our sources confirm that this is a significant find, and many eyes are on what tale the bones may tell.

THIRTY-EIGHT

Herculaneum, AD 65

Julia gazed out at the spectacular view of the turquoise sea below, sparkling in the early morning sun. She shifted her gaze to the lurking shadow of the great mountain Vesuvius hovering black and green against an azure sky. It seemed to be a beacon opening to another world. She wrote:

We are living well here at the villa. I feel quite at ease away from Rome. The scribe is happy writing in the library, and the girls are thriving. I enjoy each day as it is. I've found that each day presents its gifts if I expect nothing and refrain from worry about tomorrow.

The scribe had recently encouraged Julia to begin a diary. She had protested, arguing that her life was unspectacular and, at age twenty-five, nearly over. He insisted that record keeping was important so that those who followed could gain perspective about life from what had gone before. He urged her to remember her early years and record her memories. Julia faced the challenge and, in time, grew to savor the moments of solitude when she could reflect on the activities of her life and her part in them.

Her daughters clattered into the room.

"Mama, Livia and I want to go outside." Flavia's exuberance never failed to amuse Julia. But it concerned her, too. Her younger daughter, at age five, had a fiery temper that sometimes got her into hot water. Julia could only hope that one day she would use her passion wisely.

"You may," Julia told her daughters. "But stay away from the cliffs." Julia raised a finger and turned particularly to Flavia. She would be the one to lure her sister to the cliffs. "I mean it."

"Oh, Mama." Flavia turned away in a huff. "We'll be careful."

"Stay away from the cliffs." Julia was adamant.

"We will, I promise." Livia said.

They're so different, Julia mused. Flavia is like fire, temperamental and impetuous. Livia is like water, quiet and calm, the peacemaker in the family. If anything is amiss in the household, Livia will do her best to set it right.

"On your way, then, but be back by lunchtime," Julia said, watching the girls scurry out.

Since their arrival in Herculaneum, it had been a time of learning for the girls. The scribe was teaching them reading, writing, and mathematics and would spend hours telling them stories about his days with Yeshua. The scribe had quickly become the girls' mentor and confidante.

Julia wrote:

Livia and Flavia are embracing the scribe's teachings of Yeshua quite completely. How could they not when the older man, with his smooth voice, reads to them Yeshua's own words. It didn't take Yeshua to open my eyes to the inequality among peoples, though. I learned that lesson through Milo when he spoke to me of his family in Gaul. That was a shock, but also a great awakening. While I recognize that there will always be social structure, I know that there must be fairness and recognition that no man is less than another, even the most evil.

The scribe interrupted Julia's writing. He entered the room with a sheaf of papyrus tucked under his arm.

"How are we going to get these to Rome?" he asked. His missives were meant for the Christian communities, but the ongoing threat of Nero's soldiers who, for their own amusement, were still seeking Christians to brutalize, presented a continuing danger.

"I suppose we'll need a messenger," Julia said. "But I don't know who we could send. If a messenger were stopped and found with these things, he would be forced to betray us, and if he didn't he would be killed. And those receiving these letters, if discovered, would have their homes raided."

The scribe studied Julia's face. "There is only one person who could undertake this mission with relative safety. There would be risk, but we could minimize it."

Julia looked puzzled, thought for a moment, and then exclaimed, "You're not suggesting I do it, are you?"

The scribe simply gazed at Julia.

"But I..." she sputtered. "Think of Livia and Flavia. They depend on me. They need me to be here for them and not in danger. Surely...well, absolutely not."

The lunch bell sounded. Julia looked out the window. Livia and Flavia were nowhere in sight. "Those girls," she muttered. Then she turned again to the scribe. "I love Yeshua's words. You know I do, but in no way will I take your scrolls to Rome." She bustled out and left the scribe in her wake, a defeated expression on his face.

"Where are you, Cassia?" Julia said under her breath. *Nothing seems to be going easily today*, she thought, just as Cassia rounded a doorway from the kitchen, blotting her forehead with a damp cloth.

"Ah, there you are," Julia said. "Will you go look for the girls? They haven't come back yet. I'm going to help Cook put the finishing touches on lunch. Oh, and don't bother with the cliffs. They won't be there." Julia gave a quick second glance at Cassia's flushed face. "Are you unwell?"

Cassia smiled. "I'm fine. Just tossed and turned a little last night." She turned back into the kitchen, stepped outside, and headed straight for the cliffs. It was the girls' favorite place to play, and they weren't above outsmarting their mother.

As Cassia disappeared from sight, Livia and Flavia scrambled back into the villa through a side door. They were both drenched.

"Just look at you. Where have you been?" Julia demanded. She glanced outside. The earlier light drizzle had turned into heavy rain. "Go. Get cleaned up for lunch."

Half an hour later, Julia, Milo, and the two girls assembled at the lunch table.

"Where's Cassia?" Livia asked.

Julia and Milo shot questioning glances at each other.

"Didn't she fetch you?" Julia asked.

"No, we haven't seen her," Flavia responded.

"I assumed she sent you back indoors. Milo, is she in your room?"

"I'll check." Milo wasted no time getting up.

Recently, Cassia had sometimes skipped lunch and gone to her room instead for a brief afternoon rest.

"She's not there," Milo said, returning to the dining room.

Julia glared at her daughters. "If you had come home when you were told to...."

"Sorry, Mama." Livia looked stricken.

"Where would she likely look for you?" Julia stared pointedly at her daughters. Guilt showed in the high color on the girls' cheeks.

"The...the...cliffs," Flavia squeaked.

"The cliffs!" Julia gave her daughters a look of fury. She turned to Milo. "Best go look for her. The rain is coming down hard."

Milo turned on his heel.

Julia rose from the table and swiped at it with her napkin in anger. "And, you two, to your rooms."

Julia moved into the *ala,* a room with large windows, where she had the best view of the cliffs. She hadn't been there but fifteen minutes when Milo came into view, a tiny figure in the distance, lumbering toward the villa, Cassia limp in his arms.

Julia raced to the nearest door and flung it open. "Is she hurt?"

"No, no, I don't think so," Milo said. "She seems ill. She's shivering."

"Quick, get her in here." Julia pulled Milo inside as Cook appeared from the kitchen.

"Go to the girls' rooms," she ordered Cook. "Have them help you make up the room next to mine. We'll take Cassia there.

Go now." Cook turned quickly toward the stairs leading to the second floor.

"Get her out of these wet things," Julia instructed Milo. "I'll get blankets."

Once he had wrapped her in heavy woolen blankets, Milo carried Cassia into the atrium and positioned her on a couch by the hearth. Shaking with chills, she was passing in and out of consciousness.

"I'll stay with her," Julia ordered. "Go for *Dottore* Pelonius."

THIRTY-NINE

Herculaneum AD 65

"How long has she been with child?" *Dottore* Cato Pelonius, seated beside Cassia, removed his hand from Cassia's stomach and looked up at Milo standing beside him.

"With child? I…I didn't know," Milo said, dropping to his knees and grasping Cassia's hand.

"Why, I didn't, either," Julia said. "I can't think why she didn't tell me. When?"

"She is three to four months gone, but I must tell you…."

"What?" Milo's voice was sharp with anxiety.

The *dottore's* voice was soft. "Stay with your wife for a moment."

By the time the doctor arrived, Milo had moved Cassia to the upstairs bedroom adjacent to Julia's and placed her in bed on a woolen-stuffed mattress. Plump feather pillows bolstered her, and a feather-filled coverlet kept her warm.

Dottore Polonius eyed Julia and flicked his chin toward the door.

Julia followed *Dottore* Pelonius out. When they were out of earshot, he said, "I'm afraid I do not have good news for you. I believe she is suffering with a malignant tertian fever, Domina."

Julia stared at him blankly, frightened, but not quite

understanding his meaning. He saw the confusion on her face and lowered his voice. "The fever, Domina. The *febris ardens*. It is from bad air."

Julia, shocked, worriedly asked, "My girls?"

"This fever fortunately doesn't usually attack healthy children, Domina. However, there must be a pool of stagnant water nearby or perhaps a swamp on your lands. Is there?"

Julia considered for a moment. "There were heavy rains this year, so perhaps...."

"Get them drained, Domina. Immediately. You and your household must stay far away from any place where there may be *malus aria*, fouled air. Stay near the villa and make certain your water is clean. I will bring preventatives."

Julia nodded, her mouth dry. "And Cassia? What of her? What of her child?" Julia knew the dangers of this disease, particularly for pregnant women.

Dottore Pelonius shook his head sadly. "She will most likely lose the child. As to her, it is in the hands of the gods now. Pray to Febis that the fever will pass, also the goddess Lucina. I will return with medicines to ease her symptoms. Artemisia, perhaps some willow...." The *dottore's* voice trailed off.

Julia was no longer listening. "What will I tell Milo?"

"That's for you to decide." *Dottore* Pelonius turned toward the door and reentered the bedroom. He checked Cassia once more and then addressed Milo. "I'll return later."

Julia took a seat beside Cassia, who had flung off the coverlet and was tossing about in a sweat. "Cassia, can you hear me?"

Cassia uttered a low moan.

"You're going to be fine," Julia said. "You just need to rest."

Milo searched Julia's eyes. "Truly?"

Julia wasn't ready to confide *Dottore* Pelonius's words yet. "I'm going to moisten some cloths to help lessen the fever. Your touch will ease her."

Julia got up and headed for the door. As she opened it, she found her daughters hovering just outside. Livia was awash in tears.

"What is this?" Julia demanded.

"It's all our fault," Flavia wailed. "If we hadn't gone to the cliffs, Cassia wouldn't have been out there, and she wouldn't have got sick." To the girls, Cassia was a second mother.

Julia sighed. "Come with me." She shepherded her daughters into her bedroom and sat them down in two chairs adjacent to her bed. She pulled up a chair opposite them.

"Now hear me," she told her daughters, "and hear me well. It was wrong of you to go to the cliffs when I asked you not to. But your disobedience in going there has nothing to do with Cassia's illness. She did not catch a fever because she was out in the cold. Cassia was already ill when she went out. Do you understand?"

"Is Cassia going to get well?" Livia swiped a hand across her tear-stained cheeks.

"Let us hope so. Now, you two can make yourselves useful. Go to the kitchen, and help Cook. Perhaps Cassia can take a bit of broth."

Livia and Flavia rose as one and made haste for the kitchen.

Julia sat for a moment, a thousand thoughts racing through her mind. Uppermost was what to tell Milo. *I must be honest with him, entirely so,* she thought, *though I wish I didn't have to.*

After the girls had gone to bed and Cassia was sleeping, although fitfully, Julia coaxed Milo from Cassia's bedside to the dining room, where they usually met to discuss household matters.

"I didn't know she was expecting." Milo's face was drawn and pale. "How will this illness affect the baby?"

"Milo," Julia said gently, "let's not think just yet about the baby. Cassia is very ill." Julia stopped to let the words sink in.

"No, she can't be. It's just a fever. Yes, a bad one, but surely…" Milo dropped his head into his hands.

"We can hope for the best, and there is a chance she will come through this."

Milo's grim expression told that he knew well what the outcome might likely be. "What can we do?"

"Really, there is little we can do except to keep her comfortable and let her try to heal."

Cassia's fever would begin to subside, and then it would return, higher than before, and with each turn, Milo refused to leave her side even for a moment. When finally Cassia slipped into a coma, and then breathed her last breath, an anguished Milo still couldn't tear himself from his wife's bedside. He remained there for the next half-day. When Julia sent in the women to prepare Cassia's body, Milo would have none of it.

"Go away," he said despondently.

Julia returned to the room. "Milo, come with me, please. Let the women do their work."

"I must do it," he responded. "Please go."

Milo carefully tended his wife, bathing and dressing her in a fine white tunic. When he'd finished, he placed a coin under her tongue and one over each eyelid so that she could pay Charon, the ferryman, to row her to the land of the dead.

Cassia's body was taken to a funeral pyre. When the flames rose up, consuming her body, perfumes and incense were thrown into the fire, and when the fire burned down, wine doused the embers. Her ashes were gathered, placed in an urn, and taken to the *columbarium* outside the city. Milo placed a small stone epitaph with the simple inscription: *Cassia and baby yet to be born. Beloved are they.*

Milo's mourning seemed never ending, and a pall settled over the villa in Herculaneum for months. Julia knew that she must be patient, but as the first anniversary of Cassia's death approached, she decided that something must change

She summoned the scribe.

"I'm ready to undertake your mission," she told him.

"Oh?" The scribe was mystified. "What—"

"I will take your messages to Rome."

The scribe's eyes opened wide, and the trace of a smile crossed his face. "Very well. Very well indeed."

FORTY

The scribe was both wise and experienced and intent on developing a strategy that would keep Julia safe on her three-day journey to Rome. After all, he himself had traveled dangerous terrain in the days of Yeshua, and he knew what precautions to take.

Two weeks later, with the girls being looked after by the scribe, Julia set out with Milo by her side. He had built a false bottom in the family cart for concealment purposes, and then covered it with cloth and containers of homemade honey and wine. They had made but a half-day's journey when two soldiers stopped them.

The soldiers circled the cart. Dust kicked up from their horses' hooves. They peered inside at the contents. Domina, may we ask where you are going?" one said solicitously, as the other poked about in the back of the wagon.

"I am Julia Lucinia, traveling to see my husband, Marcus Aquillius, who serves as magistrate for the Imperial Council. This is my servant." She gestured toward Milo.

"Is that so? A magistrate's wife. Then I am sure you will not mind if we take a closer look. It's the law, Domina. The soldiers jumped down from their horses and leaped onto the cart. Tossing the honey and wine to one side, they yanked off the false bottom. "What is this? More honey and wine?" one of them said.

"Some gifts for my friends," Julia replied. "Ah, would you like some? I would be pleased to share with you. After all, our villa produces some of the finest honey in the province. And you'll find the wine to be first rate. Please take some, but…." Julia fluttered a handkerchief in front of her face as if she were about to faint. "Hurry up about it. We must be on our way. I am feeling unwell, and my husband is expecting us." Julia's manner was congenial, but her bearing was haughty, and the soldiers knew well enough the dangers of an angered noblewoman with a powerful husband.

The soldiers grabbed some of the wine and honey and jumped off the cart. "Good journey, Domina. Be careful on the road ahead. If you run into any more patrols, let them know Marcellus has already inspected your carts."

The diversion had worked. In truth, the scribe had hidden twelve scrolls in a hollowed-out compartment in the side of the cart. Milo had carved a wooden cover that slid invisibly over the opening.

The rest of the day brought no further trouble, and by the end of it, they rested at an inn. On the third day, as they approached Rome, they knew they weren't safe yet. They'd need to be especially circumspect in Rome, where the eyes of Nero were everywhere.

Julia and Milo visited several households and delivered their gifts. Then at the last house, Julia uttered the words, "I bring you good news." When the host replied, "You honor our home," she knew it was safe to hand over the scribe's documents and head for her home in Rome.

Milo went to the servant's quarters while Julia headed for the front door. Exhausted, she anticipated a good night's sleep and a hearty breakfast before traveling back to Herculaneum. She didn't know whether she would encounter her husband, but it didn't matter.

As she opened the door, a new houseboy met her.

"Take the horses to the stables," she instructed him as the boy looked curiously at a woman he had never seen before. From her authoritative tone, the boy dared not challenge her. He headed for the horses.

Seeing no one else around, Julia made her way to her bedchamber. Hearing voices as she passed by Marcus's room, she entered, took in the scene, and promptly but quietly walked out.

Julia recognized the woman in Marcus's bed. Scribonia had a reputation for sleeping with other women's husbands, and her last husband had divorced her on those grounds. Her family, however, was wealthy beyond imagining, and Scribonia was known to be a generous patron to her lovers.

They're perfect for each other, Julia thought. Scribonia had hated Julia from the first moment they met, and Julia certainly held no warmth for Scribonia.

Julia called for the houseboy to bring the horses around. "And wake my servant. Tell him to prepare to leave." As she reached the front door ready to exit, Marcus rushed to meet her. He was bare-chested, with a wrap circling his waist.

"This is as good a time as any," he sneered. "I mean to divorce you and marry Scribonia. I want you never to return here."

Julia stared at her husband.

Marcus intended for his bite to sting. "You've been a failure to me. You've provided me with no male heirs and have compromised my status with your newfound cult. Go back to Herculaneum. At least there you will be no further bother to me. I expect that this is the last time we shall meet."

"As you wish," Julia responded with reserve, though she was trying hard to suppress her laughter at his pomposity.

She wasn't in the least surprised by his aggression. Adultery in Rome was a serious legal offense, and he'd been caught in the act. She was no longer the innocent young wife so easily intimidated by a bully. This new information could be invaluable.

Julia turned and walked away from a husband she had barely known. She had suffered at Marcus's hands. He had mocked, insulted, belittled, and ignored her, but she was smart enough to know that this was his way of exerting dominance over a woman he knew was cleverer than he.

As she returned to the villa in Herculaneum, Julia felt quite lighthearted.

Two months passed peaceably. During this time, Julia hadn't given two thoughts to Marcus and her marriage, but that changed when she received the divorce papers.

Soon after, a knock on the door propelled her into a battle she didn't want to fight but knew she could not escape.

Julia opened the door to a gangly man she recognized as Gaius Fabii, her husband's legal representative. He explained that he had come to Herculaneum for a holiday with his family, but before he left Rome, Marcus gave him a letter to deliver. He handed it to Julia.

"I'll wait for your response," Gaius said.

"Please come in." She directed the man into the *tablinum* and called for Cook to prepare a refreshment. Then she took the letter to her bedroom. Opening it, Julia read the one and only line:

You are ordered to vacate the villa within two weeks or I will have you removed.

Marcus

Julia raced back into the *tablinum*. "What is the meaning of this, pray? Do you know? Marcus asked me to live here, after all."

Gaius had always had a soft spot for Julia—indeed, he had never much liked Marcus—and was not averse to confiding details to her. "Marcus and Scribonia have married. She has decided to spend the summer here, and Marcus has agreed to it. I am sorry."

A steely-eyed, angry Julia faced the attorney in silence.

"He has the right," Gaius said. "I'm sorry, but the villa is his. I'm afraid he'll get a court order if you don't comply with his wishes."

"So, my husband would see his wife and children on the street.

Is that what I hear you telling me? Ha," she said. "We'll just see about that." Julia turned to steel. "You tell Marcus I'll see him in court."

FORTY-ONE

Rome, AD 67

Spectators jammed the basilica in a half-circle as the settlement hearing between Marcus Aquillius and Julia Lucinia got underway on a late summer morning. They had shown up to see the fireworks between the handsome, well-known magistrate and his beautiful ex-wife seated opposite each other on benches with their solicitors beside them.

From his position on a high dais, the judge—a small, thin man with heavy, dark brows and a fringe of curly hair surrounding a bald pate—frowned down at the plaintiff and defendant, Julia Lucinia, a tiny figure in the landscape, and Marcus Aquillius, a picture of confidence with his head held high.

"Lucinia versus Aquillius." The judge looked again from one side to the other. "Seems someone's made a mess of it. Proceed." He nodded toward the petitioner's table.

Julia's attorney, Admilius Paullus, rose. "I have the briefest opening statement."

"A fine thing," the judge chortled. "Let's be thankful for brevity."

A rumble in the crowd set the judge's teeth on edge, but he remained silent for the moment.

"Sir, Julia Lucinia has been denied monies from her

ex-husband, who has stolen what is rightfully hers, and she now finds herself destitute. We will prove that such is the case and submit that these monies must be returned to her." He sat down and whispered to Julia.

The spectators roared their objection, and this time the judge leaped to his feet, shouting, "There will be silence or you will all go."

The gallery of spectators settled down, but they were siding with Marcus, who was decked out in his finest gold-embroidered toga, a gift from his new wife, Scribonia. After all, he held a responsible, high government position, while his wife had renounced him and high society in favor of following a cult.

The judge sat down and considered Julia, who was dressed in her finest linens.

Then he turned his attention to the defense. "Proceed."

Marcus's attorney, Gaius Fabii, rose. "What the plaintiff claims is pure fabrication, a lie, to put it in basic terms. This fine man has performed many years of impeccable public service, and not once has he come under scrutiny for misdeeds."

The judge kept his eye on the watchers who were ready to erupt again.

"We will show how this pretender," Gaius nodded toward Julia, "was no wife at all to her husband, and indeed has no right to claim any part of his estate."

"Hear, hear!" the watchers yelled.

The judge was on his feet again, and as soon as he was, a hush settled over the place. "Your witness."

Admilius nodded to Julia, who rose to her feet. "What led you to challenge the terms of your divorce contract with your husband?"

"Through a letter you sent to me while I was residing in Asia." Admilius had represented Julia's parents at the time.

"What did that letter say?"

"My parents had died, and your letter stated that upon their deaths, Marcus would cease control of their lands and turn them over to me. I was to inherit their entire estate."

"As is the custom under our laws," Admilius said, and with a scowl, turned toward Marcus.

"Yes," Julia said.

"That was some time back. Why have you just come forward?"

"I had no need of the property until now."

"And why was that?"

"My husband...my ex-husband...had provided me with a place to live. I had no need to challenge him on financial matters."

"And now?"

"Marcus has ordered me and my daughters—his daughters—off the property we live in."

"That would be the villa in Herculaneum?"

"Yes."

"Why?"

"He said he wanted to vacation there with his, er, new wife."

"And what would that mean to you?"

"I would have no place to go and no resources. Marcus has refused to give me back my parents' property, and he has refused to return my dowry."

"Do you concede that the villa belongs to Marcus and not to you?"

"I do."

"What did you do in the circumstances?"

"I contacted Marcus and demanded that he return the lands and my dowry, intact."

Marcus glowered at Julia from across the room. She cringed at first, but then extended her long, slender neck and stood ramrod straight.

"Based on the letter you received from me," Admilius continued, "did you at least ask your husband for income from the Lucinii lands?"

"I did."

"And?"

"Marcus refused me all of what is rightfully mine."

"Madame, hold your tongue! We have not yet determined what is and is not yours," the judge said.

Julia stood up even straighter in defiance.

Marcus sat shifting and red-faced, hating his former wife. His attorney, Gaius, rose. "Indeed. Thank you, Judge, for it has not yet been determined that those incomes belong to Julia Lucinia. Indeed, they belong to Marcus. He managed and oversaw the property."

"You're out of order. Sit down," the judge admonished Gaius.

"Not so, Judge," Admilius yelled out. "The money does not belong to Marcus Aquillius."

"Shut up," the judge snarled. "Now, move on."

The audience rumble was getting louder.

The judge admonished them again. "Quiet."

"That will be all." Admilius nodded toward Marcus's attorney, Gaius.

Gaius wasted no time popping up to his feet to cross-examine Julia. "Is it true that you have produced only two children for your husband?"

"That is true, but I have given him two beautiful daughters, whom he disdains," Julia said.

Gaius turned toward the judge. "Well, I never, Judge. That she would say a thing like that! Such a lie. What man disdains his children? None does, I say, especially our daughters. Especially Marcus Aquillius. Our daughters are precious to us."

"Move on," the judge said.

Admilius raised a cautionary hand. He had instructed Julia to answer questions simply with no embellishment.

Gaius turned to Julia. "Indeed. Is that so? You think your husband disdains his own daughters...."

Julia opened her mouth to answer, but Gaius cut her off. "Isn't it also true that you deserted your husband when you moved to Herculaneum, leaving him without a consort and hostess?"

"Oh, I've never doubted Marcus's abilities to find himself suitable...ah...*consorts* whenever it suited his purposes."

Scribonia jumped to her feet, red faced, fists clenched.

The gallery tittered.

"Quiet," the judge shouted. His countenance darkened.

"And, by the way, when you were living together, did you not fail in your duties as his hostess, preferring instead to cavort with a fringe element of society?" Gaius asked.

"I would not say so, no," Julia answered.

"This so-called Christian—"

Admilius jumped to his feet. "No, Judge. Julia Lucinia's friends and the way she lives her life are not relevant here. There is no law—"

The judge interrupted and speculated, "While I would like to learn more about this group we're hearing so much about, and while I cannot say I like what I already know, I am afraid the law does not allow delving into that subject in this matter."

"I have nothing further for this woman. I believe her moral standard is plain for all to see." Gaius returned to his chair and the audience exchanged looks and whispered words.

It was up to Admilius to call his only other witness.

"Marcus Aquillius, please."

FORTY-TWO

Rome AD 67

Marcus rose, glancing back at Scribonia. The two then sent a bitter glare Julia's way.

"Marcus Aquillius, is that right?" Admilius asked.

"Yes."

"Magistrate of Rome?"

Marcus puffed up. "Yes."

"What assets have you?"

"Aside from my salary as a magistrate, I own my home in Rome, the properties of my forefathers, and I own the villa in Herculaneum. My ex-wife's properties, placed in my hands to manage, barely cover their own costs," Marcus lied.

"Have you recently sold off part of the holdings of your own family?" Admilius asked.

Marcus hesitated and then said, "I have."

"In fact, nearly all of those holdings?"

"Not all."

"But almost. And why is that?"

"The lands have become too cumbersome for me to handle with my government responsibilities," Marcus said. "Good help is hard to find, and I thought it fitting."

Members of the gallery nodded and mumbled their approval.

"Isn't it true," Admilius went on, "that in truth you sold the lands to satisfy certain, ah, debts?"

"Well, yes. Nothing wrong with that," Marcus sniffed.

"And were those gambling debts?"

Marcus, seething, refused to answer.

The judge took a deep breath, put his chin on his fist, and considered Marcus. "Answer the question."

Marcus looked toward Julia with hate. "Yes."

"Thank you for being so honest with us," Admilius said with irony. "Now, can I ask you why you haven't sold the Lucinius property?"

"What?" Marcus didn't like where this was heading. "I...."

"Isn't it true that the Lucinius property isn't yours to sell?"

"It is mine. I run it."

"Then why didn't you sell it? Surely that would be preferable to selling your own parents' lands?"

"It was simply easier to negotiate the sale of my parents' property."

"Isn't it true that you didn't sell the Lucinius lands because you don't own them?" Before Marcus could respond, Admilius changed direction. "Have you ever seen a copy of Gavius's and Vesia's will?"

"I—"

"It was addressed to Julia Lucinia Aquillius and delivered to your home in Asia after Gavius Lucinius died."

"I'm not sure. I receive many documents and cannot remember them all."

"Isn't it true that you read the will and never showed it to Julia?"

"I never—"

"Isn't it true that you disregarded turning the will over to her because you wanted to keep her inheritance for yourself? You know perfectly well that under our laws, the property belonged to Julia with or without a will. Clearly the Lucinius family did not trust you to follow our laws and customs! Good thing I sent that letter to Julia. You might have got away with this."

"That's an outrage!" Marcus's face looked set on fire.

"Did you hope that your wife wouldn't *notice* that you'd stolen her inheritance?"

Another rumble broke out among the spectators, but this time the judge ignored it, so fascinated was he with the answers he was hearing.

"Judge, I offer the court a copy of the Lucinius will granting their daughter, Julia Lucinia Aquillius, their sole heir, all of their property. And may I state, Judge, that when I explained to the Lucinii that a will wasn't necessary, they expressed their distrust of their son-in-law and wanted a will in writing that would supersede any forged document that Marcus Aquillius might present to the court."

Gaius leaped up from his chair. "How dare you. My client would never...how do we know that this will is just and true? Perhaps they name Marcus as their heir...."

The judge pounded his gavel. "Out of order."

"The original will is filed in the House of the Vestals, Judge," Admilius said. "Before the Lucinii filed it, they had it signed by two witnesses, who are here to attest to the fact that the signatures are theirs and that the will's authors are Gavius Lucinius and Vesia Lucinia."

This time, the fickle spectators booed their scorn toward Marcus, who sank into his chair and tried but failed to adjust his finery. A drop of sweat rolled down his cheek.

"I'm not finished," Admilius shouted above the crowd. "Isn't it true also that you refused to return Julia's dowry after your divorce, as required by law?"

Marcus didn't answer.

"Isn't it?" Admilius insisted.

"Stand up and answer," the judge ordered.

Marcus dragged himself to his feet, his finery in disarray. "I just hadn't gotten around to it," he said petulantly.

When the spectators realized that this case was all but over, they began to file out. But the loud shout of "Wait!" caused them to turn around and scurry back to their seats.

The shout had come from Marcus. He had a card to play. He didn't know where it would lead, but it was all he had.

"Judge," he said, "I cared for my wife and tended to her as a good Roman husband should, but she would not obey me. She turned herself to cultish ways and shamed me. I could not have it. I sent her away, yet she will not cease to associate with this rubbish. I could not have a wife who cavorts with slaves."

The spectators were titillated by this admission. Of course, they'd heard the rumors.

"Are you accusing your wife of adultery, sir?" The judge's eyes narrowed to slits.

Marcus hesitated, knowing he'd be on thin ice if he made such an accusation. It was well known that *he* was the adulterer. It was common knowledge that he'd been with Scribonia before he'd had done with Julia.

"Uh…no, Judge."

"Then this court is not concerned with such frivolities," the judge said. "Had she committed adultery, you would be entitled to a share of her dowry. This is a civil court. If you'd like to denounce your wife for heresy, take it up with Nero."

As much as Marcus would have liked to denounce Julia, he needed to think of his position. A man known to be unable to control his household would not go far, so he changed tactics.

He turned and pointed to his ex-wife. Unable to maintain his prior self-control, he bellowed, "She has the children, and I want them back. I own them. And I demand that she never see them again."

The judge jumped to his feet, pounded his gavel five times, and bellowed, "You are out of order, sir. Sit down now."

Julia ignored the judge and, in turn, jumped to her feet. "Marcus, you can't do this," she shouted. "You can't. And you will never have them. Never." She made a move toward Marcus, but Admilius caught her by the shoulders. He didn't know what she might do given the ferocious state she was in.

The courtroom erupted into pandemonium. Everyone leaped to their feet. A fistfight broke out between two women who disagreed about who should get the money and the children, while the others raised their fists and shouted obscenities.

The judge turned cherry red in fury and pounded his gavel unceasingly. "Sit down, sit down, sit down," he shrieked. "I demand decorum!" Then he slumped back into his chair.

When the courtroom finally settled down, the judge said to Marcus and Julia in an exhausted whisper, "I'm tempted to hold you both in contempt…but I'm done here." He barreled out of the courtroom to consider his ruling.

As upset as Julia was, she knew that she had to calm down and think fast. Marcus had every right to the children under Roman law, but she could not let that happen. He could not take possession of them.

As soon as she had her wits about her, an idea came. She felt it would work because she knew her husband all too well. But she would wait for just the right moment to reveal it.

It was a good four hours before the judge returned to the courtroom. He faced only the principal players because he had banned the audience from further proceedings.

The judge glared at Marcus. "Marcus Aquillius, you will return to your ex-wife her dowry and her inheritance by the end of the day. As is both our law and custom, the Lucinius estate belongs to the last surviving child."

He turned to Julia. "Julia Lucinia, I give you three weeks to vacate the Aquillius property in Herculaneum and turn your children over to your ex-husband. Is there anything else?"

A sneering Marcus turned toward his ex-wife, expecting to see a face drawn in agony at the idea of losing her children, but he was puzzled to note that she was smiling, almost. His attention turned toward his lawyer who had risen to his feet.

"Ah, Judge," Gaius said, "it will be difficult for my client to return the dowry in so short a time."

The judge glowered. "And why is that?"

"Could we be granted additional time?" Gaius glanced down at Marcus.

"The order stands. By the end of the day."

"Judge," Gaius stammered, "my client has not the means at this time to return his ex-wife's dowry."

"Is that so?" the judge scowled. "I have no sympathy for your client's circumstances. If he cannot return what is not his by the end of the day, he will be placed under house arrest, and the court will confiscate what property he has left." The judge got up to leave.

Now, Julia thought. She whispered into Admilius's ear.

Admilius drew back and gave Julia a long look. "I understand." Then he said, "Judge, if I may?"

The judge sat back down. "Go ahead," he said, blotting his face with a cloth.

Admilius rose and approached Gaius. "My client has an offer." The two of them moved to a far corner, where they put their heads together.

Scribonia glared with hate, this time not at Julia but at her husband, who had brought shame on her by making her look ridiculous. Word about the proceedings would soon spread among their friends that Marcus Aquillius had squandered his fortune and couldn't pay his debts. It would look to them as if he had married the wealthy Scribonia only because she could bail him out of his tight fixes. But Scribonia did not intend to subject herself to further humiliation. She abruptly got up and stalked out.

Julia sat very still. She still smiled with confidence.

The two solicitors returned to their respective benches. As Gaius whispered Julia's terms to Marcus, he brightened.

Several days later, Julia returned home to the villa in Herculaneum—*her* villa—in a state of joy. She had won it in exchange for her inheritance: her family's lands. The agreement wasn't a fair exchange, as the lands far exceeded the value of the villa, but she loved it here and felt satisfied with the deal she had made. After some scrambling by Marcus to come up with the funds, her dowry had been returned. It would keep her and her household supported, if not rich.

The real win had to do with the girls. The deal gave Julia permanent custody of and all decision-making powers for her girls. In exchange, Julia agreed not to name Marcus an adulterer and his new wife a whore in front of his peers. Also part of the bargain, Marcus was forced to sign a new, irrevocable trust to assure that the Lucinius lands could not be sold and would return to Livia and Flavia after his death. Finally, Marcus was never to contact Julia or his daughters again.

"We leave in a few weeks," Julia said to Milo from her place in the dining room, where they always met to plan for the week ahead. "The scribe has written several more manuscripts and made numerous copies. He'd like us to make sure they are shared with the brethren.

"Domina, are you sure that is wise? Marcus announced to all of Rome that you are with us. Surely you'll be watched."

"Nonsense. No one has the least interest in us any longer. They are too busy warring among themselves."

Civil wars had broken out throughout the empire. Nero had been tried in absentia and had committed suicide rather than be captured and executed. As one faction or another attempted to seize power, any thoughts of suppressing a minority cult made up of Jews and slaves had, for the meantime, vanished. In this absence of attention, Christianity flourished.

The Roman legions were busy quelling rebellions on numerous fronts. Julia and Milo encountered no danger on the road to Rome in the many more trips they made. While a few minor functionaries employed to know the goings-on within the empire did get wind of Yeshua's teachings reaching Christian homes in Rome, it was a minor footnote in their daily reports. It was known that a Julia Lucinia of Herculaneum was involved, but as she paid her taxes and caused no disruptions, no one cared. For Rome's Christians, the Year of the Four Emperors would prove to be a time of relative peace and safety.

FORTY-THREE

Herculaneum, AD 68

Julia was tending her garden as a carriage made its way along the road toward the villa, its iron wheels raising a racket along the cobbled stone pathway. The elegant, arch-roofed carriage was pulled by four large draft horses with two drivers controlling the eight reins and two footmen riding astern. Two liveried slaves rode behind, leading an extra draft horse and a pack mule.

Julia brushed off her hands, pulled her veil over her head, and hurried back toward the villa. No doubt this was trouble, sent by Marcus.

Expecting the worst, Julia was surprised and elated as the footman opened the carriage door and Prisca stepped down, followed by two handmaidens whom Julia had never seen.

Julia rushed into her friend's arms. Before she had the chance to express her astonishment, not only at her friend's arrival but also at her apparently newfound wealth, Prisca began her introductions.

The drivers, the footmen, the two women were all leaders of the movement, men and women known to Julia through letters and messages, but none whom she'd had the pleasure of meeting firsthand.

"Another carriage will be coming later, brethren who came by sea," Prisca said. "We'll be fifteen in all."

Julia welcomed the newcomers, then summoned Milo. "Go fetch Crispus and Aelia, and ask them to prepare for anything."

"We knew we couldn't just march in here altogether to see you," Prisca explained. "We know you're being watched. But no one would think to question a wealthy Roman matron coming to join you for a season." She grinned.

Prisca pulled Julia aside as the group filed into the atrium. "Without Peter, we're having a terrible time carrying on, and some of the communities are in quite an uproar. Each community has its own ideas about how to worship and what to teach. They're squabbling incessantly, with the Jewish followers insisting their way is best, and the Gentile followers wanting to continue to worship their own gods while still following *the way* and looking down on those they call 'foreigners.' Some of the men are insisting that they will no longer attend houses where women speak. It's chaos. Linus is doing his best to cool the unrest, but he's only one person and cannot be everywhere. We thought if anyone could guide us, it would be the scribe. He knew Peter's mind."

Julia nodded her understanding.

By late afternoon, everyone had arrived. Julia and Prisca followed the group into the atrium. With a rustle of garments, everyone settled onto couches and chairs. Each one sat up straight and looked directly at the scribe, who seemed quite befuddled.

The Patriarch Linus, first among equals, sat silently looking thoughtful, his elbows resting on the arm of the massive chair he occupied, his fingers forming a steeple just below his chin.

Simeon, who had come from Jerusalem, brimmed with pent-up energy. "Scribe, you know there are many disagreements about how we're to worship, and now we've got thousands of confused members arguing all the time."

"And this is only the beginning," said an incensed Irenius from Lyons in Gaul. "Everyone is scuttling about, eating differently, dressing in all manners of garb, and laying down their own rules. We must address the question about how we are going to live our daily lives. We must all have the same purpose. Our mission must be the same!"

Bricius, leader of the Christians in Colonia, added, "This has gone on far too long, and the quibbling must stop. We have decided that all of the assemblies must adhere to the same beliefs. Therefore a—what shall we call it—a directive must be written that would allow all the rules for worship and guidelines for living to be consistent one with another. And, Scribe, you must write it, of course."

"And just what is it you wish me to write?" The scribe, with a touch of humor in his voice, couldn't help but be amused by all the ruffled feathers.

The room fell silent as the speakers exchanged dubious glances and waited for someone to answer.

"Well, uh," Judah, matriarch of the Judea region, replied hesitantly, "we're not exactly sure."

"Then it looks as if you've got your work cut out for you and you won't need me." The scribe, smiling, gradually rose to his feet to leave.

Linus decided it was time to step in. "Quite right, Scribe. Now, sit back down." He frowned as he faced the others. "We have many things to discuss. We are all of many lands with diverse cultures. Our customs are unique. We live our lives differently. What is important to some will not be so to others. We will not see eye to eye in all things, but in the end, I decree that we will find unity in the word of Yeshua."

The scribe watched, his interest growing.

Linus continued, "Scribe, you are instrumental in our discussions. We trust that you will guide us as Peter would and record what is said objectively, as you have always done." And turning to Julia, he said, "Julia, you are instrumental as well. You two are closest to Yeshua's own true words."

Word had spread within the communities about Julia's bravery in traveling repeatedly against dangerous odds to take the scribe's documents to Rome. Her visibility was rising, and respect for her was budding.

Linus turned to the group once again and finished by adding, "These decisions will not be mine alone. The majority will rule. If we come to a stalemate on any issue, I will break the impasse."

Fifteen visitors gathered that night in the *triclinum* for a hastily prepared dinner. Along with her daughters and the scribe, Julia joined her guests. Milo stood at the side prepared to attend to any needs that might arise. Julia felt the air tense with anticipation, but the conversation was of menial things. Nothing further of an official nature would be discussed this night. After dinner, guests would be shown to bedrooms, and after breakfast, the discourse would begin.

Gathering in the atrium after the morning meal, the group assembled for what would be the first of many spirited, and sometimes irksome, debates.

Linus offered a prayer asking God to provide each member especially—and when he uttered the word "especially," he gave an audible sigh—"Patience."

Then he addressed the group. "We come together to take up the conflicts that have arisen in our communities, to discuss openly all feelings related to these issues, and to come to an accord. Each of you may not be completely satisfied with our solutions, but I ask that you look beyond your personal view and consider the greatest good, the one that is in alignment with the teachings of Yeshua."

"We moved back to Rome from Ephesus not long after you did," Prisca said during a break in the proceedings. "But when I tried to find you, I learned that you had traveled here to Herculaneum. No one seemed to know when you would be back. Then, of course, we learned more about what you are doing, as word of it spread."

"Oh, Prisca, I help only in small ways." Julia didn't want to go into detail about her work with the scribe. "But what of you?" she said, changing the subject. "I know so little."

"I'm worried about my husband," Prisca confided. "Aquila has not been feeling well, yet he tries to do so much. I don't know how to slow him down."

Julia smiled. "A common grievance among women, but I do hope he will attend to your cautions."

"And what of Marcus, Julia?"

"Oh, Prisca, we always lived separate lives, as you know." Julia took a deep breath. "We're divorced."

Prisca took Julia's hand. "I'm so sorry." Since Prisca had lived a marriage of love with Aquila for so many years, she considered that Julia's life could only be miserable without a loving husband by her side.

"I'm happy, Prisca, truly. Do not worry about me."

Prisca eyed Julia without conviction, and then gave her hand a squeeze.

The group met for many days. In the end, they agreed on parameters for a document called the *Didache*. It would be a pastoral manual derived from the teachings of Yeshua to be put into practice at religious rites. It would detail consistent approaches for implementing a Christian way of life.

Though the discussions spent had been arduous, Julia was sorry to see the convocation end. The scribe, however, was not. He had worked hard and needed some rest before finishing his work. He would have to complete the manuscript, and then it had to be reproduced. And this time, the message would be written on sheets of vellum, not scrolls, and on both sides of a page. This would be a new form of writing, with the sheets sown at the edge and bound together in book form.

Julia's days as a courier, then, would not end. She would once again travel the road to Rome so that the new manuscript of tradition, custom, and practice could be circulated throughout the empire.

FORTY-FOUR

Herculaneum AD 68

As Julia was helping the servants clean up after the guests departed, she spotted in the distance an old woman with long, gray hair.

"I seek the scribe," the old woman said as Julia opened the front door and observed her quizzically. "I am Mary of Magdala."

Mary! Everyone knew of Mary Magdala, certainly, but no one had known her whereabouts for some time now. She seemed to have disappeared.

Julia immediately wrapped her arm around Mary's waist and assisted her into the atrium.

"Please sit down," Julia said. "I do not know from where you have come, but you must be very tired. I'll bring you some hot broth. Please, just rest now." Her visitor sank gratefully into the cushions.

Flustered completely, Julia had forgotten her manners. "I am Julia. Yes, please, just rest. I will return momentarily."

Julia dashed out of the atrium in a mad search for Milo. When she found him, she could barely speak and sputtered breathlessly that Mary of Magdala had just arrived at the front door.

At his amazed look, Julia said, "Please, please, Milo, let us do all we can to make her comfortable. She is very, very old now and seems exhausted. She is asking for the scribe."

The scribe had revealed much to Julia about his travels with Yeshua, of course. Of Mary, he had little to say, not because he was reticent but because Mary had been.

The life of Mary of Magdala was a bit of a mystery to them all. Julia knew only the basics. She had been born into a merchant family in Magdala. Her father had taught her to read and write in order for her to keep the accounts for his business. After her father died, she had taken over, expanded the enterprise, and become quite prosperous in the process.

Somewhere along the way, Mary had learned of Yeshua and sought him out. Everyone knew the rest of that story, as far as it went. The two had become inseparable friends, and she had been his most beloved disciple.

Why Mary had come, Julia could not imagine. She hurried to the library.

"Mary, dearest Mary," the scribe said. He stood before her and took both of her hands in his.

Julia could see him holding back tears. "It has been such a long time."

"Yes," she said simply.

Mary and the scribe withdrew to a small side chamber for privacy. Julia saw to a meal for the two of them. Shortly afterward, she showed Mary to a bedroom, where she retired for the night.

Mary's arrival had stunned the scribe, and when he sought out Julia later that evening, he still seemed astonished.

"Mary has always been reluctant to speak about herself," the scribe said. "But now she feels it is the moment, for as she says, her time is short."

The scribe paused, a faraway look in his eye. "I wish you could have seen her then. She took everyone's breath away. She was so lovely."

Smiling, he recalled, "I remember a time when Yeshua purchased a wooden flute for John because John was a very good player and Yeshua loved listening to him. One night, when many of us were gathered, Yeshua asked him to play, and John burst into a lively folk song. The crowd applauded in appreciation, and then they began to clap in rhythm. Several of the women rose to dance. John was playing with great relish, his fingers moving deftly up and down the open holes.

"Mary rose. When she did, the others stopped and formed a circle around her, and it was obvious why. She was so elegant. Her body swayed so gracefully. Her arms moved with fluidity, and her hands were like the agile wings of a bird. Her cheeks flushed red, and her smile widened as she moved. Then she seemed to catch herself, and she suddenly stopped and moved off to the side. I noticed the goatish expressions on the faces of some of the men, and I noted Mary's discomfort. The smile on Yeshua's face seemed to imply that she ought not to feel embarrassed, that her dance was a gift."

The scribe continued, "Mary and I became friends. She was so beautiful she took my breath away, but this wasn't the most attractive thing. Her mind. Her spirit. She understood Yeshua and his teachings in a way that none of the rest of us could grasp. She was the best of all of us. But she was so elusive. I wanted to know her story from her point of view, but whenever I tried to find out more about her, she would move away from me, claiming she did not merit a place in my writing. Of course she did. Her close and mysteriously silent communication with Yeshua was indeed something unique and memorable."

Looking wistful, the scribe softly said, "Truly, during those years, no one touched my heart—with the exception of Yeshua—more than Mary. I was bewitched by every aspect of her, the huskiness of her voice, the way she tilted her head down when she spoke, the rush of those black curls that always pressed against her cheek. She was a strong, exciting, intelligent woman like none I had known before. I have always wanted to write her story. Now, it seems, I have the chance."

For two weeks, Mary and the scribe met together behind the closed doors of his library. Then one morning when Julia woke, she discovered that Mary had gone. Neither the scribe nor Julia ever saw her again.

Of what Mary and the scribe spoke, Julia knew not. Of what was written, she had no idea. The scribe never revealed a single detail of their exchanges. But one day not long after Mary's departure, as Julia entered the library to summon the scribe to lunch, she saw him attaching a leather tag to the top corner of a scroll. She saw that it read MM.

FORTY-FIVE

J acques, Philippe, Anna-Marie, and Carol went home.
Yigael decided to stay for a time in Rome.
Giuseppe found himself alone again.
Cardinal Ricci, holed up alone, maintained a low profile. While he had embarrassed his peers and humiliated himself, still the research had to be done, and it could still bend to his favor.

Valentina and Erika got to work.

Three years back, when their business started to take off as their reputation and the demand for their services grew, the two had founded their own laboratory. Having Valeri Laboratorio di Conservazione also meant they would no longer need to wait for results as was so common when using university or private testing labs.

Their lab rivaled that of many university departments, from electron microscopes through digital cameras to carbon dating units and tweezers to hooks for lab coats. What they lacked but were intent on purchasing—the current cost was a small fortune—was an X-ray microscope, which could allow them to see through delicate parchments and scrolls without risk of destroying them.

Ordinarily artifacts were cleaned and documented on site. This time, though, the scholars wanted only their hands on the precious objects.

"Any guesses?" Erika asked Valentina as they peered through a container at the scroll found among Julia's bones.

"We can hope it contains what Livia had scratched into the epitaph—her life story," Valentina said. "Whatever it is, it comes first."

The two women then looked into the travel boxes. One of the scrolls was rolled tightly and looked the most weathered. The other was a thin codex, a parchment folded, sewn, and sandwiched between two wooden covers.

"This is wonderful," Erika said. "This might be the earliest codex I've ever seen!" She took a peek and spent a few moments silently translating some of its words. "It looks like an epistle."

"We'll get to it later," Valentina said.

They added more cushioning to the scroll and codex and stored them in a climate-controlled room adjacent to their workspace. Before doing the same with the artifacts, they took a good look at a bronze inkwell with basket handles and two styluses that looked to be made of palm leaf.

"We don't see these very often. I haven't seen a stylus since Qumran." Erika referred to the Dead Sea Scrolls find, a subject on which she was an expert. "And here we have two of them," she added. "Look, this one has a bit of dried ink on the tip." She wrapped the objects and placed them back in the box.

The women placed the scraps of Julia's ornately embroidered *stola* aside. They carefully boxed her signet ring in a padded container.

Valentina and Erika hadn't known what to make of the curious little stone cup Yigael had spotted on the shelf in Julia's tomb. Why such a seemingly obscure object had been saved, they couldn't figure. It certainly didn't look like much, just an old cup, common enough in many households of the time. They would clean and study it later. Valentina wrapped it and placed it in the storage room.

The women removed their latex gloves and put on white cotton gloves. Working with a scroll was always tricky, and Erika always felt nervous beforehand. The scroll had been wrapped inside several layers of oiled leather. As they unwrapped the leathers, the ancient hides disintegrated at their most delicate touch. Erika took a deep breath as a miraculously intact parchment with bits of dried flower petals stuck to it was revealed under the layers of protective coverings. She began to unfurl the first of the scrolls while Valentina placed cloth weights at the top. The scroll unrolled with surprising ease, and it stretched the length of one long table.

Once they had begun to read, Julia's life took over, consuming them for the next three weeks.

Then, on a Tuesday morning at 11:40, they looked up, locked eyes, and together looked back down at the diary before them.

"Can you believe that?" Valentina said breathlessly.

Erika read again. "No, I can't."

They stared at the scroll for several moments.

"Mary Magdalene visits Julia's villa in Herculaneum?" A dazed look filled Valentina's widened eyes.

"Can this be real?" Erika couldn't take her eyes away from what she was reading.

"Mary closeted with the scribe telling him her life story?" Valentina said.

"And then she leaves and they never see her again?" Erika said.

"Look here. Julia sees the scroll that the scribe wrote her story on, or at least she thinks she did…because of the tag she sees the scribe attach to it."

"With the initials MM. This is astounding," Erika said. "You don't think…."

"We have the Magdalene scroll? It's too much to hope for." Both women looked toward the storage locker where the other scroll was sitting. "We'll need to send it out. If it is, we don't even want to risk touching it." In her mind, Valentina was already on the phone, arranging for Yigael to get the scroll to the IAA labs.

The mention of the enigmatic Mary Magdalene always

resulted in a flurry of activity among biblical scholars because they knew so little of her. An original scroll with Mary's own words, with documentation, would be the find of a lifetime.

"Wonder if there's something more," Erika said.

"Let's see." Valentina lowered her glasses, got to her feet, and began shifting the scroll's position.

The two read for several hours, during which they spoke not a word.

"Here's something," Erika said.

"Let me look," Valentina said. "Wow."

"Here's what Julia says." Erika read out loud, "'As we left Herculaneum on that fateful day, the scribe handed me a scroll and asked me to keep it safe from harm. He seemed quite anxious about it, given the look in his eye. I saw that it bore the tag MM, Mary's scroll presumably. I told him that I wasn't sure what lay ahead, but I would do my best to care for it.'"

The two women rose as one and made a beeline for the storage room. Removing the crate from the storeroom, they carefully and deliberately set it on an adjacent work table. Valentina opened the lid and stared at the two objects inside. She peered intently to get a closer look at the rolled scroll and saw a tiny piece of leather lying separately from the scroll, but it was mostly hidden underneath it. "Dare we risk it?"

"What?" Erika said in a tone that demanded more.

"I can see a piece of the tag. It's pretty well hidden, but I'm pretty sure of it. What do you think?"

"We need to make sure. And pray it doesn't disintegrate. Hang on for a minute." Erika scurried away, returning with a pair of tweezers. After bending over to get a close look, she pulled a piece of cushioning out and laid the tweezers down as close to the object as she could without touching it.

"Just prod it out, slow, slow, slow."

Erika pushed the tweezers closer to the tag but instead of clasping it, she nudged it out from under the scroll.

"So far, so good." Erika took a long look at the tag. "Nothing on this side. We'll have to turn it over."

"Oh, great. More chance that it will fall apart."

"Do you want to do it?" Erika said.

"Either way. Go ahead if you want." Valentina said.

Erika took hold of the tag lightly with the tweezers and picked it up. A tiny shred fell off the edge and turned to ash as it fell back onto the table. She held the tag steady and then flipped it with precision and set it down.

Valentina looked over. Her words were a whisper. "There it is."

Erika gasped. In a fine tight hand were written two letters: MM

FORTY-SIX

The Bay of Neapolis, AD 79

Julia looked across the bay at the shoreline homes where the wealthy traveled to escape the heat and turmoil of Rome and she thought, *Holy God, what is ahead for us?* She glanced at Milo herding Livia and Flavia toward the edge of the small boat, where they could sit and hold on to the side to secure themselves against the sway.

They were all in shock and speechless. Just moments before, Vesuvius had blanketed Herculaneum with ash, destroying everything beneath it. Their home gone. Their friend, the scribe, dead.

Clutching her cloth bag, Julia gazed at her daughters and wondered distractedly, *Where have the years gone? The girls have grown up, almost outside my notice.*

Livia, now twenty-one years of age, favored her father. She was tall and thin-boned, with dark brown eyes and hair. Deliberate with her speech, she continued to be diplomatic with all. From the time the scribe had begun to teach the girls, Livia had been the more scholarly, deeply inspired by the scribe's writings and interested in reaching his level of achievement.

Flavia, twenty, was petite, with features like her mother. Her vivacious personality had not settled down over the years. Still spontaneous and opinionated, Flavia invited herself into any conversation with anyone at any time, chattering away with no restraint. She was not as intellectually gifted as her older sister, and, as Julia noted in her diary, sometimes she would throw up her arms in frustration from the strain of learning something new.

They are still as unalike in personality as they could possibly be. Livia, always so eager to please, always satisfied with whatever is on her plate, not at all needing others to keep her occupied. She seems so content, but is she?

And Flavia, what of her? She's always seeking excitement and so often breaking the rules. I'll never forget finding her up in the loft of the old barn with the Roman soldier she hoped to marry. When he went off to marry another, it broke her heart. She never speaks of it, of course. But I see the sadness in her eyes even when she is with her friends. She is very good at acting the part of ebullient party-goer. I wonder whether her friends see through her.

Why do we mothers know difficulty with our daughters? Yet I am grateful for them. They have filled my life as nothing else has.

Julia's mind jumped back to the present. She was struck with one idea about what they might do next, but they needed rest before heading out.

They stayed two nights in Neapolis, and then paid a driver to take them to Rome. On their second day there, Julia wrote in her diary,

When I set eyes on Prisca, I fell into her arms, sobbing. Thankfully we are on safe ground now. I am ashamed to say it, but the shock and grief I feel over the loss of everything in Herculaneum—most importantly my friend the scribe—has immobilized me. I can barely lift a finger.

Prisca immediately offered refuge to the tired travelers and saw to settling them in. Aquila had leased a large storehouse, where the couple continued to manufacture and sell leather goods. Their property featured living quarters on either side of a workspace, and Prisca assigned one side with two rooms to Julia and the girls. A small hut was out back. Milo would settle there for the time being.

Julia's room had a single bed with a table beside it. She sat on the edge of her new bed and looked inside her cloth bag. She withdrew the few personal items she had been able to gather before leaving and then tucked the bag containing the scroll underneath her bed.

Julia wanted one remembrance from home to look at, and with care, she put the cup that had adorned her mantelpiece for so long on the table. This was the cup the scribe had brought with him when he came to live with her, the one he had promised to tell them all about in times to come.

Julia remembered when he finally had done so. The account had come one night during story time when her girls were once again at Scribe's feet in front of the fire and Julia was busy at her needlework. The scribe had confided the events of that somber night when Yeshua had supped for the last time and a cup—this one—had been passed among his friends.

Julia's return to Rome marked a period of great upheaval. The eruption of Vesuvius required massive relief efforts from untold numbers of people. The disruption swelled the population of Rome, causing food shortages, overcrowding, and misery. Julia helped where she could, but the poor and desperate seemed without number. Then, in the spring of AD 80, another fire broke out in Rome, consuming large parts of the city, destroying temples and public buildings, killing those who could not escape, and leaving the rest without shelter. The squalid living conditions led to an outbreak of the plague, leaving thousands more men, women, and children dead, orphaned, or destitute. For an inexplicable reason, the Black Death passed over Prisca and Aquila's household.

"What could possibly happen next?" Julia asked Prisca as she rushed through the front door.

"Emperor Titus has died. That's what's happened next," Prisca exclaimed. "He's to be replaced by Domitian, God help us."

Fortunately, the tyrant Domitian had his mind on matters other than religious persecutions. He needed workers to clean up after the natural disasters and didn't see much advantage in persecuting able-bodied citizens who could take on the work.

The exception was the Jews. After Titus sacked the temple in Jerusalem in AD 70, they continued to be victimized while the Christians of Rome were left in relative peace. Still, though, the Christian movement was legally forbidden, and the converts had to be careful.

While the sense of community enriched Julia's life and gave her purpose, her sadness set in once more.

"We must leave here," Prisca announced one morning at the breakfast table.

Julia wasn't surprised to hear it. Aquila had become ill, and the couple needed their children. Julia reached out and took Prisca's hand.

"We'll be moving back to Ephesus," Prisca said.

Julia blinked away tears as she held her friend's hand.

Julia had been paying her part of Aquila's and Prisca's rent since they arrived, and she could well afford to pay the full amount so they could stay on.

When the day came to say goodbye, she let the tears stream down as she watched her friends depart, but she consoled herself with the thought that Milo could now move from his piecemeal accommodation in the shed into the main house. *We can establish a household and truly be a family*, she thought.

Just as Prisca and Aquila disappeared from view, Julia was in for another surprise, as she noted in her diary. Her younger daughter, Flavia, announced that she would marry a childhood friend. Julia had doubts about the union.

Poor Tycho. I wonder whether he knows what he's in for. It's too late now. The marriage ceremony is done. I am not thrilled as I should be that Flavia has married Tycho. I see no sign that she is in love with the man. She likes him well enough. After all, they were playmates as children. But unlike with Livia, I have always been able to read Flavia. (Perhaps it is because she is so much like me!) And I know that she is using him as a means to an end. She has always had an itch to be on her own, but she knows that she cannot go without a man beside her. I fear for her. But they are gone now. She has set up her household on the other side of Rome, where the population is denser and, fervent Christian that she is, she can gather new converts in greater numbers. I suppose I shouldn't be shocked. Flavia is the most dedicated Christian among us and she sees herself as a leader. I can only hope for the best for her. At least Livia is staying. Thank goodness for that.

Julia's life seemed to be settling down after many years of turbulence, making what would soon come even more of a shock.

FORTY-SEVEN

Rome, AD 81

Christian hope for a continuing peaceful reign under Emperor Domitian ended when he had himself officially titled "God the Lord" and insisted that the people greet him with shouts of "Lord of the earth," "Invincible," "Glory," "Holy," and "Thou Alone." Those who balked at these proclamations were targeted, harassed, beaten, exiled, and subjected to a usurious level of taxation known as the *Fiscus Iudaicus*, a tax levied on Jews and now on Christians, and increased to a ruinous level.

Additionally, Domitian targeted Jewish Christians and all Christians by ordering a purge of those not following Roman paganism, and he introduced an inventive way to persecute them: he went after their leaders. His soldiers invaded house assemblies, arrested those in charge, and told the others that if they renounced their religion and returned to pagan ways, their lives would be spared. However, to avoid execution, they had also to turn in others of their faith. Many obviously chose life over death.

Domitian was particularly intolerant of those among Rome's nobility who had embraced the new faith. He accused them of atheism or "lapsing into Jewish custom," and he made it his mission to hunt them down, labeling them traitors and heretics, taking their lands, and exiling them under threat of death.

As both a Roman noble and now a recognized leader of the movement, Julia had been named by more than one frightened arrestee. She had gone into hiding and was regularly moved from one safe house to another. Domitian was keen to make an example of her as a warning to any other Roman ladies who might be tempted to become involved with the Christian scum.

"My lady," Milo said, bursting through the front door just as Julia was finishing lunch. His face was contorted with fear and grief. "I come with terrible news."

"What?" Julia rose looking alarmed, a napkin still in her hand.

"The Romans have raided Flavia's community. They took all the members into custody, all except Flavia and Tycho. They...." Milo's voice trailed off in despair.

"They what?" Julia asked, gripping the sides of the table.

"They murdered both of them," Milo said, his voice nearly a whisper, his head downcast.

"What do you mean, 'they murdered...?'" Julia responded, clearly not taking in Milo's words.

Milo lifted his head and looked into her eyes. He spoke with steadiness and fervency. "Roman soldiers were looking for you. They found Flavia and her assembly and pressed the group to disclose your location. No one would say where you were. That is when the soldiers slew Flavia and Tycho and arrested the others."

Julia's knees buckled. Milo caught her before she fell and half-carried her to a chair.

"How?" Julia asked in the smallest voice, still not fully comprehending his words.

With his pain evident, Milo said only, "She is dead." He would not reveal the terrible truth that when nobody would reveal Julia's whereabouts, the soldiers had ripped off Flavia's garments and whipped her until she was covered in blood and lay unconscious. When she came to, they forced her to watch as they executed her husband, Tycho. Finally, they took a knife to Flavia's throat as the example to the others who would defy them.

"Where is she?" Julia asked him. "Where are they, I mean?"

He shook his head. "The Romans have claimed their bodies."

Beginning to tremble, she said, "I do not understand."

"I am so sorry." Milo fought tears, but his restraint failed him as he erupted into a sob.

"I must go to her," Julia said as she tried to lift herself out of her chair. "Yes, I will go to her. It will be all right. Help me up, Milo, please."

Milo knew that he was not getting through to Julia, and he needed her attention. He kneeled before her, grabbed her hands, and shook her. "Julia." He rarely called his mistress by her given name. "You must listen to me. Hear me. Flavia and Tycho have been murdered by the Romans."

"No, no, no!" Julia's keening howl drew neighbors out of their houses.

Milo shook Julia again to get her attention. "They are in search of you. You and Livia are next."

Julia gasped. "How do you know?"

"Word from a friend. Tullus. He warned me that his master is ordered to arrest you and Livia. The soldiers are on their way. They will find you. Please hear me, for you do not want to lose your other daughter. Come. Now."

Lose my other daughter. Those words brought Julia back to the present and startled her into action. She began again to rise from her chair. Milo helped Julia stand and all but lifted her out the front door. Livia, already aware of her sister's death, had just passed by curious neighbors and pulled up with a rented cart. There was no time for conversation. They had to leave instantly.

Milo gave a dazed Julia a boost onto the cart, and then bolted back into the house, emerging with Julia's cloth bag in one hand, the cup in the other. He stuffed the cup into the bag, sprang onto the cart, and seized the reins.

Then, with all possible speed, they fled, the three of them.

Julia, Livia, and Milo escaped by traveling overnight on the Via del Mara. They found safe haven on a small farm just outside of Ostia. Then, they moved on and stayed overnight with friends in the town. Ostia was not all that far from Rome, and Milo could not be certain that they would be safe. But they stayed out of sight, and the Roman soldiers did not show up looking for them.

They traveled on to a place they hoped would provide safety for a longer time. The friends who opened their home to the three fugitives were Meshulam Ben-hadad, a wealthy merchant, and his wife, Emet, who lived on an island just offshore.

Julia and Emet had become friends in the early days of their marriages. Emet had never liked Marcus, and many times after the divorce, she had said that she admired Julia's fortitude and independence but worried that she might find herself destitute. Julia continually had to assure her friend that her dowry allowed her to live comfortably.

Emet and her husband had moved out of Rome to the island of Isola Sacra, which lay between the cities of Portus and Ostia. Emet felt that Julia would be out of harm's way on the island. The Ben-hadad villa was beautiful and tranquil. Surrounded by green fields and facing the shoreline with a natural bay, Julia should have found peace there, but she did not.

My grief knows no bounds. Adding up my divorce, the loss of my home in Herculaneum, and the death of the scribe, all three together do not equal the sorrow and anguish I feel at losing my beloved Flavia. And Tycho, of course. Yet all through these years, I knew there was danger. How could I have so ignored it and put my family at risk? I regret ever hearing about these Christians, let alone becoming part of them. If I had not, my daughter would still be with me. I am so angry. How bitter I am.

Meshulam and Emet were Jews who worshipped at the synagogue in Ostia. They knew of Julia's involvement with the followers, and now that she was with them, they invited her to share Yeshua's words at their temple.

She refused. But after being asked again and again, she relented. "I won't speak Yeshua's words, though," she told Emet. "I will speak my own."

When Julia walked to a dais at the front of the sanctuary for the first time, facing people she had never seen before, she showed no hesitation.

"I am broken," Julia said. In a monotone, she told the congregants about the disintegration of her marriage, of life with the scribe and his end in Herculaneum, and the loss of her daughter. She figured that her vulnerability would put off these people, and they would never ask her to speak again. But she was wrong. Her burdens drew them to her instead.

Newcomers came to hear her, and the telling and retelling of her life story propelled others to share their hurts and misfortunes. Ultimately, Julia found peace. And somewhere along the way, she added to her story, "The Messiah has come."

Julia had stepped to the forefront of Christianity. Much to her surprise, it had not escaped the notice of the patriarch in Rome.

FORTY-EIGHT

Rome, AD 88

Pope Clement had a problem on his hands. He'd heard rumors that some of the new leaders in the Roman community were looting the coffers. He considered it scandalous that parishioners' contributions meant for the poor were being taken by so-called men of God. At the same time, he was leery of interrogating and perhaps offending those who may not have been at fault. Worse, though, the thieves, if caught, might well turn their leader in to the Romans in order to protect themselves. If they could steal, they certainly could arrange for their leader's demise. That's what Clement thought, though, so he felt helpless to confront and change this state of affairs.

Making things even more difficult was the pressure of keeping the faithful safe from Rome's relentless pursuit of them. Rome had shown no letup in persecuting Christians over the past ten years, and the Christian population still operated underground, quite literally in Clement's case. He had managed to stay out of harm's way by leading religious services secretly in below-ground family vaults at the homes of some of Rome's wealthy citizens.

Word had reached Clement about the growing movement in Ostia with Julia at the helm and, improbably, in strife-free conditions. *How does she do it?* Clement wondered. He decided to turn to her for help in the matter of the monies. Because of the short distance between Rome and Ostia, it would not be difficult to communicate back and forth.

Clement's letter to Julia surprised her. As she wrote in her journal,

A letter has arrived on a matter of some secrecy. (I trust his secretary is discreet.) Clement confides to me his perplexity in suspecting that someone is stealing from the Church treasury. Clement is asking me to consider how money collected can be accounted for and properly distributed. The answer is simple.

Clement was pleased with Julia's response and asked her to compose a decree requiring all monies to be handled simultaneously by two, and only two, appointed members from each community. With two at the till, neither could pilfer a coin without being observed.

Ten years passed, during which Julia and Clement exchanged letters but never met. Then, in the year 96, Domitian died, and the moderate Marcus Cocceius Nerva took over as emperor. Nerva reversed the hated Domitian's policies of persecutions. He released prisoners detained unjustly and stopped executions. No longer had Christians to fear for their lives.

Clement had been in hiding and holding secret meetings at the upscale home of Priscilla, whose husband had been killed by Domitian. Now that the persecutions were over—for the time being—Clement could emerge and lead his flock openly.

The faith spread faster and became more popular, especially among slaves and the poor. These circumstances led to needs that Clement couldn't fulfill just with his current advisers.

He summoned Julia to Rome.

When she arrived at Priscilla's home, Clement was astonished to note Julia's tiny physical frame, given the scope of her large endeavors. But seeing the intelligence reflected in her huge, brown eyes, he felt assured that she would be up to any task required. He only hoped that she would be willing.

"I have asked you here on a matter of some urgency," Clement said as he looked at Julia directly.

Julia considered the man before her. Far from handsome, Clement was slight of build, with a crooked nose, his hair and beard long and graying. His dark-brown eyes, set beneath thick, gray brows, were sometimes piercingly direct, at other times pleasingly soft and kind. She knew he lacked formal education, but in his letters to her in Ostia, his thoughts were clear-cut, his ideas refined. "Yes, er, Your Excellency?"

"To you, I am Brother. Please call me that."

"And how can I help?" Julia felt a flutter in her heart as her natural instinct to come forward took hold and she began to feel enthusiastic.

Clement explained bluntly, "We need money."

Julia raised her eyebrows and looked mystified.

"I know your background," Clement said. "I need someone with your influence to seek out and bring the affluent to our congregations. Once there, we hope to persuade them to join in our movement and add to our coffers."

As quickly as Julia had brimmed with enthusiasm, her heart sank.

Clement went on impulsively, "You can move here. We will assemble your friends and prevail upon them to support our movement."

Ask for money? Julia thought indignantly. *How vulgar. I will have nothing to do with this.*

Over the years, Julia had tamed her temper and learned the art of diplomacy. To avoid offending the Christian leader, she said nearly apologetically, "Brother, I have little to do with my former friends. I do not think they remember me anymore, or if they do, they undoubtedly have critical views about my life now. No, I could not possibly go to them. I am sorry."

"Nonsense." Clement wasn't about to spare her this task. "The climate has changed. The upper-echelon Romans think it is fashionable to seize on the latest vogue. And anyway, as always, they will never decline an invitation to a lavish banquet. Please reconsider."

"But my efforts have been to help…uh…elsewhere," Julia argued. "I would be no good at this."

"Did I not hear what a compelling and coveted hostess you once were?" Clement persisted slyly. "Hmm?"

"But those days…."

In the end, Julia bowed to Clement's wishes and moved into Priscilla's *domus*. Livia and Milo followed.

Julia reached out to her former friends and organized weekly get-togethers to enlist monetary support in order to keep the movement growing. Feeling she was being used, she did it with a touch of resentment, but nonetheless, she did it.

As she settled into life at Priscilla's, Julia began taking care of Clement's letters. Her knowledge of several languages made her an invaluable helpmate to his need for communication with the outside communities. Soon, she and Clement had developed a close relationship, and during meetings of the elders, she sat at his right, the only woman present. As Clement relied on her more and more, he gave her additional responsibilities. One was to arbitrate disputes among leaders. This put her at odds with the men of power, especially when her word was final against theirs. Julia noted naively in her diary:

I suppose he has assigned me these duties because I have built a reputation for fairness and diplomacy. At least, that is what he has told me, and I will not argue. My association with Clement is very rewarding and gratifying.

As the years wore on and unknown to Julia, her visibility was wearing on the elders, and their grumblings about the woman who had their leader's ear were escalating in tone and intensity.

But Clement knew nothing of that. To him, Julia had served Christianity for years, successfully recruiting, opening assemblies, raising money, even putting herself in danger. By the late 90s, he decided that her position ought to be elevated.

FORTY-NINE

Rome, AD 97

Julia's investiture as bishop was taken under the disapproving sneers of the male pecking order. As she was presented with an ornately embroidered *stola* of office and her pastoral ring of chased silver, her enemies were secretly devising ways to bring her down. As Porcius, bishop of the Esquiline district, watched from the wings, he thought, *We'll see about this.*

On this day, though, Julia had no thought of who might be against her.

I was quite astonished when Clement summoned me to say that I had been chosen bishop. I could barely believe such a thing. He told me I well deserved it for the many ways I've served Christianity. That may well be part of it, but I am under no illusion about the real reason: I was able to raise substantial contributions.

I suppose I must actually think of myself as a Christian now. I resisted the nomenclature for so long because I am resistant to being labeled, but I am also ever so mindful of the scribe's words that it is not important to become a Christian but, rather, to be a Christian.

Clement has made me head of the Trastevere district in Rome. Trastevere crosses the Tiber by the Pons Aemilius, the large stone bridge built about 300 years ago. It will be easy for me to stay in close touch with Clement.

The allies and co-conspirators of Porcius were Terentius of the Aventunus district and Lexus, bishop of the church of San Saba, which was a center of banking for Rome's Christian community. Each had a different reason for wanting Julia out.

Terentius was jealous, believing that Julia had usurped his position as right hand to Clement, and he seethed under the fact of it. Lexus, a Jew, considered it unnatural for a woman to worship alongside men.

Porcius was harder to read. A tall, sinewy, icy man, he had a reputation for lewd conduct and a bent for violence. When his vicious temper erupted, the red strawberry-like spot on the right side of his forehead seemed to pulsate frenetically.

Mysteriously quiet about his objections to Julia's position, he nonetheless was the clear danger to her because he realized that she could well be the one, if she found out, to blow the whistle on the trio's scandalous activities.

The three had built for themselves a life of luxury by extorting money from worshippers. Their ploy was to specify in letters to communities that tithes to the Church be sent directly to themselves. Of course, they kept most of the funds, turning over to the Church just enough *denarii* to hold suspicion at bay. Each, then, was able to build a lavish home with slaves and mistresses to serve him. Some of their peers were none the wiser. Others turned the other cheek.

With Julia tucked away and busy in Trastevere, Porcius saw that she was no threat to them at the moment. They could leave her alone and turn their attention elsewhere. In a brazen attempt to gain even more power and lock in their lofty positions, they devised a scurrilous plan to control their congregants. But their plan would necessitate skewing Yeshua's words and undermining his message.

After Aquila's death, Prisca had once more returned to Rome to help the movement grow. She'd been dismayed after her arrival that the home churches had moved so far from Paul's intentions. Her husband had served as bishop in Ephesus, anointed by Paul himself, and she knew the thoughts of Paul as if he'd been her own brother.

The small home churches led by simple people were giving way to larger congregations, being led by men who ignored Yeshua's teachings. Elderships and overseer positions were being purchased through bribes. Women, who had once been leaders of the movement, were increasingly being silenced.

But *this* had gone too far.

Prisca held the letter in her hand, and she was shaking with rage.

"This is not legitimate!" she remarked to Christa, looking her friend straight in the eye.

"It says that they are speaking with the authority of Clement!" Christa took the letter back and reviewed it with knitted brows.

With a dark look, Prisca fumed. "I know Clement. He would never sanction such a thing. This must be stopped. We need to speak to him, and we need to do it now!"

"I don't know that we can get near him, Prisca," Christa remarked. "He is surrounded by secretaries and hangers-on. Whenever he is seen in public, he is surrounded by goons."

A look of alarm passed over Prisca's face. "That poor man. He was always too holy for his own good."

The next morning, Prisca made her way across Rome...to Julia.

"This is preposterous," Julia said, taking her eyes from the letter and looking directly at Prisca. "I can barely believe what I'm reading." Julia looked again at the page and re-read the letter.

To the Christians under the Authority of the Esquiline Hills,

I bring you the good news that you can enter the kingdom of God through instructions from your Holy Father in Rome. As heaven has a hierarchy, so too must we honor the Lord's hierarchy on earth. Just as you are subject to the rule of the blessed Nerva who has been appointed above us all, it is also befitting that you should in every way be subject to your bishop, who has been appointed by our Father and is to be your divine representative of heaven on earth. Do so, and in return, you may in all respects be sanctified.

It is manifest that you should revere your bishop and look upon him, even as you would upon the Lord Himself. I commend your good order that you live according to this and that no secret have any dwelling place within you.

Peace be to the brethren from the fathers of the Church of Rome. Porcius, an apostle by the will of God, Bishop of Esquiline in Rome.

Julia looked up again at Prisca. "This directive has nothing to do with Yeshua's intent. This is outrageous."

"No, indeed it doesn't have anything to do with Yeshua and his mission," Prisca replied. "In fact, it's a contradiction of everything Yeshua taught. They are appointing themselves little Caesars, claiming temporal powers over the followers. How could Clement allow this?"

Julia shrugged. "These men have powerful friends in the Senate. Porcius and Lexus have even been licensed to open an *argentarium*, allegedly for the Christians. He is using Christian money to make loans to Roman officials, and he charges interest. When Clement argued with him, Porcius convinced him that it was necessary to have Romans in his debt, for Clement's own safety."

Prisca blanched. "That sounds like a threat!"

"Yes," Julia agreed. "Let's see how far this edict has spread. Maybe Porcius is just shaking down his own district. Come with me." She headed for the doorway.

Julia and Prisca left the Trastevere and made their way to

Clement's small palace. No one was about at this time of day. Prisca followed Julia into the *scriptorium*. It didn't take Julia long to find what she was looking for, and she could not stomach what she saw. Identical transcripts had been signed by Terentius, Lexus, and three other new bishops. Clement was clearly in danger from the men he had appointed.

FIFTY

Rome AD 97

Porcius, Terentius, and Lexus sat across from Julia and Clement on stone benches in the assembly hall.

"Just what is this about?" Lexus asked Clement. "And why is she here?" He glowered at Julia.

With all of her glowing qualities, Julia, Clement conceded, was not always the easiest elder to work with. With a constant barrage of tribulations to deal with, many leaders of the Church, including the mild-mannered Clement himself, simply ignored them and hoped that they would go away. But when Julia was involved, she always faced them down, no matter whose feathers she ruffled. Clement sighed, hoping that her mission this time would really be only a minor administrative matter. He would have to wait and see.

Julia winced at the vile-smelling Lexus facing her.

"Julia has requested this meeting," Clement said. "I, too, do not know why we are here. Perhaps, Julia, you can explain."

For just a moment, Julia recalled the feisty, opinionated young girl she had been, always blurting out spontaneously whatever was on her mind. That fiery young girl had turned into a woman with the same determination, but a more tempered approach.

"I have evidence against the three of you of corruption and

false teachings." Julia hadn't lost *all* of her ability to be blunt. At the same time, she was calm and confident.

Porcius jumped to his feet ready to react.

But Clement spoke first. "Are you quite certain of what you say, Sister? What evidence of such an accusation do you have?"

Julia knew then that she would be getting no cheers from the man who had made her a bishop—he didn't like trouble. She felt she was already losing the battle, but she forged ahead nonetheless. "I have proof that they are stealing money from their parishioners to pad their own pockets."

And then she faced the bishops. "Unfortunately for you three, I have inquired of the parishes about the monies sent, and I have compared those to what the Church has received. The numbers do not match."

"And just where is your proof?" Lexus interrupted.

"I have the documents, and I will produce them," Julia said.

"You have no such proof," Lexus said, slurring his words.

"I do, and it is easy to see where the money has gone. I have seen where you live. I know that you could not maintain your quarters with the money provided you by the Church."

Terentius stopped her and jumped up. "You know not of what you speak. You accuse us only to gain power. Our homes come from the wealth of our families, who have purchased the properties for us. It is necessary for us to live in a style that will draw the prosperous to our faith. It is not a crime to live as we do." He sat back down with a thump, crossed his legs, and turned sharply in his chair, away from Julia's probing stare. He hoped that Clement would appreciate that he was being candid and declare the matter dropped.

When that failed to move Clement, Lexus went on the attack. "Who is she, Brother, but a Roman woman?" Lexus said. "We do not follow women. They are subject to us—men."

Julia was hardly surprised by the accusations, and paying them no mind whatever, simply moved on. "I also have the letters you sent to your parishes, apprising your parishioners of new rules and regulations you have set forth. These so-called policies have been devised for no other reason than to promote your own power. You have made your own brethren answerable to you in a quest to seize complete control over them. All of these run counter to Yeshua's words and to the spirit of Paul's instructions for the ordination of bishops and elders. Why, you are no better than false prophets."

"Blasphemer!" shouted a shaken Lexus.

Clement's face registered shock, but it was quickly replaced by acquiescence when Terentius exclaimed, "Folly. The letter you refer to has been redacted. It is false, as you know. The message was written to encourage all members to pay respect to the bishops and especially their leader, Clement. All of your accusations have been a malicious attempt to attack those who serve the Church, as appointed by Clement. All of your accusations are typical of your gender. Listen to Paul. '*For from garments cometh a moth, and from women wickedness.*'"

Porcius, who had said nothing during the exchange, tried to put an end to the meeting. "We will listen to no more."

In a quandary about what to do in this messy state of affairs, Clement called for calm. "I will consider the matter and deliver a verdict sometime in the future."

Porcius decided then that the time for action against Julia had come, but he had to bide his time and wait for the right moment. The three bishops walked out.

Weeks later, before ruling on the matter, Clement was hauled off by guards under the new Roman regime of Emperor Trajan, tied to an anchor, and flung into the sea.

FIFTY-ONE

The cunning Aristus followed Clement as the new Christian patriarch in Rome, and when he appointed Julia's old foe, Porcius, as his top aide and henchman, she feared her days as a bishop were numbered. *Is it not enough that we have to deal with the wrath of the Romans, but now must fear the new so-called Christian leaders as well?* she thought. *They're far from Christians. They're really interlopers.*

Aristus was a mysterious man—proud, ambitious, and fierce. Julia thought he displayed the worst traits an elder could possess. Where Paul had written that an elder must be a man above reproach, faithful to his wife, sober, and no lover of money, this Aristus had not only married a woman while taking her daughter as his mistress, but he was enriching his relatives at the expense of the Church while waging relentless war against any rivals to his authority. In her journal, Julia wrote,

These things are awful enough, but when I found that he was betraying those who do not agree with him by turning them in to the Romans, I felt I must go and speak with him privately, as Yeshua taught. I asked for a meeting with Aristus. Milo cautioned me not to undertake such an action, but I ignored his warning and went to make my appeal to the new patriarch.

The meeting proved both fruitless and forbidding. An incensed Julia demanded of Aristus how he could collaborate with the Romans to destroy his fellow Christians. The only response she got was a stone face and the words, "Get out."

Julia wrote,

I realize I have been stupid and naïve to think I can change anything with this man. He is not one of us, but simply a man who saw the opportunity to profit through our movement, or perhaps he's an agent of Rome who has insinuated himself into our company. Through his unworthy and evil acts, Aristus has proven to be dangerous indeed, and I am under no illusion that I am safe from his brand of terror. The scribe taught us that Yeshua had warned against this very thing. Many would come, bearing his name, but they would be wolves in sheep's clothing. I fear I have walked unawares into the wolf's den. I know I don't have much time, but I need to take a step further. I must expose him to others.

Still a bishop with all the rights afforded to her as such, Julia distributed a message to the Christian communities telling them that Aristus had blinded the minds of the bishops and impugned the underpinnings of their faith by using his key of power to contradict the truth. She then proposed corrections to Aristus's abuses. First, citing Paul's many letters to the communities, she demanded that Aristus cease elevating immoral men into positions of authority and instead appoint only those of upright character. Second, she called for the bishops and deacons of the far-flung communities to guard against and denounce those who would profit from their positions, recover any monies illegally gained, and for the miscreants to confess and atone for their wrongs.

Aristus was furious when he learned what Julia had done, but he did not exact retribution immediately. He was busy elsewhere.

Aristus was determined to bring all of Rome's believers to heel. To that end, he placed each of Rome's many *domus ecclesiae* under his own authority, and overruling tradition placed presbyters and deacons of his own choosing in each home church. He then forged ahead with the same demands outside of Rome.

Julia knew that the lowest point had been reached when Aristus stripped all female Church leaders of their offices.

I am sad to say that Aristus has relegated us to traditional feminine duties of servitude. The deaconesses have been reduced to serving only as midwives, and the prophetesses have been silenced. He has gathered and destroyed all the documents written by women, and that includes mine. Well, not quite all of mine. I still have my cloth bag. I have added some new documents I came upon that show how twisted Yeshua's teachings have become. I hope they will someday be discovered. And I have this, my diary. Still, I am afraid that if these new documents are found, they will be destroyed. I am telling Milo to hide them all well.

Three years later, Aristus accused Julia of false prophecy and demanded her exile and excommunication. Knowing his penchant for turning believers over to the Roman authorities, Julia fled Rome. She, Livia, and Milo returned to Ostia and settled into a small house. She'd told few people where she was going and determined to live in silence and obscurity. She'd agreed to obey Aristus and leave Rome, rather than put her other daughter at risk to these men and their ambitions.

As Aristus and his handpicked henchmen tightened their control over Rome, the people remembered Julia's warnings. While her reputation for speaking truth to the powerful had made her many important enemies, it had also made her beloved by many of the followers. In her absence, her reputation grew, and her courage in standing up to Aristus was beginning to inspire rebellion, with followers starting to abandon the houses under Aristus's control and choosing instead to meet again in secret. Julia received a warning from Rome that her very life might be in danger.

Though they have not heard a word from me in more than two years, it appears that my silence isn't enough for them. They want blood. I cannot think what they may have in mind. I'm not much of a threat to them anymore. I am, after all, an old woman now. What could I do to them? But I cannot care about these things. My life has been my life, and it stands for itself. I do not apologize to anyone.

On a mild, sunny spring afternoon, a tall, austere figure with a noticeable red splotch on his forehead entered the marketplace in Ostia. He eyed the shoppers until he spotted the woman with a red ribbon attached to the handle of her shopping basket. He approached the woman, who looked around furtively for possible watchers. The man, too, looked around as he guided the woman to the far edge of the market. There, the two spoke in whispers as the man handed over to the woman a small packet that she tucked into the bottom of her basket. Taking a last look around, the man skirted the outside of the stalls then disappeared back into the crowd. The woman resumed her shopping.

Drusilla, the cook, extracted the small package from her basket, opened it, and added a pinch of the poisonous white false hellebore to Julia's honeyed wine.

Julia noted the acrid, bitter taste of the wine she was given, and after she drank it, she doubled over in pain. Milo sent for *Dottoressa* Arsinoe, an Egyptian woman, who could not explain Julia's malady. Julia became weaker, and she knew why.

Ah, so that is it. I am being poisoned. What should have been obvious has come to my mind too late. I should not be surprised, for there are many who would want to see me dead. Livia and Milo do not suspect, and I shall not tell them. My time is coming. I know it, and it is all right. I have lived long.

I see now that the retaliations done to those of us who wanted only to carry Yeshua's message will endure for a very long time, perhaps for centuries, and I am sorry for it.

I am so very tired....

FIFTY-TWO

The Vatican
Present Day

"And what *are* your conclusions?" Cardinal Ricci asked Valentina when she called. Pacing the floor of his office, he wondered what other unpleasant surprises she might have in store for him.

"There is so much to talk about, Cardinal, that I think it's best done face-to-face. I've reserved a conference room in the archives for a meeting on Thursday at eleven."

"I'm expecting good news, you know." Ricci moved toward a window overlooking the Vatican gardens, but he failed to notice the beauty there.

"I have some very comprehensive information for you," Valentina stated.

"And I trust it's *good* news," the cardinal repeated, his voice tensing. "I'd hate to see your career derailed."

"Yes, Cardinal," Valentina said as politely as she could manage.

Father Orio Rinaldi waddled into the conference room at 11:03, feeling quite self-important. For once, he was being included in what could be a monumental meeting, even if he was there only as his boss's minion. Rinaldi no longer wondered what all the secrecy was about. The ill-fated press conference had enlightened him completely, making him secretly elated that his boss had so humiliated himself. He was beside himself with anticipation about how this meeting would turn out.

Just as Father Rinaldi took a seat in the middle of a maple table large enough to seat twelve, Cardinal Antonio Ricci entered the room. He stopped and frowned in perturbation. *What are all these people doing here?*

Already assembled were Valentina, Erika, Anna-Marie, and Yigael. Anna-Marie and Yigael would answer questions about the search and the dig site.

Another man present was Cardinal Justin Parina, the Vatican librarian. He was required to attend because he would take charge of the three sets of original photos shot at the scene and in the women's lab. His job would be to distribute them for safekeeping to three different secured locations. This was nothing new. Valentina and Erika had many times, according to protocol, submitted photos to the prefect of the archives.

Valentina and the others rose to their feet as Cardinal Ricci walked quickly to his seat. He nodded in Valentina's direction, muttering, "*Dottoressa*," and inclining his head, indicating they could be seated. *High and mighty she is*, Ricci thought while noting the curve of the jacket covering her bosom. *She thinks she can protect herself by performing in front of an audience. She doesn't realize who she's playing with.*

Ricci had envisioned a one-on-one with Valentina, listening to what she had and then using it to his own purposes. If he heard something he didn't like, he would simply have omitted it from any public announcement. No, things were not going the way he had planned, but in the circumstances, he had no choice but to bide his time. *Well, if she's decided to play hardball, she should have chosen a lesser opponent.*

His annoyance was furthered by the ordinariness of this conference room. Instead of furnishing the space with the usual elaborate, showy fittings that would inspire reverence and adoration, the room was fitted out just like many others in ordinary office complexes, with cream-colored walls and modern sconces that added balancing light to the industrial-styled chandelier over the table. A printer sitting next to a copier had just finished churning out pages, which Erika got up to collect. The cardinal frowned.

"Shall we begin?" Valentina rose to a simultaneous knock on the door.

A priest Cardinal Ricci recognized as an aide to the pope poked his head through.

"Why, come in, Father," Valentina said. "May I help you?"

"His Holiness will be joining you momentarily," the pope's aide said, addressing Cardinal Ricci. "Will you please wait for him?"

"Of course," Cardinal Ricci said.

Dumbstruck, Valentina sat down. She certainly had not expected to be presenting to the pope. Visibly shaken, Valentina gave a worried glance to Erika and then to Yigael, who nodded almost imperceptibly. He seemed to be saying, "There is nothing you can do about it."

Father Rinaldi was temporarily speechless himself. *I've never even met the pope,* he thought, looking around nervously.

Anna-Marie flushed.

Erika looked apprehensive.

Yigael appeared unperturbed, and amused. He certainly was not awestruck by the notion of a pope's presence.

Cardinal Ricci felt the rug slip from under his feet. Now everything was out of his control. He abruptly rose to his feet and rounded the table to confront Valentina. Turning his back to the others, he hissed, "Did you know of His Holiness's visit?"

"Of course not, Cardinal. I'm just as much in the dark as you are," Valentina whispered.

With his frown deepening, Ricci returned to his seat.

Everyone had the same thought: How could the pope have known of this meeting?

Pope Augustine, followed by his secretary, arrived in the conference room at ten past

Nearly apoplectic at the sight of His Holiness, Father Rinaldi took it into his mind to hold a chair for him, so as the others were settling in their seats, he leaped up instead, knocking his to the floor, and raced around the table, his cassock flying at odd angles. Just as he was about to collide with the pope, Augustine deftly stepped aside. Rinaldi tripped on his robe, stumbled, and then losing his footing completely, went down in a heap.

Cardinal Ricci put his head in his hands.

"Well, this is an auspicious beginning," Yigael chortled under his breath.

Cardinal Parina rose and hoisted the maladroit priest to his feet. As he helped Rinaldi back to his chair, which Anna-Marie had turned upright, the pope moved toward a seat at the end of the table. His secretary took a seat to his left. The rest sat frozen in anticipation for what could possibly happen next.

Pope Augustine was far from immune to human reactions to the ridiculous, and it was all he could do to hold back his mirth. However, he had honed his skills as a diplomat and instead said soberly, "Thank you, Father, for your intended…mm…kindness. I trust you are unhurt?"

Father Rinaldi, close to a dead faint, squeaked, "Quite unhurt, Your…Your…Holiness."

With the slightest indulgent smile, Pope Augustine turned his attention to his audience. "I do beg your indulgence, and I hope my presence will not trouble you, ah, further."

"Of course not, Your Holiness," Valentina managed to stammer.

"Good," Pope Augustine said. "I don't want to hold things up, so *Dottoressa* Vella, please proceed."

Valentina took a breath and rose again. She gave Erika a beleaguered look.

Then, she gave Ricci a quick glance and for a moment felt

empathetic. He had financed an archeological dig on the premise that it would turn up information that would favor the position of the old guard and support the status quo, and he believed with his whole heart that this was in the best interest of the Church. Of course, he also wanted to put another feather in his cap. Valentina knew that in the next few moments, all of his hopes would be dashed.

"The purpose of today's meeting," Valentina began, "as you all know, is to reveal and interpret what we uncovered in Ostia nearly eight weeks ago."

She related for all how she and Erika had been on assignment in the first-century room at the direction of Cardinal Ricci to research Church office holders in the first century.

"We came upon an original letter that seemed to be written by a bishop no one had ever heard of. Adding to that, there was some question about this individual's gender."

"Why this discrepancy? Why would you even consider that this could be a woman?" His Holiness asked.

"Holiness, a tag attached to the document noted two names, one female, the other male."

"Go ahead, *Dottoressa*," Augustine said.

Valentina traced the steps they had taken in their journey, from engaging Yigael Dorian, to ascertaining the bishop's likely whereabouts, to finally discovering the tomb in the old cemetery in the Ostia ruins.

"If I may," Pope Augustine said, "I have another question regarding the gender of this person. Is it true that somewhere along the way to locate this bishop, you learned more about whom and what you were looking for, that indeed you were certain this bishop was a woman?"

"All but certain, Holiness. We did uncover documentation that indicated with considerable certainty that we were looking for a female bishop."

"And you failed to notify Cardinal Ricci of this certainty?" Augustine frowned in Valentina's direction.

Valentina blushed and looked down at the table. "Yes, Your

Holiness." Valentina knew very well not to try to make excuses.

Cardinal Ricci knew it would not benefit him to add his views at that moment. *Don't pop the balloon.*

Gauging the mood, Erika waited for several moments, and then got up as unobtrusively as she could, walked around the conference table, and handed out a single sheet of paper to Augustine and Cardinals Ricci and Parina. With no top heading, it was a simple list of the crucial contents of the tomb.

The deceased's journal/diary

The deceased's obituary

A Church epistle

Another's biography (only a shred is readable)

Various other artifacts

The three Church leaders scanned the list and looked up.

"We are still mystified as to why this bishop was interred in another family's crypt," Valentina went on. "It's possible that friends saw to her burial there. But why? We are still looking for an answer to that question."

Valentina paused and then continued, "When we entered the crypt, we saw an image of a menorah painted on a side wall and five ossuaries in alcoves in a main chamber. We saw the human bones lying on a slab in a small cutout to the side of the ossuaries. The epitaph there told us we had likely found what we were seeking.

"We removed the bones and sent them to osteoarchaeologists." Holding up a multipage document, she said, "I have a report from the lab detailing their results. I will convey their findings in a moment."

Valentina continued, "Right beside the bones in the tomb was a scroll. Because of its positioning, we felt it must be important. And it was. That document turned out to be a diary of the bishop's life."

This news touched off a rustle of garments. Cardinal Parina murmured, "Extraordinary…well done."

"You know how rare a find such as this is, and I can assure you that we have a wealth of detail about the bishop's life."

She went on, "All of the remaining contents, which you see on your list, were packed and delivered to *Dottoressa* Simone and me at our lab, and we began study immediately. I can say without doubt that there is a rich accumulation of information that weaves an original and telling tale of the undercurrents of social, religious, and family life during the course of the first century.

"Your Holiness, Cardinal Ricci, Cardinal Parina," Valentina said, looking at each, "the scientists did determine that the bones they tested showed that this bishop was a female. She lived beyond the age of sixty. There was no injury apparent to her bones, indicating that she was privileged, not of the working class.

Cardinal Ricci sank back in his chair and dropped his head to his chest.

"Okay, now back to the diary." Valentina looked down at her notes. "What we deciphered is the life story of a woman who was born in the year AD 40 and who lived a privileged, married life in Rome as Christianity was emerging onto the world stage. Then as a young adult, she was introduced to Yeshua's teachings and eventually became a Christian, acting over the years as recruiter, teacher, writer, and record keeper, and counting as friends Peter and Paul. Appointed bishop by the fourth patriarch, Clement, she journeyed over an uneven path in Church service. She endured persecutions, even banishment. In the end, she simply vanished. Until now."

"Her name?" Augustine asked.

"Julia, Your Holiness. Julia Lucinia Aquilleia Episcopa. Julia Episcopa."

FIFTY-THREE

"So it's true," Cardinal Ricci commented, quietly seething, unwilling to let the subject of gender go. "You told me that a Bishop Julius was named on a letter found in the archives and that was whom you would be researching."

"Your Eminence, we apologize. The tag was marked 'Julius Episcopus,' but we spotted that underneath the masculine form, the feminine form was clearly written. We believed we had a new bishop either way."

"Did you deliberately lie to me?" Ricci said, turning to the pope, whose mild, calm façade had turned slightly darker.

"Cardinal, we were called to find a first-century leader," Valentina said. She struggled for her next words. She didn't want to indict the cardinal on his bias in this roomful of people, point him out as someone who, suspecting a female would be found, would end the search and bury the facts. "Ah…we feared that the subject of a female leader would be awkward for the Holy Office, and we determined to find out first. What we would actually find, we didn't know."

Cardinal Ricci was distinctly unimpressed with Valentina's explanation.

"Again, Cardinal, our apologies for keeping the truth from you. I am sorry," Valentina said.

Yigael Dorian's head was tilted slightly to the side. His half-closed eyes gave no hint of what he was thinking.

Pope Augustine spoke up. "*Dottoressa* Vella, can you explain the details of this so-called name change to us?"

"If you don't mind, Your Holiness, *Dottoressa* Simone will address your question. She's an expert in the nuances of the ancient writings."

"Of course." His Holiness gestured for Erika to begin.

Staying seated and looking directly at the pope, Erika explained, "In fact, Holy Father, we have seen rewording in texts many times. The most common instance of a scratch-over occurs when a scribe makes an error and must correct it. In this case, however, we see two different hands. The scratch-over was clearly written by someone who was not a scribe by training, or we might never have caught it. Whoever it was must have assumed a mistake had been made, and decided to fix it. Otherwise, a document written by a female might simply have been destroyed."

Cardinal Ricci leaped do his feet "How dare you imply that we would...."

Pope Augustine made a slight hand gesture, and Cardinal Ricci slumped back into his chair.

Cardinal Ricci exclaimed, still hopeful, "You could have it wrong."

After a moment of silence, Valentina said, "Your Holiness, the document is signed Julia Episcopa. There's no doubt."

A cloud covered the sun and cast a shadow through the only window in the room.

Pope Augustine remained unreadable, while Cardinal Ricci sank even lower in his chair, mumbling insistently under his breath, "A hoax."

"You say you can substantiate that she was indeed a bishop?" the pope asked.

"We believe so, Holy Father," Valentina answered, entering the conversation again.

"In that case, why do we know nothing of her, *Dottoressa*? There is no mention of her in any other records. Other Christian women, less important than an alleged bishop, have left deep historical footprints. A woman of such import couldn't simply disappear, *Dottoressa*."

At the pope's words, Cardinal Ricci began to look less glum.

Cardinal Parina looked on with interest.

"Your Holiness, Julia's own words say that she was stripped of her title and condemned for heresy. Erika and I think that it's logical to assume that, in light of that disclosure, whoever wanted her gone also wanted any traces of her to disappear. Somehow, this letter must have slipped by."

"What's in this letter anyway?" Cardinal Parina asked. "We haven't heard."

"I was just getting to that, Your Eminence," Valentina said. "In considering the content of the letter, we determined that whether the document was a simple grocery list or something more important didn't matter. The signature alone was enough for us to investigate." She peered at Augustine to gauge his reaction so far, but saw nothing.

"As it happens," she went on, "the content was far more compelling. Julia's words were a request to Pope Clement for a meeting with three other bishops on a matter she called 'of some gravity.' She didn't explain the reason in the letter, but later in her diary, she wrote of the three men 'editing' Yeshua's words for their convenience and ordering Church contributions circumvented to their personal accounts. This letter certainly establishes Julia as equal in stature to the men."

While Pope Augustine's face masked any reaction to Valentina's words, Cardinal Ricci could take no more, though he tempered his tone. "Unbelievable. Then she must have been the wife of a deacon or a bishop writing on his behalf," he said, tightly gripping the arms of his chair.

"If I may, Cardinal," Erika interjected, "Julia's husband was a Roman senator. It wouldn't be likely he served the Church as a bishop. Not only that, Julia speaks of other women she served with, other women who were leaders in their community. The way she writes of them, it seems that there wasn't anything so extraordinary about female leadership in the early Church.

Ricci's eyebrows arched with anger, and his face reddened. *How dare she contradict me,* he thought. Then he sputtered, "But this means nothing, nothing at all. First you tell us that you've found a female bishop. Then you say that she was only one of many? Rubbish."

"Holiness, Your Eminences," Valentina said, "Modern scholars have made a very strong case that around the end of the third century, a deliberate attempt was made to remove women as leaders in the Church, remove and erase them. There is some evidence that some of this erasure may have started earlier, at the end of the first century. Why, over the last few decades, your own predecessor, Your Holiness, has apologized for the Church's treatment of women."

Cardinal Ricci's next words were almost a sneer. "Are you challenging the authority of the Council of Nicaea? Women leaders were heretics, and they were justly put out of business."

Valentina said, "I don't think so, Cardinal. If you'll allow me, we have other evidence that supports our theory."

"Please, enlighten us," His Holiness said noncommittally as the sun emerged from behind the clouds and spread a glow into the room.

FIFTY-FOUR

"Actually, we have three pieces of compelling evidence," Valentina responded. "First, we have it in Julia's own words. For now, I'll repeat that her diary is an account of her life as she evolved from a well-to-do Roman matriarch to an early Church mother and then as a Christian who rose to a position of authority before eventually falling out of favor." Valentina searched out her audience. Her eyes landed on Father Rinaldi, whose eyelids drooped dangerously toward sleep.

"Second we have it in writings found in her tomb. The third, we'll get to in due course.

"We found some original epistles that Julia had preserved," Valentina went on. "They were authored mostly by Paul. Along with these originals, Julia collected copies of these epistles that we can gauge were written decades later, in the 90s, just before the turn of the century. So, each original epistle had a copy attached to it."

"So?" Cardinal Ricci said.

"Eminence, when *Dottoressa* Simone and I studied them, we could see that the copies differed from the originals. New phrases and words had been incorporated into the copies. We noted that the changes on the copies altered the meaning and intent of the originals."

The pope shifted slightly, but did not stop looking at Valentina. Father Rinaldi's chin now rested on his chest.

"Now, here is where Julia was very clever," Valentina said. "*Dottoressa* Simone and I surmise that this woman, who carried Yeshua's word far and wide, must have recognized the deception inherent in these altered copies. She knew she could do nothing about it at the time, but she wanted to make as certain as she could that one day, Paul's original intent would be discovered. That is why—and this is our best theory of her intent—she kept the two documents together, the original and the copy, and saved them. If her story is to be believed, and we have no reason not to believe it, many of the changes to these original texts were purposeful."

"Come now," Cardinal Parina interjected. "You know very well that these were living documents, necessarily copied over and over again. It isn't as if they had fax machines. Letters were mistranslated, enhanced, and edited all the time. What sort of changes are you speaking of?"

"Cardinal, we're not talking of simple changes or mistranslations here," Valentina replied. "Of course, we can assume that some of the changes are quite innocent, made by those wanting simply to clarify a passage. But we are seeing substantive changes in a number of areas, changes that pervert the meaning of what we believe to be the original texts, changes that are reflective of an ulterior motive, political motives rather than spiritual motives."

"An example?" the pope inquired.

This time, Erika took the question. "Your Holiness, the Church often cites 1st Timothy as justification for excluding women from positions of authority, quoting Paul when he forbids women from holding authority over men."

Pope Augustine nodded, listening intently.

Ericka continued, "Holy Father, we have two copies of Paul's epistle to Timothy, one that we can date to around AD 60, the other to near the end of the first century. They are substantially different." She waited a moment, allowing the significance to sink in. "Paul's authorship of 1 Timothy has long been in dispute, with most scholars attributing the pastoral letter to one of his later disciples."

Cardinal Ricci could no longer hold his tongue. "This is nonsense. How dare you presume to teach *us* theology? The Bible is clear. Pauline doctrine forbade women to hold authority, period."

Valentina ignored him and reached into her folder, bringing out scans of the two documents, with side-by-side translations. "If I may, Holy Father?"

Augustine nodded and Valentina approached the pope. She placed the first document in front of him.

Augustine put on his eyeglasses and scanned the text. "This is the text we are familiar with, the widely accepted translation of 1st Timothy, 2:9-12.

"'Therefore I want the men everywhere to pray, lifting up holy hands without anger or disputing. I also want the women to dress modestly, with decency and propriety, adorning themselves, not with elaborate hairstyles or gold or pearls or expensive clothes, but with good deeds, appropriate for women who profess to worship God. A woman should learn in quietness and full submission. I do not permit a woman to teach or to assume authority over a man; she must be quiet.'"

Then, Valentina lay down the accompanying document, directing his attention to it. "This document is far older. We can date a papyrus manuscript simply by looking at the way it's written."

Pope Augustine nodded, for the moment taking her at her word.

"Look here, Holy Father." With this, her finger scrolled to an additional sentence, absent in the other missive. "In this earlier version Paul writes,

"'Brothers and Sisters, I implore you to not allow Pagan heresies to take root in your communities. You may know these pagans by their indecent dress, their elaborate hairstyles, their gold and pearls and expensive raiment. Do not be deceived, for they worship not our God but are declared in the name of the idolaters.

"'Our brothers and sisters in Yeshua are to dress modestly and learn

in quietness and submission to the word of Yeshua. Should they seek to learn, welcome them but do not permit these newcomers to teach or usurp authority over our brethren.'"

Silence fell over the room as all absorbed what Valentina had said.

Softly, she added, "Your Holiness, Paul's instruction was not meant to apply to women, but to the pagan population in that region, and I would suggest he was referring the Goddess cults that were predominant in Asia Minor in those times. And if you consider all the letters Saint Paul wrote, commending women for their work—Phoebe, Appia, Prisca, Nypha, and Lydia—it's clear that Paul held no ill will toward women leaders. This letter, which we believe to be the original, is far more in line with his other writings."

With this, Valentina returned to her seat.

"What you are alleging amounts to a willful conspiracy against women," Cardinal Parina mused.

"We think it's possible," Erika said.

"We found something else, as well, Holiness. It's not much, but it is profound."

FIFTY-FIVE

The Vatican

"Go on," His Holiness prodded reluctantly. What these two scholars had already alleged was potentially quite dangerous. He wasn't sure that he wanted to hear more.

"This is our third piece of evidence. It's the words of the woman who perhaps knew more than anyone: Mary Magdalene."

Around the table, people gasped, heads turned, eyes opened, and backs straightened.

"*Santo cielo!*" Cardinal Parina sputtered. "The words of Mary Magdalene?"

Pope Augustine raised his hand for silence. "Let's hear more." Turning to Valentina, he said, "Go on, *Dottoressa* Vella, please."

"Yes, Holiness," Valentina said. "Julia writes in her diary that Mary Magdala, as a very old woman, unexpectedly paid a visit to the villa in Herculaneum where Julia was living with her daughters and the scribe. Julia writes that Mary Magdalene wanted the scribe to record the details of her life, something she had previously refused to talk about. Whatever Mary told the scribe was never revealed, and this document remained unpublished, if you will."

A mix of skepticism and excitement filled the room.

293

"What have you found?" Cardinal Parina's eyes sparkled with interest.

"Cardinal, allow me for just a moment?" Valentina smiled warmly at the librarian.

"Of course."

"Thank you. As we just referenced," Valentina continued, "Julia lived in Herculaneum for some years. She was forced to flee when Vesuvius erupted. As she was preparing to leave, the scribe, who decided to stay behind, handed her a scroll to take with her. She writes that she recognized it as Mary's because it bore a tag reading *MM*." Valentina took a breath. "The path it took from then up until the time Erika and I opened a cedar box and saw it inside is anyone's guess. By the time it got to us, it was all but destroyed by time and the elements."

"Well, but…" said a bewildered Cardinal Parina.

"We dared not open it," Valentina went on. "It would have crumbled before our eyes. But technology is a wonderful thing, and we sent it out to see if it could be deciphered using the newest scientific methods."

Pope Augustine's eyes opened wide. "You put it in the mail?" he asked.

Cardinal Parina hid a small smile. As the Vatican librarian, he knew well what steps Valentina and Erika had taken.

With his ancient history background, Cardinal Ricci knew, too, but was giving nothing away, not with a smile, not with a frown.

"No, Holy Father, we didn't send it out in that way. Yigael, er, Dorian hand-carried the scroll to the Israel Antiquities Authority. Their labs have the equipment to digitally unwrap the scroll for us."

"Please, enlighten me about how you managed to transport this scroll out of the country?" The pope raised his eyebrows ever so slightly.

Yigael spoke for the first time. "Holiness, you may not want to delve too closely into that matter. But I can tell you that the scroll is safely back in Rome, no worse for its travels."

The pope's expression became calm once again. "I see." Then he changed tack. "This was how they read that old En-Gedi scroll recently, is it not?" He looked to Yigael, and then to Valentina. "Can you explain this to me? In laymen's terms, please?"

Valentina took the question. "Your Holiness, without getting overly technical, first, we digitally scan the rolled-up scroll with an X-ray-based micro-computed tomography—we call it a micro-CT scan. It takes 3D pictures of the object. At this point, the scroll can be stored because the rest of the work is done by computer. Software programs are then used to basically unroll the scroll and flatten it out. After that, the text can be read. That's oversimplification, of course. The scroll you'd read about had been burned to a crisp, yet they were still able to read some of it. It's nearly miraculous." Valentina smiled.

"Indeed," Pope Augustine said.

"And our scroll? How did she fare?" Cardinal Parina asked.

Unfortunately, unlike the other scrolls we found, the Magdalene scroll sustained much damage before her daughter Livia so carefully stored it for us. It had been, at one time, soaked with seawater. Perhaps when Julia escaped Herculaneum."

"Yes, yes?" Cardinal Parina said.

All eyes were riveted on Valentina. Even Father Rinaldi had come awake.

She said, "In the first fragment, Mary states that Yeshua asked her to be a disciple and that he also asked Salome. And they both agreed. In another piece, Mary told the scribe that she wanted to work with the disciples after Yeshua's death, but was shunned by Peter, who resented her and sent her away."

"Quite extraordinary. This agrees with what is written in the Gnostic Apocrypha," Cardinal Parina said bemusedly. "What else about Mary?"

"Unfortunately, that's all we got," Valentina responded. "And Julia writes that she never again saw Mary after her visit to the villa."

"I don't know what to think," Cardinal Parina said, lost in thought.

While the others were also a million miles away, pondering what Valentina had just told them, the door opened and lunch was announced.

FIFTY-SIX

The Vatican

"So what remains for us to determine," Valentina said after a nearly-silent luncheon of the pope's favorite panini, "is how Julia came to be buried in another family's crypt, the Ben-hadadi mausoleum. Clearly, they were an important family, as theirs is the only tomb near the synagogue. I'm certain the IAA will want to send a team as soon as possible. She may have been buried by friends, but why there?" Valentina looked around the table, gauging reactions before ending. "That finishes my presentation. Thank you."

As Erika rose to give a copy of Julia's diary, along with the photos, to Cardinals Ricci and Parina, and the pope's secretary, Valentina turned to Pope Augustine. "Holiness, might you stay with *Dottoressa* Simone and me for a moment after the others leave?"

Pope Augustine nodded his assent, and Valentina sat down.

With curious looks and glances at one another at what more Valentina might have to say and why they would not be hearing it, the cardinals, along with the others, were halfway to standing when the pope raised a hand. They sat back down.

"I have not been unaware of the nature of your disclosures here today," His Holiness said, addressing Valentina. "Still, I wanted to hear all of what you have discovered. As of yet, I have no words to offer for your account." And then, shifting his attention to the others, he said, "I charge each of you in this room with silence on this matter."

Of course he knew, Cardinal Ricci thought. It was that scoundrel, my nephew Francesco, who tipped him off. Of course it was. I should have known.

Cardinal Ricci was mystified by the pontiff's silence in the face of these monstrous allegations. Ricci had assumed that the pope would denounce Valentina, even offer to excommunicate her should she go further in this matter. *Why hadn't he?*

The light began to dawn. When the cardinal looked around at the others departing the meeting, he sensed that the support for his position, if he'd ever had any, had vanished. Not even his hapless secretary, Father Rinaldi, had come to his aid.

Cardinal Ricci rose from his seat. There was heaviness in his bearing as he slowly walked out, shocked that for the first time, he was losing the battle and fearing that his reputation would be forever tainted and his career destroyed.

When the door closed behind Yigael, the last one to leave, Valentina said, "Holy Father, may I read to you the scribe's own words?"

Pope Augustine nodded to indicate his permission.

"*This passage comes from the scribe's final days with Yeshua. 'I wondered why he had to speak of death on this celebratory occasion. He talked about the bread as though it was a part of his body. Did he honestly expect anyone to believe that? I looked around the room and saw everyone eating, all eyes grave. I looked at my piece and suddenly felt the urge to eat it immediately. I looked at Yeshua, his hair like black silk under the light of the lanterns. I love you. You cannot die, for we cannot exist without you. I reached for my bread and ate quickly. Suddenly it made sense. With the bread inside my body, I could hold on to the man. The cup of red wine, which was passed for each of us to drink from, marked a profoundly overpowering moment. I suppose that was why, as the last one to drink, I gripped the cup in my hand, and, unaware that I did, mindlessly took it with me as we left on that night.'*"

A fully-alert Pope Augustine immediately grasped the reference to the elusive Holy Grail.

Erika fetched a box that had been resting beside the printer behind the two scholars. She opened it and, reaching inside with care, freed from its protective padding an ancient stone cup. She set it on the table for Pope Augustine to see.

The cup was crude, hand-carved in stone, probably crafted from the soft, chalky rock common to an area in the Galilee. It was similar in style to those used in ordinary first-century households. What set it apart was an inscription sharply etched onto the side.

Stone-still, the Holy Father watched in fascination, his breath catching with thoughts of the impossible.

Nobody spoke for several moments, and then Erika picked up the cup. Cradling it in both hands, she passed it into Valentina's cupped hands.

Valentina stood and with her hands outstretched walked slowly to the end of the table.

"Holy Father," she said in a near whisper with tears glistening, "please…." She offered the cup to the pope.

The Holy Father raised his hands to receive the offering, his bearing one of humility but also confusion. "You have more to tell."

"I do, Holy Father." Valentina returned to her chair. "If you'll allow me…."

The pope nodded. "Of course."

"In her diary, Julia writes, 'Last night, when I was embroidering a decoration on Flavia's tunic and the girls were once again begging the scribe for a story, he told us how he came to have the cup that he brought to our house and which now sits on the mantelpiece. He said the cup was passed from Yeshua to his friends on the last night they dined together.'"

His Holiness held his breath.

Valentina looked up at Augustine. "Later, Julia fled Herculaneum because Mt. Vesuvius verged on eruption. When she made it to Rome, she entered the following into her diary: 'I didn't have time to carry much with me, but as I prepared to leave the villa, I spotted the cup on the mantelpiece and I grabbed it and added it to my bag. And I'm glad I did. That it could have been buried after the devastation of Vesuvius is beyond thinking. To me, this is the cup of Yeshua. It is magic. When it is with me, I am safe.'"

"Could it be?" Pope Augustine whispered, his eyes gleaming with tears. "After all this time?" He clutched the cup, unable to keep his eyes off of it.

All was silence in this profound moment. None of the three seemed able to break the spell of the mystery. Each had private thoughts. Erika wondered at all the rituals 2,000 years ago that this cup might have been part of. Valentina held a vivid picture in her mind's eye of Yeshua raising this cup and of his disciples, in misery, fearing what might come. Pope Augustine recalled the myths and legends from a time long past and the many who had died looking for what he now held.

The three were brought back to the moment when Pope Augustine placed the cup on the table.

"*Dottoressa* Vella?" the pope said simply.

"Holy Father," Valentina said in a shaky voice, "the provenance seems reliable. We know that the diary is not a forgery. It was written by Julia in the first century. There is absolutely no evidence that either the tomb or Julia's remains had been disturbed."

"Can you be more specific about the diary's authenticity?" Pope Augustine asked.

"Yes, Your Holiness. We rejected carbon-14 dating because it would have required us to destroy part of the scroll in order to date it, and the dating could be off by one hundred years or so. We chose instead to study the papyrus, the script, the ink, and even the handwriting, all of which change over time. We were able to match what we had with what was common usage to that specific time. When we came to our conclusion, we called Yigael Dorian to verify. He examined it using his technology processes, and we all agreed that the manuscript is authentic and was written by Julia."

A shaft of light pierced through the room's only window and lit the cup in a dazzling glow. Then, as fast as it had beamed in, the light faded.

Did I really see that? Valentina wondered. A look at Erika's bright wide eyes told her she did.

Pope Augustine's expression again was unreadable. "The words?" he asked. "What do the words say?" He traced a finger across the letters: ῥαββουνί.

"The letters are Hebrew." Erika blushed, realizing that the Holy Father recognized the lettering as Hebrew. "And they translate to *rabbouni*…'my great one' or 'my teacher.'"

"*Rabbouni*," His Holiness whispered. "Mary Magdalene called Yeshua *Rabbouni* when he rose from the grave."

As His Holiness took a long, silent breath and lifted his eyes to the sky, Valentina felt him moved beyond words. She dared not intrude on the moment.

Several more seconds passed and Pope Augustine asked, "Who would have inscribed this cup? One of the apostles? Mary?"

"We cannot be sure, Your Holiness, because there is no mention of the inscription in Julia's diary. Perhaps it was a gift from one of the disciples, or perhaps the scribe had it done after he took it. We can't be sure." Valentina took her own deep breath at the power of the words being spoken.

It didn't need to be said that Pope Augustine would take possession of the cup. Erika stood, took the box, and packed the cup back into it. And then she handed it to the pope.

Pope Augustine rose. The conference room door opened as if by magic, and His Holiness disappeared through it, the box containing the cup clutched in both hands.

The two scientists, exhausted by the day's events, slumped in their chairs.

"*Ho bisogno di rilassarsi,*" Valentina said. I need to chill out.

"*Ho bisogno di un bere,*" Erika said. I need a drink.

In her bed that night, Valentina's feelings of kinship with the woman, Julia, rose to the surface. *I hope that, somehow, her story gets out.*

FIFTY-SEVEN

Rome

Valentina ran fingers through her hair as she shook the cobwebs of a deep sleep from her foggy mind. She rose and dressed in yoga pants, a tank top, and a lightweight zip-up jacket, then ventured out for a predawn walk in St. Peter's Square. Few people were out at this hour. The only sound was of noisy trucks making early bread deliveries to the nearby bars and restaurants.

The day promised to be hot, and Valentina realized that it was now late July, nearly four months since the discovery of Julia's letter in the archives and a day after her presentation to the pope. *However did I work up the nerve to present to Augustine?* she wondered. *And however did I have the cheek to call his office afterward?* She winced thinking about it.

Across the street, she saw a dozen novitiates on the move. She watched as they entered the lower level at the side of the largest church in the world. She observed how young they were and how innocent they seemed. For a moment, Valentina wished that she could be one of them. And then she thought of her lover, Luca, and chuckled to herself. But she decided to follow them inside.

She trailed behind the group of young women as they progressed through an unmarked door leading to a stairway down to a section of the Church she had never been in before. At the base of the steps lay the tombs of the popes. As they entered a small chapel, several of the young girls eyed her with curiosity before stepping into the pews and kneeling for morning prayers.

Valentina thought, The Roman Church has been here in one form or another for 1,600 years and I love it for its progressive views on education, science, and the arts, all of it. But what tales it has to tell, of scandal, of bloodletting, and cover-up. What a dichotomy. And who are these young women? They are likely well educated. They can do most anything they want…most anything, yet they are here.

A young priest emerged and walked to the altar.

Valentina wondered, Would any of these young women want to be standing where the priest is?

Back outside, the sun was up, and the plaza was teeming with people darting about in all directions. On her way home, Valentina approached a newspaper kiosk, glanced at the morning *La Carta,* and saw the small headline in the fourth column of the front page just above the fold: "Controversial Cardinal Dies Suddenly."

She paid the vendor, bent to pick up the newspaper, and stopped in her tracks at the first sight of his name. Valentina folded the paper crisply, tucked it into her shoulder bag, and headed to a coffee bar. After ordering a cappuccino, she reopened her newspaper:

Rome—Cardinal Antonio Ricci, sixty-six, died yesterday at his office in Vatican City of an apparent heart attack.

Cardinal Ricci was born January 3, 1945, in Novara, Italy. He studied at the Pontifical Gregorian University, where he earned a licentiate in theology. He was ordained a priest on April 29, 1970, and then entered the University of Munich, where he studied for doctorates in history and canon law. He spoke Italian, German, English, and French. Ricci was appointed to the College of Cardinals by John Paul II.

Ricci articulated a conservative case for the Church's positions on contraception, sexuality, the role of women, and clergy sexual abuse. He was seen as an advocate of orthodoxy.

Cardinal Ricci is survived by a brother, Massimo Ricci of Novara, and a, Father Francesco Ricci of Ostia.

I saw him only yesterday, Valentina thought through tears. She left her cappuccino untouched and sped home.

Pushing open her apartment door, she heard the sharp *ring-ring* of her house phone. Breathless, she picked up the handset and listened to the pope's secretary telling her to be at the *appartamento pontificio* at three sharp for her requested meeting with His Holiness. She changed into a long-sleeved black blouse, a mid-calf black skirt, and matching jacket. She slid into low-heeled pumps and added a single-strand pearl choker. From her drawer, she pulled out a black silk scarf to cover her head. She checked her outfit in the tall standing mirror in her bedroom and then set out for the Vatican.

Valentina felt awestruck upon entering the pope's private study, but when she caught sight of the pontiff, she forgot all about her surroundings and dropped to her knees to kiss his ring. Then she rose. "Holy Father, Cardinal Ricci is dead."

"Yes, I am saddened to say," Pope Augustine said.

"Holiness, I feel as if I murdered the man. During our meeting yesterday, I challenged everything he thought and believed. He seemed so upset. It must have been too much for him. And I knew very well where he stood. I should have had more sensitivity. I should have told him the truth in the beginning. And Erika—I just spoke with her—is beside herself with grief. This is very, very hard." Valentina gulped, trying to hold back tears, which were getting the better of her.

Pope Augustine gave Valentina a consoling smile. "Do you not think that perhaps you take too much on yourself? This is not your doing. You know it's not. It's God's doing. Now, you may mourn our friend, but you may not blame yourself. That would be an insult to God, who," he said with a look of understanding, "is in charge, after all."

The pope summoned his secretary and ordered tea for the two of them. Valentina continued to be dazed by this turn of events, but as she sipped her tea and listened to the pope's soothing words, she settled down. Still, she continued feeling strangely conflicted and walking a tightrope somewhere between grief and reprieve.

"Now," His Holiness said, "you are here for quite another reason. Hmm?"

"Yes, Your Holiness. It's about the woman, Julia. I have come to feel such a strong bond with this woman as I've learned about her, that I think that her life should be celebrated now as it was not in her day. At our meeting, I presented a summary of the find in Ostia, but there is very much more to consider where the subject of women is concerned."

"Indeed," Pope Augustine said.

"Holiness, the Bible speaks of dozens of women who walked with Yeshua, hundreds who spread his word, and thousands who gave their lives and died for him. Yeshua considered women his equal and he treated them as such. So why should we women be subservient to men?"

Valentina swallowed hard and continued to look directly at the pope. "To me, there is unfairness in this. I'm sorry, Holiness," she said softly, looking down for a moment.

"It would seem that the Church hates women, Your Holiness." Valentina raised her eyes again to his.

"The Church doesn't hate women."

"Then why, Holiness?"

"The *men* of the Church are afraid of women. That is the crux of the problem."

"But why?" Valentina asked.

"For all the talents and intuitive abilities that men do not believe they themselves possess. They are afraid. In some ways, men of the Church are afraid of life. So you see how complex this all is."

"Holy Father, women in the world today practice law and medicine. They are scientists and philosophers, great thinkers, and world leaders. Why, women are ordained in nearly every other denomination. Why not ours?" Valentina feared that he would give her the pat, standard answer—Yeshua had twelve apostles and they were all men—but Pope Augustine didn't answer.

Valentina said, "Please, Holiness, at least let us publicize Julia."

"*Dottoressa* Vella, leave it. You don't know the danger you could bring upon yourself." Augustine gave Valentina a stern look. "There is nothing you can do that would not put you at risk. You must leave this to me."

Valentina left for her office with the hope of being consoled by Erika, but when she got there, Erika was oblivious to Valentina's mood.

"I just found something else in the cedar box."

Valentina was in no mood for games. "Yeah, right. No way. We emptied it out."

"As it happens, we didn't. I was moving the box to another shelf when I heard a rattling inside. When I opened the box, a thin piece of wood was lying on the bottom. It had fallen from the ceiling of the box and was concealing this."

"What?"

Erika pointed to a sheet of papyrus on the table. "I can't believe it. The papyrus was pressed between the ceiling of the box and this piece of wood. The wood just gave way."

Valentina's pique turned to curiosity, "Well, what is it? What does it say?"

"It answers our only remaining question about Julia," Erika said.

"What happened to her?" Valentina asked.

"Yes, it describes her final days."

"It's what we've been waiting for," Valentina said, sitting down to read.

FIFTY-EIGHT

Ostia, AD 104

My mother *died with Emet and Meshulam, Milo, and me at her bedside. Early that morning, Milo had summoned the medica, Kiya Arsinoe. The good doctor saw that my mother was beyond help, but was mystified as to why she would succumb to what seemed like a simple stomach ailment.*

Milo knew, though. Too late, he suspected the truth. Through his sources, Milo had picked up rumors that powerful men had been planning my mother's demise.

He never could pin down specifically who was involved in the plotting, but he understood finally that she had been given somehow lethal doses of white false hellebore.

In our household, there were only Drusilla, our cook, and the servant girl who had taken my mother her meals. They could not be suspect, could they?

On whose authority was she murdered? I doubt we will find out.

I don't think Milo will ever come to terms with the fact he was so helpless to keep my mother safe from harm. I haven't seen him like this since Cassia died. So distraught.

Milo and I are afraid that those who feared my mother will come to claim her body so that they can dispose of it in a way that no trace of her existence will ever be found. We and the Ben-hadadi are discussing what to do.

Obviously, we must have my mother buried in a place where no one would think to look, and the burial must take place in secrecy and with great haste.

It took only a moment for Emet to come up with the solution.

The Ben-hadad family had gifted the land for the synagogue, but had kept its family crypt on the periphery of the grounds, far enough away to be in accord with Jewish custom.

That singular honor would allow us to hide her body and her papers far away from the necropoli. We have adapted the Jewish custom of internment and will not allow her to be cremated as our enemies do with their dead.

My mother was entombed in the Ben-hadad family crypt in Ostia just as darkness was descending.

The burial ceremony was brief and attended only by Emet and Meshulam, Milo, and myself.

Milo dressed my mother in fine robes with the symbols of her position, and I placed the signet ring on her finger. While she had been stripped of her title and was in principle no longer a bishop, it wouldn't do for her to be without these marks of her work.

I took great pains with her papers in the hope that far into the future, her life work would be known. When I was a child, the scribe told us tales from Egypt, of how the Pharaohs preserved their works for the afterlife. He told us that what was buried with a Pharaoh would last until the end of time. We have carefully wrapped my mother's cloth bag and the scrolls she was able to harbor to hold out the water, using layers of waxed skins. We have nestled them in sand to keep out insects. We placed these in a cedar box.

I carried the cup and my mother's diary to her funeral service, and when our words were spoken, I placed the diary in my mother's arms and the cup on a shelf. I thought it fitting to place the cup there, because it had always rested on a mantelpiece at the villa in Herculaneum. Even after all these years, I still think of the villa as home.

We left the tomb quickly and the Ben-hadadi returned to their island.

If the Roman elders arrive to take my mother's body, they will find only cinders where a small house once stood. They will see that a blaze consumed the structure, and they may assume it consumed my mother's body with it.

Whatever they think, Milo and I will not be there to explain.

Milo and I are in hiding now. We plan to return to my mother's tomb in a few days. We will go under the cloak of darkness and hope that nobody sees us. Milo and I together have had a plaque carved that we will place at the entrance to her tomb.

I have not had time to properly preserve the letter I write now. I'll have to protect it as best I can inside the cedar box. Milo says it may be preserved by placing it between two pieces of wood. I will have to trust that one day, all will know of my mother and her life and steadfast dedication to the true teachings of Yeshua.

Milo and I must leave this place soon. Where we will go, we do not know.

Livia Marca Aquilleia

FIFTY-NINE

Rome
Present Day

It wasn't often that Valentina or Erika caught sight of Cardinal Justin Parina at the archives, but as they packed up their few belongings, they saw him approach.

"For all your work, I'm sorry things have ended this way," Parina said.

"Truly?" Erika sputtered. "Do you mean that you would have liked to see our find go public?"

It had been one month since Valentina had met with Pope Augustine, and the lid was still fastened tight on the subject of Bishop Julia.

Parina smiled but didn't answer. Instead, he said, "Come. I have something to show you."

"What could this mystery be about?" Valentina said with a smile.

Cardinal Parina led the way to the far end of the archive's second level and past many rows of shelves. At the end of the last row, there was a door with a sign reading *Locum Patrum.* Room of the Fathers. Pulling a key from the right pocket slit of his cassock, he slid it into the keyhole and jiggled the lock several times until it released. He opened the door, and Valentina and Erika followed the cardinal inside.

"I don't come in here often," Cardinal Parina said, "but I know what's here."

Valentina and Erika looked around and marveled at the wood-paneled walls and the many volumes in handcrafted cabinets. It looked like a place forgotten in time.

Cardinal Parina said, "Thousands of our most private documents are stored here—codices of the popes' formal letters and decrees and papal financial records. But this is what I thought you would be interested in." He gestured to a table along the left wall. "I'll leave you to look through what we have here."

The cardinal reopened the door to leave. "I'll be back after a while."

It didn't take Valentina and Erika long to realize Parina's intent. A stack of bound documents lay on top of the table. Fingering through them, they saw the names of the earliest writers. They included Polycarp, Irenaeus, Jacques of Antioch, and Clement of Rome. Looking further, they came upon meticulously detailed lists of early congregations. The lists were indistinguishable one from another. It looked as if this record keeping had followed a specific blueprint. They all added up to an accounting of meeting places—homes—in the first centuries in Rome.

Each sheet began by naming the owner of the house and, beside it, the date at which that home became a Christian gathering place. Directly under the owner's identity was the name of the Church leader presiding at that specific house and then a listing, in no particular order, of the attendants.

In the quiet, Valentina and Erika counted dozens of houses apparently operating as churches at the time.

"So detailed, so comprehensive," Valentina said. "Much more so than records of today, it would seem."

"Do you see this?" Erika asked. "How many places list a woman as the teacher? Quite amazing. Just think what it would have meant if we had come across this earlier and shown it to Cardinal Ricci."

"Erika, the Church has always had these records," Valentina responded. "They already knew."

Erika glanced up at a painting on the wall. The rendering was of a woman dressed head to toe in a long, dark red robe, a ring of light circling her crown, an arm bent with fingers pointing upward. The woman faced eleven men, nearly all bearded, all with halos of light. They leaned forward to hear her. "Look at that," she said.

Valentina followed her friend's gaze. Her eyes came to rest on the plaque naming the portrait: *Mary Magdalene Teaching the Apostles*.

"Yeah, before they tossed her out," Erika said with an acidic tone.

The two women had just ordered salads at the counter in a noisy café when Erika's phone chimed. As she reached into her pocket, Valentina spotted an empty table and sped toward it. They took seats.

Erika read her display and answered. "Paula?"

Valentina raised her eyebrows at hearing the name.

"Yep, it's me, and you're in demand again."

"Oh?" Erika responded.

"I'd like for you and Val to present at the conference." Paula was referring to the annual International Conference on Patristic Studies held yearly in Oxford.

"When is it?"

"Two months down the track. Plenty of time to prepare. I can send you the particulars," Paula said.

"Topic?" Erika put Paula on speaker, but turned down the volume so that the other diners couldn't hear their conversation.

"We've invited the Americans who developed the software for virtually unrolling and reading the oldest scrolls. They'll explain the technology, and we want you to follow with some examples of how you've used the technology—what you've been able to decipher that otherwise would have been lost. Bring some sexy examples."

Valentina and Erika gave knowing looks to each other.

"Not Julia," Valentina mouthed silently to Erika.

Erika frowned as if to say, "Of course not." Then she said to Paula, "Putting you on hold for just a minute."

"Okay."

"What do you think?" Erika asked Valentina.

"Why not, now that we're officially unemployed. Maybe pick up some work."

Back on the phone, Erika said, "Paula?"

"Yeah."

"Okay, we'll do it. I'll have to browse through some stuff."

"Yeah, okay, just get back to me with your title."

"Will do. Bye."

Paula Kirkpatrick pulled on black leggings, a yellow tank top, and her sky-blue Nike running shoes and headed for the front door. She opened it and came face-to-face with the postal carrier.

"Here you are", he said to Paula. A tiny box sat atop her stack of mail.

Paula looked at the little square package tied with twine. "Thanks," she said.

Paula mail into her flat, looked at the box. And then she went out for her run. Halfway through her jog, Paula stopped, stretched, and turned back. Her curiosity about the contents of the box had got the better of her.

Entering her flat, she went straight to the counter, picked up the box, and took it to her home office, where she cut the twine, tore off the plain brown wrapping paper, and took the lid off the box. *Whatever is this?* she wondered, lifting out the box's only item: a flash drive.

Paula pushed the stick into her computer and watched as her screen came alive.

"What the…?" she gasped.

SIXTY

"Let's walk," Valentina said as she stepped off the train in Oxford. "I'm tired of sitting." With their bags rolling along behind them, she and Erika set out on foot on this warm fall day for their hotel in Oxford's city center, ten minutes away.

That night Valentina dreamed.

The shelves went on forever. She couldn't find the book she wanted. It was a very early edition and nowhere to be found.

Ah, there it is, she thought. She read the title and reached for it.

Then a voice called out, "Not that one."

She turned. A tiny woman, barely five feet tall, stood before her. Her hair was parted in the middle, wound into a knot in back, and fastened with a delicately carved ivory hairpin. Her garment was a simple draping of ankle-length linen fabric.

The tiny woman said, "The book you seek is not here."

"Then where is it?"

"The story you seek is the one you will reveal."

"Who are you?" As she asked, Valentina felt warmth envelop her.

"Valentina, you know me," the tiny woman said. "I am many women."

Valentina responded, "What do you want?"

After a long pause, the tiny woman said, "That the mothers take their seat so that all are joined at God's table."

Valentina stirred. With her eyes still closed, she thought, *Just how do I accomplish that?*

～～～～

The two scholars arrived at the Examination Schools on the Oxford University campus Friday morning to set up for their presentation. The technical staff had assembled a laptop and projector on a table at the foot of the stage. A large screen was set at the rear. Erika inserted the flash drive containing their PowerPoint presentation into the USB port. They would manage the slides on stage by remote control.

"Let's try it out. We don't want any screw-ups," Erika said.

"Right, go ahead."

Erika picked up the remote. "It's got a laser pointer, great."

Theirs would be the last lecture of the conference. Their talk was titled "*Cyber-Archaeology in the Holy Land: The Future of the Past.*" Valentina would open with a slide of a blackened scroll resembling a burnt log overlaid with readable pages of the same scroll. This particular scroll was a letter circa AD 15 detailing a family's wedding festivities. One could imagine that perhaps it had been sent to a relative who couldn't attend the ceremony. It described the wedding ceremony in detail and would demonstrate just how important this new technology was.

～～～～

At three o'clock, Valentina and Erika waited in the wings as Paula introduced the two scientists to 1,200 scholars.

Light applause greeted the pair as they walked onto the brightly-lit stage.

"Thank you," Valentina said, smiling down at the audience. "Emerging technologies are allowing us to know more than ever about the daily lives of those who came before us. Our ancestors are literally getting to speak for themselves."

"We have so much to be grateful for," Erika added. "So, let's begin."

Valentina nodded to the stage manager to lower the lights, then she and Erika moved back to the side of the screen.

Erika clicked and they both gave a start.

A picture of a gravesite came into view, a site they were all too familiar with.

How did that get on there? they both thought.

"Sorry," Valentina said. "We seem to have an errant slide here." She nodded to Erika as if to say, "Just get rid of it."

Erika clicked again with the hope that the correct slide would appear.

But it didn't.

The second slide showed the same burial site with a plaque superimposed over it. The plaque was carved in Greek. The English translation was captioned at the bottom: *Here lies Julia Episcopa.*

Erika fast-clicked three more times. Three more slides of the Ostia excavation.

Erika clicked off.

Valentina moved toward the mic at the front of the stage. "I don't know what to say, but it seems that our presentation has gone missing. I don't know what we have here." As Valentina fumbled for what to say next, Paula emerged from behind the curtain.

Still standing beside the screen, Erika was beginning to see the light, and she didn't like the light she saw. Where Paula had got these photos, Erika couldn't imagine, but she knew that she and Valentina had been tricked.

As Paula took the mic, Valentina stepped aside.

"I invited these two phenomenal archaeologists here on false pretenses." Paula flashed a smile and nodded to an assistant who stepped forward with a small plaque. "Our work in archaeology frequently goes unacknowledged, and sometimes our most important discoveries go unpublished when our funders don't like what we've found."

The members of the audience chuckled and whispered among themselves. They all knew the truth of that.

"However, we take care of our own," Paula went on. "I would like to award Doctor Valentina Vella and Doctor Erika Simone our department's top award in the field of archaeology for their discovery of the first confirmed female bishop in Western Christendom."

Paula pressed the small, leather-framed plaque into Valentina's unwilling hands as the audience exploded in cheers.

Valentina felt fury building within her. How dare she? I gave my word to the pope. Augustine will never forgive me.

Erika's face had gone white. This was the height of academic malfeasance! This is my fault…. I never should have let her see that tag. She's using us to settle her own grudges.

"Despite the wishes of those who want to keep the discovery quiet, this revelation will be made public one way or another, as it is too large a story to bury." Still smiling, Paula turned toward Erika, still at the back of the stage, and then Valentina. "Erika, Valentina, congratulations on the find of the century. Tell us, what methods did you use to find the location of Bishop Julia? And what challenges have you faced in authenticating your discovery?"

Valentina put up her hands and took the mic. "I'm sorry, but there is nothing I can say at this time." She glanced back at Erika, who had not moved from her place beside the screen. Erika gave Valentina a sharp nod of agreement.

"I *am* sorry," Valentina said again. And then she walked off the stage.

Erika followed.

"Luca, I'm so sorry, *amore*. It's just not going to work," Valentina said to Luca half an hour later.

Luca had flown to London for a series of meetings on climate change and planned to drive to Oxford to spend the night with Valentina before returning to Vienna. "What's wrong, Cara? Did something happen?" He knew she would never cancel for no reason. He could hear the tension in her voice. And he was worried.

"*Grande disastro,*" Valentina said, "and I have to figure out what to do about it."

"I don't understand. You were just there for a conference," Luca said.

Valentina swallowed something between a sob and a sigh. "Paula sucker-punched us, Luca. She replaced our presentation with one of her own. She somehow put together the story of Julia and presented her to the world. She had slides of our photos and Julia's diary. She had nearly all of our work. I refused to talk about it and left the stage, but Erika and I are going to get the blame anyway. She knew damned well that this would be politically explosive. She knew she would be risking our reputations. And she didn't care. We'll be lucky to get hired at a high school after this is over."

"*Dio Mio.* My God. I am so sorry, Valentina," Luca said. He was furious on Valentina's behalf, and he knew exactly how serious this situation could get. Valentina wasn't a politician, she was a scientist and she had just been hurled deep into diplomatic waters.

"You sure you don't want me to come up? I can be there in a few hours."

"No, Luca. I have to think. Erika and I need to see if we can't find a way out of this."

"Okay. I'll get down to Rome as soon as I can. In the meantime, let me make some calls, try and get out ahead of this for you.

Who would you like me to call first? I can try some diplomatic backchannels, and I can get you any attorney in Rome."

Valentina thought for a moment. "I don't think a lawyer can do much at this point. But if you could check with some of your counterparts in the Nuncio's office, find out how fast this thing is moving, what the mood is...." Her voice choked a bit, and she stopped speaking.

"Look, try not to worry," Luca said. "It's possible no one knows about this yet. I have fairly long arms into the Vatican. Maybe I can tamp it down before anyone starts chewing on it. At least, I'll see what I can do."

Valentina closed her eyes, daring to hope.

SIXTY-ONE

Valentina and Erika sat at a round table in a busy and dark Oxford bar Friday night, fuming. They had changed into jeans and held double martinis in their hands.

"How could she? She has no idea what she's done!" Valentina said, slapping a hand on the tabletop.

"I forgot how she is when she gets something in her mind to do. There's no stopping her," Erika said. "You know, I always believed her to be the victim of the big bad Church story, but maybe they had a point. She just threw us under the bus to further her own goddamned agenda! She doesn't care who gets hurts as long as she gets her payback," Erika said bitterly. "To think she once told me she loved me. I trusted her."

"Wait until I get my hands on her," Valentina said. "I'll rip her to shreds."

"No. Let me," Erika said.

"You sure?" Valentina added as delicately as she could, "She's always been able to make you see things her way...."

"Not this time," Erika said. "Never again." She drained her martini and slammed the empty glass down just as her phone chimed. She looked at the display and answered. "What?"

"Breakfast tomorrow?" Paula asked.

"You bet," Erika responded without a trace of warmth.

At first, after Paula's presentation, the news of Julia didn't make headlines in the world press. *La Carta* released the story on page three of the first section. But the Associated Press and Reuters picked up the story, and by noon, it was in the hands of news bureaus worldwide. Even so, only a few news radio stations mentioned the story, and it was entirely ignored on cable news in favor of panel free-for-alls about the possible impeachment of a president that numerous renowned psychiatrists had called clearly demented.

But the story did cause rumblings among the faithful and the religious news blogs both right and left. It was gaining traction on chat and social networking sites in all corners of the globe. It made a little more noise in Oxford.

Erika and Paula sat at a table in the front window of an organic café. Paula perused the menu. Erika's lay flat and unread. Tension played at the corners of Paula's mouth at the sight of her glare.

"What are you having?" Paula asked as she peered over the top of her menu.

"You've ruined us, you know that?" Erika said with a frightening stillness. "What right did you have to betray us?"

"The story had to come out." Paula shrugged indifferently.

"It wasn't your story to tell," Erika growled between clenched teeth.

"Somebody had to tell it, and you two weren't going to do it," Paula said.

"How did you get it?" Erika asked in a demanding tone.

"A box delivered in the mail with a flash drive inside. The translation of Julia's diary and all the photos were on it. I have no idea who sent it to me. Really, I don't. There was no return address, but it was postmarked Rome." Paula refused to meet Erika's eyes.

"You know who they'll think sent it, though, don't you?" Erika said.

"So what? You didn't," Paula said.

"You know very well that we're going to be blamed for this." Erika kept her voice low but her steely look said her anger had not diminished.

"There are things more important than your reputations. The truth, for one thing," Paula said with a measure of self-righteousness.

A short-skirted, ponytailed server appeared at their table with a cheerful, "What can I get for you?"

"Nothing for me, thanks." Erika gave Paula a last scathing look. "I'm done here." Then she gave the table a hostile shove in Paula's direction, got up, and walked out.

Valentina sat on her hotel bed, fresh from a shower. She perused through the emails and texts that had piled up overnight on her tablet. As she thumbed through them, she was pleased to see many messages of support. She was shocked and dismayed, however, by some of the more venomous and even threatening emails. They were repulsive to read, and some—sent anonymously, of course— were terrifying. A tap at the door brought Erika in, clutching her tablet.

"How'd it go?" Valentina asked.

Erika shrugged. "What you'd expect. She was unapologetic."

"Would she reveal how she got hold of the photos and the diary?" Valentina asked.

"She said she had no idea. A plain-wrap package came from Rome. No return address, of course," Erika said. "I believe her on this."

"Well, I'm going to investigate as soon as we get back, and I'm going to nail the SOB. But first things first." Valentina nodded toward Erika's tablet. "Any messages?"

"Heaps. Many good, some bad, a couple even scary. Heard from Luca yet? Anyone?"

"Not..." Her phone chimed. "It's him." She picked up. "*Ciao,* Luca."

Valentina went quiet for several minutes and then, "I know what I want to do. I'll talk with Erika and let you know. *Grazie, caro.*"

"Pins and needles here," Erika said. "What—"

"It didn't take them long at the Vat. Word's out all over the place. The right-wing press is calling for our heads, their own so-called academics are trying to discredit Julia's diary, we're being smeared as shoddy scholars and, to cap things off, we're accused of being man-hating feminists. They are going to do their best to blackball us as scientists who ignore science in order to further our 'political agendas.' Luca spoke to the apostolic diplomats and the Vatican press office, but it's already out of their hands. He couldn't stop it."

Erika had fire in her eyes. "No one is ever going to hire us again. Christ, and who can blame them? If they believe we leaked this against our employers wishes...we're finished."

"Augustine warned me, and he was right," Valentina said.

"I hate to say it, but evidently Paula unleashed a sleeping tiger. Most of our colleagues are on our side, though, and they're pretty pissed that the Church would bury this." Erika noted her partner's faraway look. "What are you thinking?" Erika pursed her lips and cocked her head.

"I'm thinking about what we have to lose. Our life's work is going to be called into question...I think we need to fight back. We've got a fair number of people on our side, so we don't have to fight alone. History is written by the winners. If we fight, and if we win in the court of public opinion, at least this won't have been for nothing." Valentina folded her arms across her chest and looked directly at Erika.

"What? What do you mean? What do you have in mind?" Erika asked.

When Valentina told Erika what she was shooting for, the

two circumvented Paula and sent out a mass email to all the con-
ference-goers announcing a follow-up meeting. Many decided
to attend, so the two embattled women extended their stays in
Oxford by half a day.

Valentina and Erika faced 150 people in a conference hall at
Magdalen College on Saturday afternoon. As with the original
conference, they were professors, historians, and theologians
who represented numerous organizations, many of which had
fought the Holy Office valiantly but futilely for women's equality.
Most who came were women, including the uninvited Paula
Kirkpatrick, who sat in an aisle seat in the back row. But there
were men, too, one of whom was Cardinal Justin Parina.

"The time for letter writing is over," Valentina told the crowd.

Then, she rolled out a specific plan for immediate action that
would turn the tables on the Holy Office. Her idea was simple
and could be organized quickly, though she would need help. Her
proposal would make a statement that could not be ignored.

SIXTY-TWO

"I don't know what we'll serve His Holiness this evening," Sister Birgitta remarked to Sister Ursula while opening a large refrigerator and peering inside. "We're running out of vegetables, and you know how he is about anything that isn't fresh."

The two German Benedictine nuns ran the kitchen in the papal household. They were always mindful of the pope's favorite dishes, which tended to be simple, but had to be impeccably prepared.

Sister Ursula looked skyward and sighed.

Two weeks earlier at the follow-up meeting in Oxford, with Valentina and Erika at the helm, plans had gotten off the ground for a vigil in St. Peter's Square. They called on their reliable problem solver, Yigael Dorian, to devise the master plan and coordinate a mass demonstration. A date was set for one week hence. Word about *Project Julia* had spread, like a widening spider web, via social media. People scrambled to catch planes and board trains to get to Rome for what was to be a showdown with the Vatican.

As Piazza San Pietro in Vatican City began to fill with tens of thousands of protesters from all over the world, with men and women from every walk of life taking part, Valentina and Erika, who had figuratively, and perhaps literally, put their lives on the line, stepped into the background. They realized that the confrontation they had precipitated had taken on a life of its own, and their job was done here.

The square, always a center for the faithful to cheer the pope, had become quite something else: an arena of eerie silence, where all eyes were trained on the third-floor logia where the pope appeared on Sundays to bless the masses.

It was Saturday. The demonstrators had maintained absolute quiet for six days, and there was no sign that they were planning to leave anytime soon. Occasionally, groups of counter-protesters would show up, waving placards and banners and seeking a confrontation, but they left quickly in the face of the still and silent throng.

Inside the Vatican, the cardinals were at a loss, in several ways.

The discovery of Julia Episcopa and her story had sparked something in the human imagination, and she became front page news. *Frontline* was planning a documentary, and Hollywood was vying for the movie rights. The internet had gone wild, and suppressed anger at the Church came to a head, with long-forgotten injustices and ridiculously false conspiracies being dredged up and shared by an army of keyboard warriors.

Inside the Vatican, the cardinals were at a loss. The Holy Office had wasted its time debating about which way to turn. At first, they ignored the story, and then they tried to minimize it. When this hadn't worked, they'd tried to embrace Julia as a sainted one-off, but by this time, it was simply too late. The Church was in chaos.

And then this collection of humanity, absolutely silent and bearing lighted candles, had turned up outside. As the cardinals peered out from behind curtained windows, they trembled. This silent witness was something they'd never expected, not from their pliant and obedient sheep. In their experience, nothing like this had ever happened before.

"What's the world coming to?" muttered one eighty-two-year-old.

The Vatican offices were in complete disorder, the cardinals' comfortable lives thrown into disarray. The massive numbers pushing into the square and surrounding Vatican City had jammed service entrances, stopping deliveries and cutting off supplies. To add to that confusion, the lights went out. With no provisions being delivered and a power failure blacking out the place, the Holy Office froze, and some cardinals were approaching panic. No one knew the state of the papal apartments.

The Swiss Guard came to the rescue, using flashlights and emergency generators to lead the cardinals slowly toward the Sistine Chapel, where they would consider the state of affairs.

Cardinal Carlos Diaz, a moderate progressive, was the first to speak. "God's other face, Mother Mary, has too long been overlooked. I believe that this Julia Episcopa has shown us that *certain* women *might* be considered for higher office."

Diaz was interrupted by Cardinal Fionghan McInryre. "Our Church has stood for 2,000 years because of its adherence to tradition."

Senior among them, Cardinal Carlo Lavoti, held his tongue. As the cardinals continued to fight amongst themselves, he slipped out of the chapel and made his way to the papal apartments. It was time to confront Augustine, and put an end to this chaos one way or another.

"What now, Holy Father?" Lavoti asked the pope. "It doesn't look like they're going home anytime soon."

"We must speak to them," the pope responded.

"But *we* lay down the law, not these unwashed masses," Lavoti insisted. "We cannot answer to them. It would be very bad precedent."

"It would change things," the pope said mildly, "but we must speak. I will address them tomorrow."

"Good. Order them to disperse, under threat of excommunication!" Lavoti's face grew dark as he hunched over.

Augustine considered how the two of them had been at odds

always. Could he trust the prefect to obey him in this? Probably not, but he felt a responsibility to inform him ahead of the announcement. "I am issuing an encyclical. I was working on it well before that crowd came upon us. The Church will change its rule regarding women's ordination. It is time we join the modern world."

Cardinal Lavoti broke out in a sweat. "Your Holiness, the leadership will not stand for it. You'll destroy us all if you do this."

Augustine knew that the Holy Office could, probably would, undermine any decision he might make. "Look out that window," he said. "Are the cardinals willing to risk the Church collapsing under the strain of this fight? Our children are crying for justice. Not just our daughters, our sons as well."

"The Holy Office is accountable to no one," Lavoti dared to say.

Augustine gave him a cold glare. "You are accountable to the Lord your God. And I, not you, am his bishop. For God's sake, you are all wedded to times-gone-by. Your misguided leadership is archaic, and the Holy Office will fall due to your ineptitude."

Lavoti slowly shook his head.

"Look, my son, do you not think that I have considered all sides of this? I have sat three days in prayer, and the answer I receive is clear to me," Augustine said. "We have been wrong. Who are we to waylay any whom God has called to His service? It is clear to me that God's daughters deserve an equal place next to their brothers in the Church."

Lovoti quailed, his face draining of color. *He's invoking extraordinary magisterium. Papal infallibility! This cannot be.* With his mind running amok, Lavoti was seeing hordes of women invading the Holy See. As he took his leave, he thought, *For God's sake, what about the papal conclave? Where will these women sleep?*

Lavoti hurried to track down the man he turned to when he needed things handled. *May God forgive me.*

The next day, Sunday, just prior to noon, the sun shone on the crowd in St. Peter's Square.

The crowd, still silent, waited.

Cardinal Carlo Lavoti stepped out onto Pope Augustine's balcony.

SIXTY-THREE

Rome
Six Days Later

T
he papal *corteggio* made its way past the grand obelisk through the colonnade-skirted gates of Vatican City and toward the Ponte San Angelo. From there, the pope's body would be carried through the streets of Rome, giving the faithful a last view of their beloved Holy Father before reaching the distant Archbasilica of St. John Lateran where Pope Augustine I would be interred.

His death had been unexpected. While elderly, Augustine was reputed to be in excellent health when he reportedly suffered the fatal myocardial infarction.

When *"Il Papa è morto"* headlined the world's newspapers and scrolled across television screens, the name Julia Episcopa virtually disappeared from the respectable press. Upon hearing the news, Valentina had dissolved in inconsolable tears. She feared that her discovery had murdered the blessed Papa Augustine, just as it had Cardinal Ricci.

Cardinal Carlo Lavoti gazed out onto the square in smug satisfaction. As dean of the College of Cardinals, Lavoti would conduct the funeral Mass before Augustine would join the six other popes entombed at St. John Lateran. The last pope to be laid to rest there had been at the turn of the last century, but Lavoti had put out that this had been Augustine's dying wish. *Lontano dagli occhi, lontano dal cuore.* Out of sight, out of mind. Augustine would soon be forgotten.

As Lavoti stepped out into the procession, his face at once grim and holy, he was the very picture of true suffering. After all, some two billion people worldwide were watching. Heads of state had been in attendance all week long, and every news channel in the world was tuned in with minute-to-minute coverage of the funeral of the now deceased pope.

Of course, arrangements had needed to be made. The cardinal Camerlengo, the acting head of Vatican City now that Augustine was dead, had been bought off with enough cash to keep him and his bastard children, grandchildren, and great-grandchildren comfortable for life. The Guard had been a little more difficult, but, after all, they had failed to protect their pope. Would they want that to be made common knowledge? The pope's doctor was a doddering old fool whose predilection for the caresses of other men had made him an easy target for blackmail.

Upon the pope's death, the interregnum had begun, and while the holy seat was vacant, the College of Cardinals ruled the Church. It would do so for at least the next nine days, the *Novendiales*, until conclave was called. Lavoti would spend this time wisely, greasing the right palms, stroking the correct egos, and finding cause to blackmail or threaten any of the College foolish enough to stand in his way.

As the *corteggio* wound its way past the Castel Sant'Angelo, Lavoti reminded himself that he would need to alert his shoe-maker to re-measure his feet. It would not be seemly to have his new red shoes leave blisters as he was breaking them in.

What he did not know was that Augustine's encyclical, stamped for the last time with Augustine's Ring of the Fisher-man, was tucked away safely in a mendicant's priory less than an hour outside of Rome.

SIXTY-FOUR

The two travel bags sat at the back door of Valeri Laboratorio de Conservazione.

Valentina still had not shaken the conviction that Augustine's blood was on her hands.

"Val, come on. He could have died of natural causes like they said. You didn't cause this!" Erika was beginning to lose patience, as they'd been over this a million times before.

Valentina just looked at Erika glumly as her colleague and friend handed her a latte and sat down across from her. Erika began again.

"Valentina, you have got to stop blaming yourself. We did all the right things. We can do *if only* forever. *If only* we hadn't found that letter, *if only* we hadn't chased Julia...."

"If only Julia's story hadn't been leaked and Paula hadn't outed us," Valentina interrupted. "I'm still frustrated that I've gotten nowhere with the leak. It seems there are walls up everywhere I look."

"It wasn't *any* of us, Val. It was someone on their side," Erika said.

"We know that," Valentina answered. "To me, it had to be someone in that room. Someone *else* in that room at our show and tell. Father Rinaldi hated his boss and would have been happy to undercut him. Cardinal Parina wanted the story out."

"Even Augustine," Erika said. "The more I think about him, the more likely it seems he was the one."

Valentina, on the edge of tears, looked at Erika. "If so, he paid a very high price."

The two women slipped into silence. A horn beeped outside.

"My cab," Erika said. She was off for a short getaway in Barcelona.

Valentina got up and gave her friend a hug. She was getting away too, but first, she had a stop to make.

As the months passed and interest in Julia Episcopa surged again after the pope's death, her burial place was becoming a popular tourist attraction. A fence had been built around the perimeter of her tomb, and the doorway had been enlarged and reinforced. Inside, a copy of the cedar box stood in the position of its original. Julia's bones lay within a shatterproof glass enclosure, and replicas of the artifacts they'd uncovered were on display in museum cases. The Church had, of course, tried to prevent this, but the park lay in municipal grounds, and local officials were far more willing to listen to the quiet words of Father Francesco than they were to obey edicts from Rome.

Of the stone cup, there was no sign. If there was any news to be had about it, it had yet to be revealed.

When the tomb opened to the public, Giuseppe Benoni led tourists inside to see exactly what the excavation team had discovered.

Giuseppe's duties had multiplied at the old cemetery, and he had become something of a celebrity. Plucking facts from his remarkable memory, he was able to regale visitors with anecdotes about the place. In return, he was awarded the title "Docent of the Julia Episcopa Historical Site" and paid a modest stipend that, thanks to Yigael Dorian, who had overseen the negotiation, would continue until Giuseppe's death.

The sky was overcast with a soft drizzle driving the usual tourists indoors. Valentina had Julia's tomb to herself. She stepped inside and gazed at Julia's remains. She'd brought flowers, and added them to the collection atop the glass case. *We did our best, Julia. We all did our best. I hope it was enough.*

She stepped outside, brushing away a tear as Father Francesco Ricci approached. "I thought it was you I spotted."

"Hello, Father." Valentina smiled. "I'm so sorry about your uncle. And you were close to Augustine, too, weren't you?"

Father Francesco smiled and looked at his shoes. "What's next for you?" he asked, looking back up.

Many thoughts floated through Valentina's mind. She really had no idea. "We'll see. For now, I'm off to Vienna."

Father Francesco returned to the chapter house. He'd had months to think about what to do with the encyclical that Pope Augustine had sent him. Clearly, this document had cost Augustine dearly. It had cost him his life. Of this, Francesco had no doubt.

Father Francesco retrieved the encyclical. Making sure that his office door was closed, he stepped to his scanner and copied the document page by page. Placing the original back into its hiding place, he slid the copy into a plain manila envelope. He attached a computer-generated address label and sealed the envelope. Later that day, he'd take the train into Rome and mail it from the Termini train station. It would not do to have this traced back to his quiet, sleepy little priory house.

A week later, *La Carta* reporter Michael Levin stared at the buff-colored envelope on his desk. After his first cup of coffee, he slit it open.

LEARN MORE!

Want to find out what happens next? Would you like to know more about the world Julia inhabits? The next book in our series will be released later this year. Check out our website, and sign up to our mailing list at VaticanChronicles.com

Note from John and Diane: Reviews are gold to authors! If you've enjoyed this book, would you consider rating it and reviewing it on www.Amazon.com?

ACKNOWLEDGEMENTS

The authors wish to thank for their insight and valuable assistance the following people: Eldon Chittick, Janet Ziegler PhD, Marilyn Ward, Sid Hollister, David Ruettiger, Pamela Desvernine, Willy Brady, Anne Murphy, Lisa Cerasoli, and JD Smith.

To our Italy connection, Shaun Loftus, publicist extraordinaire and so much more, our deepest gratitude.

Remembering our literary agent, the late Michael Hamilburg, with love and gratitude.

ABOUT THE AUTHORS

John Ignatius Rigoli's experiences as both a cradle Catholic and former US Naval officer informed his world view in a rather unexpected manner, opening his eyes to the proposition that those who seek power are the last people who should hold it. John is an unabashed social justice advocate, outspoken liberal, and a patriot – and he sees no dichotomy in this. As a talented and inquisitive amateur historian, John became interested in the stories of the earliest women in the Church, and how they have been erased. Though a work of historical fiction, The Vatican Chronicles takes its inspiration from the real women throughout history who toiled unacknowledged alongside their brothers.

Diane Cummings is a California girl, a UCLA alum, and is currently sweating in Atlanta, Georgia, with the world's smallest Persian cat. Diane has worked as a reporter and news director. Deciding that truth was too much stranger than fiction, she turned in her microphone and press pass and set about applying her passion for writing and editing to the world of literature. Diane has edited or ghostwritten more than fifty titles – and now she wants her name on the cover. The Vatican Chronicle Trilogy has encompassed six years of research, writing, and polishing and she hopes you enjoy Book 1 – The Mystery of Julia Episcopa as much as she has enjoyed writing it.

Made in the USA
Middletown, DE
18 August 2018